Distant Heart Sounds

A Nurse Morgan Series: Book One

Kate MacInnis

Distant Heart Sounds
A Nurse Morgan Series: Book 1
Copyright © 2020 Kate MacInnis
All rights reserved.

ISBN: (ebook) 978-1-949931-82-2
(print) 978-1-953335-05-0

Inkspell Publishing
207 Moonglow Circle #101
Murrells Inlet, SC 29576

Edited By Yezanira Yenecia
Cover Art By Najla Qamber

DEDICATION

This book is dedicated to the memory of Linda Walters, who was my best friend and mentor. She opened my eyes and mind to so many possibilities beyond the explainable. Also, to my husband Bill for his patience and sense of humor.

KATE MACINNIS

CHAPTER 1

Morgan jerked the covers below her chin, held her breath, and listened while her eyes searched high and low for whatever woke her in the dark bedroom. Dresser with mirror, chest with TV on top, makeup table with chair, dirty clothes on the floor around the hamper, and her queen-size bed were all in order. Nothing moved in the room. She rubbed her face with both hands, took another deep breath, and exhaled slowly. Her body ached from yet another fitful night of sleep. A foreign sound in the distance made her turn left toward the window. She sat up, tilted her head, and listened with eyes closed. It was faint and sounded like piano music. Again, she glanced around and did not see any movement or source of the sound. The music got louder—definitely a piano with a tinny tinkling quality. She slid out of bed and went to the closed window.

She pulled the frilly curtains aside and looked across the blue-collar neighborhood in which she had lived for nearly five years. She unlocked the window, opened it, and stuck her head out. The only sound was the steady hum of early morning traffic a few blocks away. Lights were on from early risers in the other small houses, who also started their workday before daylight. Morgan occasionally recognized some of them as they toiled in their yards and homes every night and all weekend. The stillness of the night felt cool and safe just as the music suddenly blasted, vibrating the window. Morgan stepped back, closed it, and turned the lock. Piano music swelled again and shook the walls while someone inside the house laughed as a champagne cork popped.

Morgan crossed the room and grabbed the baseball bat from her bedroom closet and placed it on her shoulder in a "batter up" gesture. She stepped into the dark hall outside the bedroom where a glow from the first floor of the house gave off enough light to flood the stairs. She frowned at the intense smell of freshly baked bread and rich food that made her mouth water since she could neither cook nor bake. At the top of the staircase, she crouched with her back against the wall and planted one bare foot on the first step as she leaned closer to the banister.

With the bat now cradled on her lap, she peered downstairs. In the foyer below, she counted more than thirty people gathered in the entry, library, and living room of her small home. She was sure she didn't even know that many people. The lights blazed as the revelers laughed, ate hors d'oeuvres from silver platters, smoked cigarettes, stood around the shiny black piano as they sang Cole Porter tunes, and clinked champagne glasses filled to the brim. Several people made toasts for good luck and great health. One gentleman spilled the bubbly liquid with a flourish onto the shiny marble floor as he tried to hit the target of another gentleman who lay there with his mouth wide open. A few couples snuggled into corners while others danced, shimmied, and vied for attention. Everyone was dressed in black and white silks and satins with dazzling jewels and long strings of pearls.

"I don't own a piano," Morgan said out loud. "And my house doesn't have marble floors."

The piano player stopped and looked up at her with widened eyes. His mouth opened and a loud *pop* shook the house. Every light went out on the first floor. Morgan clutched the bat to her chest and felt her heart hammer her ribs. She leaned back and felt over her head for the hall light switch. She flipped it and the illumination revealed no people, no party streamers, no wet floor, no dirty dishes, and no piano. She stared at the empty site for a moment, stood, and edged her way back to the bedroom.

Morgan sagged on the side of the bed. Sweat broke out on her forehead and upper lip. Her head pounded as hot tears scorched her eyes. The scar on her scalp, from the brain surgery performed a few weeks earlier, throbbed. She rubbed the spot and stretched her neck.

Back to work for only three days as an emergency center charge nurse at a metro Detroit hospital, Morgan survived a ruptured aneurysm deep in her brain six weeks earlier. She was fortunate to still be alive. The blowout was fixed without residual damage, at least that's what the doctors said. Morgan believed something happened on the operating table while she was under sedation. She remembered a visit from her mother, father, and sister, all of whom had passed away years before. There was also a handsome couple who hovered in the background, neither of whom she recognized. The only logical explanation was a near-death experience while under anesthesia. She asked the neurosurgeon about the incident but he dismissed her. She decided not to share this information with anyone else.

Morgan struggled to breathe normally while her heart thudded. She turned off the alarm at 4:30 a.m. and counted to ten, slowly, over and over as she rocked herself to and fro on the edge of the bed. Tears rolled down her cheeks. She reached for her cell, looked at it, and put it back on the bedside table. She choked on a sob, wiped her face with the bedsheet, and looked around.

"Douglas," she called. "Where are you?"

The white English bulldog came in from the hallway and scampered over to her. Morgan scratched his head.

"Did you sleep through the party at our house? Did you see any of the people who were here? Some guard dog you are. I am sure if they offered you cookies, you'd try to stay awake and keep an eye on them."

Douglas looked at her with soulful eyes and sniffed her hand as she reached for him. He pulled his head back and stared at her again. She helped him onto the bed and watched him get his balance. Douglas walked around, cuddled into the pillows, and snored within seconds.

"You know, Douglas, if these party people are ghosts or a figment of my imagination, at least they know how to have a good time. I like that in a hallucination." She nodded and looked around the room. Everything was in its proper place.

Morgan got out of bed and gathered clean clothes, then turned to glance at the clock on her way to the bathroom. It was early to be up as she stood in the center of the room and stared at the enormous antique clawfoot bathtub that was original to the house. As a nurse, many of Morgan's workdays were filled with blood, guts, pain, and heartache. She had spent hours in here soaking away the tension. She moved on to the separate glass shower that she added when she moved in.

After her shower, Morgan dressed in fresh scrubs and hurried downstairs to the kitchen with Douglas close on her heels. The sunny, yellow kitchen was at the back of the house with large windows on two adjoining walls that overlooked the backyard and the neighbor's house to the right. Much of the room was the original 1940s layout with new cabinets and appliances added when she bought the place. The kitchen sink was centered under the largest window for a full view of Douglas when he was outside. The door in the center of the back wall opened directly onto the porch with a couple of steps down to the fenced backyard.

The dining room was also at the back of the house on the opposite side, across from the kitchen. Same window positions as in the kitchen, but one overlooked the neighbor's house on the left. An empty, built-in corner china cabinet stood erect like a hollow sentinel between the windows.

Douglas raced outside and Morgan left the back door open for him. She searched the refrigerator and found no edible food for herself; however, she did see two bottles of liquor—one rosé and the other a cherry vodka that had chilled to perfection months before. She reached for one of the bottles, stopped short, and closed the fridge. She opened the pantry next to the outside door and grabbed a few peanut butter cracker snacks that could sustain her throughout the day.

Douglas came back into the house and looked at his bowl of food. Clearly not impressed that it was the same old fare, he shot her a dirty look, as bulldogs often do, and scampered upstairs. She grabbed her purse and keys, locked up the house, and got into the car.

The Jeep Wrangler growled to life immediately. Although early spring, it was still cold enough to have the heated seats and steering wheel activated. Morgan sighed as she felt the warmth. She pulled out of the driveway and drove along the quiet street for three blocks before she turned south on the infamous Woodward Avenue, known for being the first paved road in America. She pressed the accelerator and within minutes joined the early rush hour traffic.

A song from World War II played on the car radio. She changed the channel and the same song played. She touched another button to switch stations, but the same song played again. Morgan shivered and cranked the heat up to seventy-five degrees. The music played all the way to the local coffee shop, where she pulled in and parked.

Inside the store the baristas and customers moved along at a normal pace. Morgan felt as though she was in shock and forced to move through thick gelatin with every step, a colossal effort. She stood in line to order and rubbed the center of her breastbone where she felt a twinge deep inside her chest. Panic washed over her. The party at her house and the same song on every station of the radio were as real as the hair on her head. She knew in an instant that from that day forward, her life would never be the same, and these experiences would continue.

Morgan got her chai latte and a black coffee for her boss, then hurried back to the Jeep. She made the ten-minute trip to the hospital with the radio turned off. She pulled into the parking deck and hustled to the Emergency Center (EC) entrance as she balanced the tea, coffee, and her canvas bag stuffed with a change of street clothes and shoes. She powered through the pneumatic doors and didn't stop until she reached the whiteboard behind the main nurses' station that showed the cases currently in examination rooms.

The EC itself was well lit and the odors were distinct. There was a familiar *eau d'penicillin* combined with the metallic smell of blood intertwined with dabs of chlorine bleach. The aroma triggered the adrenaline to pump all the way into her fingertips as she stopped and counted the number of cases pending on the whiteboard. It was a good day as only half of the fifty patient rooms were filled.

Morgan looked up at the huge clock over the nurses' desk, which was the hub of the center. The EC was a large roman numeral II with two long halls, each with twenty-five total examination and trauma rooms.

The back hall was the bottom of the II and another hall across the top was the front hall or entrance. The main nursing desk was anchored in the front hall, positioned to prevent patients and visitors from entering the treatment area. It had three computers: one for the desk clerk in the center and one at each end of the counter for staff.

A waiting room off to the side of the desk was available for the public to use while they waited. This morning, some visitors paced while others texted or dozed. One child cried and asked for his mommy. His father held him close and looked exhausted and scared at the same time as he paced around the room. A huge flat-screen television with muted sound was mounted in the corner and set on a news channel. Its remote was locked away from sight to avoid conflicts. A bank of elevators stationed next to the waiting room was in constant use, and pneumatic doors to a hallway connected the EC to the rest of the hospital.

Behind the nurses' desk was a small kitchen that adjoined a slightly larger room with a few ancient magazines, rectangular table with plastic chairs, and several storage lockers with broken locks. This room was used for employee meals or just to get away for a few minutes. Morgan went into the break room, put the coffee on the table and the rest of her stuff in the closest locker before she went back to look at the patient list again on the whiteboard. She held her hot tea in both hands as she read the board.

"Morgan, flies are gonna nest in your precious mouth if you continue to stand there with it wide open," Savannah Holt, MD, said as she came from behind. "I've seen every one of the patients and most are still here waiting for consults. Actually, it's a pretty tame bunch today."

Morgan nodded and watched Savannah stifle a yawn. "There's a semi-hot coffee for you on the table."

"Well, aren't you the sweetest thing." Savannah hurried to retrieve the coffee and came back. "You look pale and washed out, Morgan. Are you sure you're ready to be back to work? Tiffany called and she'll be late, which means you have to handle the desk, phones, and public. She had personal business to take care of before work." Savvy went to the whiteboard and erased a name. "That patient went home an hour ago. No need to keep her listed up here. Her discharge papers should be around here someplace. I told the resident to drop them on the desk."

Morgan nodded as she sat in Tiffany's chair and placed

her tea on the desk.

"I don't like it when Tiff isn't here," Morgan said. "I'm not nearly as organized as she is."

"We'll manage. And by 'we'll manage,' I mean that you will." Savannah laughed.

Morgan narrowed her eyes at her boss, who moved behind Morgan's chair.

"You do know that if you need more time off to heal, you can tell me. I would take the maximum amount of time needed to protect my health, if it were me."

"Oh, as if you could ever leave the EC for more than forty-eight hours. Honestly, Savannah, this place is the child you never had. This is your weird and perverted little baby."

"You seemed in a daze a few minutes ago and now you're all über efficient. I've known you for twenty years, and I sense that you're not really your old sarcastic self. Tell me, Morgan, *is* there a problem? Don't give me one of your wiseass remarks either, just spit it out."

Morgan turned to look directly at Savannah. "I am different, Savvy. I've been through a lot, and at this point I'm not even sure *if* I will ever be the same." She stiffened and rubbed her hands together. "Look, Savvy, if at any time I can't do my job, you won't have to deal with it. I'll leave voluntarily. You won't even have to ask."

She waited for Savvy's reaction, which was a simple nod. Savvy moved away from the desk and said over her shoulder, "I will hold you to that promise, Morgan."

Morgan nodded at Savannah's back and got to work, reading through the stacks of orders, notes, and lab results left by the previous shifts. She wiped hot tears from her cheeks with the back of her hand as she looked around for a tissue. She found the box, grabbed one, and continued sorting another stack of paper.

She had already answered the phone several times when she noticed a photo tacked to the small bulletin board between the top of the desk and counter. Morgan smiled as she unpinned the picture taken at last year's office Christmas party held at her house. So much had happened since then. The picture was a group shot of her co-workers with Tiffany at the center—easy to spot with her burgundy hair and Goth lipstick.

The memory of that party triggered a sense of peace to wash over Morgan. She loved her home; it was her safe place, although it was currently threatened by unknown visitors who partied in the middle of the night. So far, they hadn't done anything to hurt or threaten her in any way, so maybe they would go away altogether if she ignored them. She kissed her finger and tapped the picture before putting it back on the wall behind the phone.

The multi-line phone rang often and she answered questions as fast as she could. As the remainder of the day shift staff arrived, they greeted her and asked about the missing Tiffany. She shared that Tiffany would be late as they were interrupted by the phone. When she was again alone at the desk, she let out a sigh before a rich, guttural moan exploded right behind her chair, causing her to duck. The noise swelled and broke apart into a collection of agonized voices in the open area in front of the desk. Some cried in high pitches as others keened in deep tones. She stiffened at the screams of small children—sweat breaking out on her head and chest. "Does anyone else hear that noise?" Morgan asked the nurses who returned to the desk from the first rounds on patients.

"What noise?" one of the nurses replied.

"Probably the pipes again. This area of the hospital is really old," said another.

The EC was part of the original hospital when it opened in the 1920s and still had the original shiny pale-green subway tiles accented with smooth, pale-yellow brick. Over the years, more rooms were added, but still there were not enough. When all the rooms were filled, carts were parked on both sides of the halls to accommodate the overflow of patients.

Morgan nodded and rolled back in the chair to face the nurses' desk. The stench of burned wires overwhelmed the area. She coughed at the acrid smell and checked for a similar reaction from the others—no one else seemed to notice. Again, she gagged right when Ellen Garcia, one of her best friends, came behind the desk.

"Hey, charge nurse, how are you? Did I just hear you gag on something?" Ellen moved closer to Morgan and patted her back. Ellen was small and wiry, with curly, dark brown hair and huge brown eyes.

"I'm fine, Ellen, thanks. How are you?"

"I'm fit and ready for duty this fine day. I sure did miss you here, just like everybody else did. Truthfully, I missed your sense of humor the most. It's so needed in the EC. Hey, it sounded like you were about to cough up a lung. You're sure you're okay?"

"Yeah, I gagged on my cold tea." Morgan held up the empty cup from earlier.

"Oh, sorry, I didn't see you take a drink. Sure glad to have you back, though."

"Wait, Ellen, have you noticed an odd smell around here?"

"Nope. What did you have in mind?" Ellen asked, grabbing the computer on wheels (COW) and pointing it toward the hall on the right.

"I don't know, like a burnt hair dryer or an overheated toaster."

Ellen shook her head, and not wanting to be scolded by Savannah, she hurried away when she saw her boss heading to the desk. It was a rule that nurses shouldn't spend time talking when there were patients to care for—unless the conversation was specifically about a patient.

"I don't want you here if you aren't well, Morgan. Not only for the safety of my patients, but for your own good." Savannah inhaled and let it out slowly. In a more relaxed voice, she continued, "Morgan, I overheard you say something about smells. Did you know that a head injury can cause your nose to be out of whack and your sense of smell can't work right?"

"Yes, I've heard about that," Morgan answered as a bright emerald light appeared all around Savannah.

"Just make sure you can handle yourself," Savvy replied.

Morgan watched as the light vibrated in rhythm with the doctor's speech pattern. At almost six feet tall, Savannah Holt was a striking woman with blonde hair and flawless porcelain skin. Morgan had heard of auras before but had never experienced seeing one. She knew immediately she had to do some research and see if this ability was also related to her surgery. She smiled thinking the aura was a nice touch to accent Savvy's green eyes.

"I'm fine, really, Dr. Holt, but I would like to get out of this chair for a while." Morgan stood and patted Savannah's arm as she looked carefully at the light around the doctor. "Honestly, Savvy, trust me."

Morgan shivered as she walked away from the desk and down the hall to the examination rooms. She turned around and said, "Hey, Savvy, how's your mom these days?"

Savannah stiffened at the comment and sat down hard in Tiffany's chair. Her emerald green glow now displayed never-ending bright yellow lightning bolts emanating from its core.

Morgan watched and mumbled, "I bet it's a safe bet those bolts aren't a positive sign."

She glanced around the EC but didn't see any other visible auras on the nurses, aides, lab techs, residents, visitors, or patients. Morgan crossed her arms over her chest as she continued down the hall.

A loud knock followed by moans and cries rang throughout the EC. It started at one end of the hall and thundered through the entire length. Morgan paced as she held her hands over her ears to block the sounds. She stopped abruptly when a storage closet door opened by itself and the soft light beckoned to her. Without a second thought, she scooted inside and leaned against a shelf where she could still hear the deafening sounds that vibrated the floors and walls.

"Our Father who art in Heaven, hallowed be thy Name," she said out loud and stopped. "Dammit, I can't think of the next line of that prayer." Her heart skittered and banged in her chest as she held her head down to concentrate. She repeated the line from the prayer several times but could not remember the next word. She closed her eyes.

"I swear I will brush up on my prayers the first chance I get."

After a few minutes in the closet, Morgan cracked the door open and peeked up and down the hall. Savannah was nowhere in sight and all was quiet. She slinked out, straightened her back, and walked remarkably close to the wall all the way down the hall.

"I am strong and I am not a victim. I can handle this," Morgan repeated to herself on the way to the nurses' station. When she arrived, no one was at the desk. Savvy left it unattended—the phone rang unanswered and more papers were in a pile. She sat immediately and answered the phone. Within seconds, Ellen was at the desk answering another line. When Morgan hung up, another rang. Both women took the calls for a few minutes until the telephone settled down.

"First few days back are rough, aren't they?" Ellen asked as she rolled her chair closer to Morgan. "And what time is Tiffany supposed to be here?"

"I'm sure she'll be in soon."

"With Tiffany, that could mean she volunteered to feed the homeless or had to appear in court for the commission of a felony. You can't tell with her," said Ellen.

Morgan nodded as several lines on the phone lit up. She stared at the phone until Ellen jumped in to help. She continued sorting orders and answering lines until it was quiet again. "You know, Ellen, I'm a little bit rusty. I was home for longer than I thought."

Before Ellen could comment, from the other end of the desk, EC physician Ted Kelly, MD, snapped, "The patient in room 2 needs help to the bathroom."

Relieved and eager for a distraction from the chaos of the phone, Morgan got up and walked quickly down the hall toward room 2.

KATE MACINNIS

CHAPTER 2

Not paying attention, Morgan walked right by room 2. Frustrated at her lack of concentration, she stopped and turned back. Entering the correct room this time, the patient looked up.

"Nurse, I need help, please." A pale, elderly man sat on the side of the bed and dangled his legs. His arm was strapped to an IV with a full bag of clear fluid connected. The room also had a small sink with a soap container and box of sterile gloves mounted to a stainless-steel holder on the wall. There was a closet for clothes and shoes and a large flat-screen television across from the bed on the opposite wall; the landline telephone was on an overbed table pushed to the side of the bed. She glanced at the whiteboard to read his diagnosis, time of arrival, and doctors on the case. His name and age were printed across the top of the board.

"Mr. Gillespie, I'm here to help." Morgan slipped on a pair of gloves and provided support for him to slide off the bed and into her arms. They walked together to the bathroom as he leaned on her for balance.

"Please, nurse, let me have some privacy," he whispered.

"Certainly, Mr. Gillespie. If you're sure you're able to handle this by yourself. I won't be far away." He nodded and gazed at the floor.

Once he was situated properly on the toilet, he waved her away, and Morgan left him alone to tend to his business.

As she waited for her patient to finish, Morgan watched through the window as scores of employees hustled from building to building. Numerous people paced back and forth in front of the imaging center while they talked on their cell phones. There were folks who raced to the main hospital with balloons, flowers, and gifts for the newest babies in their families.

"Nurse, I'm finished," Mr. Gillespie shouted from the bathroom. Morgan hurried from the window and announced herself at the bathroom door before turning the knob and entering. She gasped at the elderly man slumped over on the commode. Next to the body stood a faint outline of Mr. Gillespie: the vision smiled, waved, laughed, and disappeared into thin air in less than two seconds. Hurriedly, she reached out and touched his neck in search of a pulse. There was none.

Morgan's legs buckled but, fortunately, she fell against the wall and sank to the floor still holding onto the doorknob. After a few moments, she got up on her knees and slowly stood. Her heart hammered as she tried to breathe in deeply and swayed again. The faint figure was gone, but her patient was still slumped over.

She pushed the emergency signal button next to the toilet and help arrived within seconds. Dr. Kelly confirmed that Mr. Gillespie was, in fact, dead. Morgan pulled her gloves off, threw them in the wastebasket, and grabbed a paper towel from the dispenser to wipe her forehead as she left the room.

The tears stung her eyes as Morgan sagged against the wall.

Ellen came around the corner. "Still having a tough

day?" she asked putting her hand on Morgan's arm.

Morgan nodded and looked down at the floor. She wiped her face with the towel again.

"Look, maybe we can go to lunch and take Savannah with us. We'll buy her some decadent food and she'll be in a great mood all afternoon." Ellen put her arm around Morgan's shoulders. "Besides, you look like you need a friend with access to good food. You need Coney dogs smothered in chili and onions with a side of chili cheese fries. Wait, a big bowl of spicy hot buffalo chicken wing soup with hot buttered rye rolls is another winner."

"You know, you're right, Ellen. Our aristocratic southern belle boss, as well as me, are suckers for tasty comfort food." Morgan stretched and straightened her back. "Let's get out of here about 11:30, if Tiffany is here by then. I owe Savvy that much for the worry I've caused today."

"Sounds good to me. Hey, did you hear that the new doc is here? Savvy finally hired some hunk to help out in the EC. I've been told that the ladies in Human Resources drooled on him and one had to take an extra dose of heart medicine. And just think, he'll be all ours." Before Morgan could respond, a call light came on and Ellen hurried back down the hall, disappearing into one of the rooms.

Morgan held her hands out in front of herself to check for tremors. They shook so much, she hid them deep in the pockets of her scrubs. As she continued down the hall, she chewed her lower lip and pondered about Mr. Gillespie and his hologram. Her heart galloped when she stopped and looked again at her jittery hands. She shook her hands hard to rid them of the adrenaline overload, but not for long. The *ding* of another call light interrupted her ritual.

The light was on over room 4. As she approached, a wisp of smoke curled from the room and spun around as it spiraled upward. It grew thinner until it disappeared above the door.

Morgan muttered under her breath, "Terrific, clearly someone in that room smoked. Oxygen is used all over the place and some addict had to have a cigarette in the middle of it all."

She was convinced that no one was more of an anti-cigarette zealot than a reformed smoker, and she fell into that category. Whoever puffed away in that exam room would quite the lecture from her when she confronted them. The campus had been smoke-free for years, and there were signs all over the place that warned patients and visitors not to light up. Break the rule and suffer the wrath of Morgan Cutler, who honestly had to admit that a cigarette right now would taste and feel pretty darn good. Nonetheless, she was on a mission.

Once inside, she glanced at the man's name on the board. He was Anthony Jacobs, age eighty-five. He came in an hour or so before with shortness of breath, which was most likely from a lifetime of cigarettes. His back was to the door as he slept on his left side. A shock of white hair stuck out over the top of the blanket that covered his torso. Two women and a man stood next to his bed. They looked up as Morgan hurried in. She glanced at them as she grabbed gloves, pulled them on, and leaned over the patient to turn off the call light.

"We are so sorry, but there's no smoking in here or anywhere on the hospital grounds," Morgan said in her most officious voice. All three were elderly and could easily have been the patient's siblings. One of the women wore a dated coral Chanel suit, the other had on what her grandmother would have called a drab housedress with a faded apron over it. The man wore a suit so old the material was shiny. He held a hat that he rotated through his fingers by the brim.

The people did not speak. Morgan watched as they turned and left the room single file. She frowned even though she knew very well that folks often behave a little weird because of stress. When a loved one is in the hospital, everyone is stressed to the max physically, emotionally, and oftentimes financially. Most people don't think clearly enough to use their best judgment. The way they exited was odd, but not illegal or dangerous. Just a bit off. She shrugged and turned back to her patient.

"Mr. Jacobs, I'm Morgan, one of your nurses. How are you?" She touched his shoulder, but he didn't respond. She pulled on his shoulder and he flopped to his back with a *thud*. No cigarette there, also no breath or eye movement. Morgan inhaled and felt his neck for a carotid pulse—no pulse. For the second time that morning, she hit the call button with her other hand to alert the team to arrive immediately and administer CPR. The buzzer went off and everyone crowded into the small area. Morgan stayed out of the way and watched as the code team experts began resuscitation efforts. It suddenly hit her that there was no evidence of a cigarette and the burnt smell was gone.

After a few minutes, the code was ended by Dr. Ted Kelly. Mr. Jacobs was officially pronounced dead and the time was noted on the electronic chart. Before they left, the nurses who responded to the code picked up the heart rhythm paper strips and medication packets that were thrown on the floor as they tried to save his life. One of the nurses patted Morgan's arm as she left and muttered, "Welcome back."

Morgan stood in the doorway and leaned her head against the cool frame. She focused on deep breaths, in and out. Her head throbbed as she fought the panic.

"What was that curly smoke?" She muttered to herself and rubbed her forehead. She looked up to see a strange man across the hall in room 5 wearing a white lab coat over his scrubs. The scrubs were color-coded for identification—dark green indicated he was a physician; nurses wore royal blue scrubs. The man stepped closer and leaned against the doorframe of room 5 as he stared at her.

When the man turned to check on the patient in that room, there was a long, shiny black ponytail low on his neck. He turned back to face Morgan—his cheekbones looked like carved marble and his blue eyes were intense and sparkled. There was a scar on his chin that made his face more attractive rather than flawed. All the necessary security ID and hospital information cards dangled from a lanyard around his neck. He looked official. Morgan assumed he was the new guy that Savvy hired.

Morgan couldn't take her eyes off him. In some way, she felt he was reading her thoughts and secrets, as though looking directly into her soul. Goosebumps covered both of her arms, so she looked away from the handsome man. Wordlessly, she wrapped her arms around herself and hurried to the computer terminal at the nurses' desk to chart some of the activities of the past couple of hours.

Ellen walked by at the same time Morgan sat at the desk.

"Is that the new guy down there with the black hair and Paul Newman eyes?" Morgan asked.

"Yep, and I'd say you better put a seat belt on. He's just your type," Ellen replied on her way past the desk and down another hall.

Morgan frowned and saw Dr. Kelly at the other end of the desk as he filled out paperwork for the code and subsequent death of Mr. Jacobs. The body would be released to a funeral home as soon as the papers were finished.

"Well, Ted, I have a strange question for you," Morgan said before he had a chance to speak. Ted sighed and looked at Morgan. In the distant past, they dated for a short time and then on occasion. Morgan could barely recall any experiences with him, but she did recollect that Ted expected her to come to her senses and beg him for marriage.

Ted sighed again. "There isn't much that I would rather do than spend time in a conversation with you. Go ahead and ask me whatever you want, and I do mean whatever you'd like to know."

Morgan scrunched up her nose and continued, "Did you see anyone with a cigarette in the room with Mr. Jacobs? An item that could burn, either electrical, tobacco, or paper?"

"No, why?" Ted moved closer.

"I saw smoke outside his room and can't figure out where it came from." Morgan rolled back in her chair to avoid his proximity.

"There was no fire or smoke anywhere near that patient," Dr. Kelly spoke as he wrote more information in the chart from his notebook.

"I know what I smelled and saw, Ted, and it wasn't my imagination. What on earth could it have been?"

"I'm sure there was no fire."

They stared at each other until Ted blinked. "I was really anticipating that there might be an invitation for me to dinner or out for a drink with you."

"Ted, I'm serious here." Morgan grabbed the forms for lab and X-ray results and sorted them on her lap.

"Are you sure you're all right? Headaches? Dizziness? If you notice strange smells that no one else notices, maybe you should call your doctor. Or I could call if you'd like." Ted moved even closer.

"Ted, I'm fine. I know what I saw." Morgan used her foot to push her chair away again.

"Look, Morgan, as far as the smoke goes, I've heard people say it's the soul, if you're into that, as it leaves the body. Supposedly it happens every single time at the moment of death. Most of us are not gifted enough to see it, and maybe you're one of the lucky ones who can. Or one of the unlucky ones, I guess, since you work in an EC. We see more than our fair share of death down here. But the ability to see smoke could cause you to burn out sooner." Ted laughed at his own joke.

"I've been a nurse for years and never saw smoke like that before. Have you, Ted? Have you ever once seen that happen?"

"No, I haven't, but that doesn't mean it doesn't happen. I'm half asleep most of the time and probably miss a lot of stuff that goes on around here." He moved away from her.

Morgan stood and said, "I'll go speak to his family before they leave. One of them could have hidden a cigarette from me. They're probably still in the waiting room."

Ted jerked up from the notebook and frowned as he said, "What family? Mr. Jacobs was alone."

"There were three elderly people in his room who moved out of the way when I went to his bedside."

"Did they speak to you?" Ted took a pen from his pocket and clicked it repeatedly. "I need someone's signature to release the body, if he has family."

"No, I don't think so. Actually, I'm sure no one said a word."

"Do you get enough sleep? Have you mentioned any of these symptoms to your doctor? You weren't off that long after brain surgery. You've barely healed." Ted put his pen away, returned to the notepad, typed a few words, and electronically signed his name.

"Again, I'm fine, but thanks for the concern." Morgan went around the corner to the waiting room. She looked around and didn't see the two ladies or the elderly gentleman. They most likely left the hospital as soon as they could when they heard Mr. Jacobs had passed. People don't like to hang at the hospital longer than necessary. Morgan looked around and saw Ellen race toward her.

"You won't believe my patient in room 10. Her dog bit her. She's a little old lady, perhaps a touch senile, and her faithful companion bit her. You can't trust anybody these days." Ellen grinned.

"Why is that funny?"

"Because she thought her dog was a radio. She tried to change the channel, twisted his dials, and he bit her. Took a big chunk out of her hand, too." Ellen chuckled and continued, "They have identical Detroit Tiger baseball hats because, apparently, both of them are fans. Seriously, the little old lady and her dog have the same baseball hats. You know what his name is?"

Ellen answered immediately, "Vanessa. Yep, Vanessa. I'd bite her, too, if she gave me a name from the wrong gender, especially after she pulled on my kibbles and bits. She's lucky he didn't take her finger totally off. That little guy has an impressive male package for such a small specimen, and she called him Vanessa. That's just outright humiliation for the boy." Ellen grinned as she pulled a lab coat off the shelf and put it on over her sweater and scrubs.

"I'm frozen. I think they turned the thermostat down again around here to save money. Hey, what's the matter?" Ellen adjusted her layers of clothes.

"I thought I was the only one who was cold. No one else mentioned it," Morgan replied.

"Well, if the hospital gets so cheap, we can't have heat, we'll all have to find another way to keep warm." Ellen shivered as she pulled up her sleeves.

Morgan smiled and said, "I guess that's why you have four kids. I'd rather bring a thicker sweater tomorrow."

Ellen laughed and went back to the hall on the right. Just then, Morgan watched the new doctor walk toward the desk. When he was a few steps away, a red light pulsated all around him. He looked at her with an intense gaze and then abruptly turned around to go back to room 5.

Morgan logged into the desktop to pull up the chart on the patient in room 5. The woman had been in a car accident and the trauma surgeons were ready to whisk her to an operating room (OR) as soon as one was available and ready for another case. The space was tight in the surgical area, and it was easier to keep patients in the EC until the last minute when an operating room opened. In the meantime, she was stabilized and continued to receive fluids before surgery.

The new doctor monitored the patient while they waited for the call to surgery. She had suffered multiple traumatic injuries that required surgical repair. Once underway she would be in surgery for a few hours. Coincidentally, the elevator doors across from the desk opened and the surgical team got out to take the car accident victim to the OR. Morgan also noticed Savannah heading in her direction.

"How's your day going? Hear anything from Tiffany?" Savannah asked as she stretched her long frame.

"Oh, it's all good. No, not a word from Tiff. That probably means everything is fine. She'll come blowing in any minute." Morgan turned to face Savannah. "Savvy, do you ever think about death or life after death?"

"I think about death every single day, Morgan. Look where I work." Savannah spread out her arms. "What is your real question? Are you suddenly afraid of death, which would be a normal response to what happened to you?"

Morgan glanced at Savvy and the same green glow from before appeared with faint yellow lightning bolts. She relaxed in her chair and said, "I don't honestly know, Savvy. I can't put it into words."

"I've never known a cat or anyone else to have your tongue, woman. You generally express yourself with the utmost clarity and brevity. Tell me what's in your head."

"Death is a permanent life-changer, especially if you don't plan on it," Morgan whispered.

"Okay, sort of abstract, but I get it. You fear that when death comes again, it could actually be your turn," Savvy said as she signed some forms that were left in a stack for her.

"I don't know where to start or how to explain it, Savannah."

As luck would have it, a patient in one of the exam rooms cried out for help before she could elaborate. Savvy dropped the papers and hurried in the direction of the voice. Morgan made no attempt to follow her.

It was nearly eleven a.m. when Tiffany raced around the corner and hurried to her seat behind the desk. Without Tiffany asking, Morgan stood so she could have her chair back.

"You people always panic when I'm not here," Tiffany said as she surveyed all the papers that had accumulated. "Plus, Miss Priss on the night shift never puts stuff away. I have to come in every morning and clean up her mess first and then begin on my own work." She threw her purse in the drawer and put her keys in her pocket. She gathered up the notes, orders, and assorted debris on her desk.

Morgan stood next to the clerk and said, "Tiffany, did you ever think about the fact that we can't see germs but we know for sure that they exist and are everywhere? No one can argue that unless it's a sterile item or space. But at the same time people argue about whether or not ghosts exist because we can't see them. What if we just haven't invented the tool yet that lets us see them all the time?" Not waiting for a response, Morgan grabbed another chair and sat.

Tiffany stopped and studied Morgan's face. "Okay, good morning to you, too. Look, isn't that exactly what digital cameras are known for? I mean, aren't all those so-called orbs or disks seen on photos really the captured essences of ghosts?" Tiffany shrugged and continued to clean up the piles of paper.

Tiffany's hair was unnaturally black and spiky today, which was a change from the burgundy and spiky. She was pierced all over her face and ears, but the holes were unadorned at work. She was fastidious about her appearance, and other than the black hair and light makeup, she looked like any other young woman. If she had other pierced parts or tattoos, they were hidden and not seen by anyone at Good Samaritan Hospital during work hours.

Tiffany picked up each piece of paper, every phone message, determined its worth, and either threw it away or wrote a note on it before it was re-stacked methodically on the desk.

"I'm constantly amazed at how smart and intuitive you are. You could be a terrific nurse or doctor. You're kind, compassionate, intelligent, and far from lazy." Morgan watched the young woman carefully assess the mess.

The clerk blushed and smiled at Morgan. "It wasn't in the cards for me, boss."

"It's not too late. You're still young."

"Thanks, but I'm not that career-minded. Too restrictive."

"Okay, I'll keep my nose out of your business, but let me ask you this, and it's not work-related. If, suddenly, odd, or unusual occurrences happened in your house and there was no logical explanation, what would you do?"

Tiffany thought about the question as she sucked on her upper lip. "I think that if I'm absolutely sure odd incidents occur that are not the result of my own actions, I would contact a priest or a psychic to come and check it out. I wouldn't want to be hurt by an entity I couldn't see." Tiffany turned and concentrated on the computer screen. "Somebody on the night shift watched porn on my PC again. I just know it's that new nurse aide guy who'd love to get me in trouble."

"I thought IT blocked all that stuff." Morgan studied her fingernails.

"He gets around it somehow and leaves it for me almost every time he works. Jerk." Tiffany typed rapidly on the keyboard. "If these are selfies, I will applaud his efforts. I have a hunch it's plain old run-of-the-mill porn."

Morgan nodded and said, "Thanks for the advice, Tiffany. You're a smart young woman."

Tiffany smiled. "Good luck, Morgan. It can be very dark over there, so be careful. If you decide to contact a reputable psychic, I know people."

Morgan hurried away from the desk—chills running down her spine.

CHAPTER 3

After an enjoyable and decadent lunch, Savvy, Ellen, and Morgan relaxed in the cafeteria. This was a luxury they rarely enjoyed. Most meals were brought from home and easy to fit into pockets. The cafeteria was a break from the usual.

"When will you introduce us to the new guy?" Ellen spoke as she stuffed part of a roll into her mouth. "I assume he has a name. I've already figured out he has a right fine body and looks that cause hot flashes."

"His name is Dr. Lightfoot. Caleb Lightfoot. Don't bother him unless he asks for help," said Savvy. "He wants to get the feel of the place before he meets all of you, and I intend to respect his wishes."

"So, when is the intro?" Morgan blew on a spoonful of buffalo hot wing soup.

"Whenever he's ready. Maybe this afternoon, maybe not. Poor man must be exhausted. He came in overnight and is still here," Savvy said.

"Wow, he's back on duty in just over six hours," Morgan said as their beepers went off and all three women looked at their phones.

"Leave your trays, ladies, we have to get back to the

EC. Now." Savvy stood and hurried to the cafeteria exit with Morgan and Ellen right behind her.

They turned the corner and hit the button for the EC hall doors to *whoosh* open. Once inside, there was a palpable electric tension in the air. Techs scrambled to log blood samples they had taken, pharmacy techs hurried from room to room with new medications, and nurses took verbal orders from doctors and raced to get IVs started and consults arranged. Tiffany answered the phone lines every few seconds and wrote down instructions from the calls. Every nurse and doctor had an assigned phone so they could be reached throughout their shifts. This process eliminated overhead paging and prevented additional noise that could upset patients and families. As a result, no one could get anything done with the constant ringing in their pockets.

A multi-car accident and gunshot wound arrived at Good Sam while Savvy, Ellen, and Morgan were at lunch. Along with the patients, families, emergency medical technicians (EMTs), trauma surgeons, nurses, and techs in the EC, there were also police officers, detectives, TV and radio news crews, and newspaper reporters. Phones rang non-stop and news writers filed their stories from their phones as television people set up remote shots inside and outside the EC. Monitors beeped from every room as they recorded blood pressure, oxygenation, and heart rates.

Savvy and Ellen reacted first and reported to Dr. Lightfoot. The new doctor had taken over triage when the first victim arrived and gave orders to the trauma team, who focused on injuries that could result in immediate death while he handled the media and cops. Morgan watched Savannah for a reaction and was sure that she saw respect in Savvy's eyes.

Most of the rooms were filled with accident victims, in addition to the usual number of cases. Morgan looked around to determine where to begin when she saw Tiffany at the desk giving her a thumbs-up despite the anxious news people gathered in the space.

The most critical cases got attention first—as the rule was always to save the ones closest to death before you saved the others. With this in mind, a woman on a gurney parked around the corner at the end of the hall was loudly sobbing. Morgan turned in her direction and the closer she got, the more blood she could see on the blankets and sheet.

Hurrying to evaluate the patient, the EMT chart at the foot of the woman's bed indicated that she was only forty-five years old. Morgan noted the victim was slender, average height with long red hair and expensive jewelry on her hands and wrists. Her eyes were swollen, nose runny, and she had blood spattered over her entire face as she cried out of control. Even though her body was covered with the blanket, Morgan caught a glimpse of a beautiful designer outfit beneath. The time of death was written in red across the first page of the chart. Morgan saw the time and looked at the patient again. According to the EMT notes, the woman had been dead for over an hour.

"Who would pronounce a woman dead when she can still cry at the top of her lungs?" Morgan mumbled as she checked other pages in the chart. In disbelief, she dropped the chart on the end of the bed, grabbed the gurney, and wheeled the woman to a quieter spot.

"Why did you move me?" the woman wailed with her pretty green eyes wide open.

"I thought you'd like more privacy." Morgan locked the bed down so it wouldn't roll.

"You can hear me?"

"Well, of course I can hear you. Why wouldn't I be able to hear you? People in Ohio can hear you."

"The young man in the ambulance pronounced me dead on the way here," the woman said and again was wracked with sobs. "He kept putting that sheet over my face, and I didn't like that."

"Say that again, would you, please?" Morgan asked.

"The young man in the ambulance said I was dead and gave a time." The patient inspected her clothes, jewelry, hands, and wound.

Morgan stared at her and looked at all the blood spread around the blanket and sheets.

"This isn't fair. It just isn't fair." The redhead struggled to sit up and then poked at the gaping wound in the middle of her chest.

"I understand that life isn't fair, ma'am, but did you happen to notice that your chest wound doesn't bleed?" Morgan whispered and took two steps back from the cart so she could lean against the wall.

"There probably isn't any blood left in my chest to pour out," sighed the woman. "Ah, hell, nurse, life certainly isn't fair and, so far, death isn't fair either. This shouldn't have happened to me."

Morgan pushed the cart around the corner farther out of the way. For now, the patient was fascinated with the hole in her chest.

On her way back to the nurses' station, she felt lightheaded and dizzy. She heard Savannah call out, "Morgan, get a large blood pressure cuff for exam room 8. I can't leave this patient." Savvy stood in the doorway of a room down the hall.

Morgan froze and Savvy hurried toward her. "Morgan. Nurse Cutler," Savvy shouted. There was a large blood pressure cuff draped across a portable BP unit right outside room 3. Savvy grabbed it, glared at Morgan, and went back to room 8.

Morgan jumped when Ellen came up behind her.

"Morgan, did you order the ultrasound for room 2? How about the CAT scan for the dog lady?" Ellen asked as her cell phone rang. She checked it and groaned as she walked back in the direction she came from.

"Yes, I ordered all the tests and labs for everybody before we went to lunch," Morgan said in a loud voice. Ellen waved and proceeded toward the exam rooms as the phone in her pocket continued to ring non-stop. Morgan returned to the nurses' desk and sat at the computer while Tiffany made a cup of tea in the break room.

"You look pale," Tiffany stated as she made her way back to her chair.

"Lightheaded, a little. The world is locked in slow motion," Morgan replied.

"You're in shock of some sort, aren't you?"

Morgan looked at Tiffany and then focused on the window for a few beats before she asked, "Tiff, do you ever notice funny smells around here?"

"The burnt smell mixed in with the aromatic stench of old urine and antibiotics that have permeated the very foundation of this cement block fort? Yeah, sometimes when I go home the smell is still on me," Tiffany said between sips of tea. "For sure, if I have a date after work, I bring clean clothes."

Morgan was nodding in agreement when Savannah suddenly appeared at the desk with an unhappy look on her face and the bouncing green light still surrounding.

"I've had a rough time today," Morgan said before Savannah could speak. "I'll get my groove back."

Savannah nodded as the phone in her pocket rang once more. She sighed and ignored the call as she walked down the hall.

"Constantly calling the doctors and nurses by cell phone was a bad idea. They're so numb to the noise, they don't even hear them anymore," Tiffany whispered. "Hey, did you see the new doctor?"

"Yeah, he was in room 5 a while ago. I don't know where he is now, though," Morgan answered. "What did you think?"

"Too good to be true. I think if he takes a nap in the resident call room, I might have to go peek, but I'm afraid he'll wake up and see me. Then I'd be tagged as a stalker and out of here in no time. It would be a shame because I do still love this job." Tiffany smiled at Morgan who nodded.

"Well, keep your distance till you're introduced at least." Morgan chuckled as she walked around the station. "Savvy is supposed to do the introductions, and it'll have to be soon. The guy has to go home and get some sleep so he can come back and do it all over again tonight."

"He has a charged vibe." Tiffany smiled and pointed at Morgan with her index finger and thumb like a gun. "You're gonna like him. A lot."

Morgan stopped in front of the desk and rubbed her head. "I don't want or need a new man in my life who wants to rock my world or be the center of it. I don't have time or inclination at this point."

Tiffany smiled.

"By the way, before I forget, did you see the paperwork on the gunshot wound lady who came in same time as the car crash?" Morgan asked as she checked the message on her phone.

"Yeah, I put her file in the dead on arrival box for the morgue guys. Why?" Tiffany answered as she typed. She stopped, looked up, and added, "The air in here just changed."

Morgan felt it, too. She shivered, frowned, and reached over the counter to get the paperwork from the DOA box. Both women heard the pneumatic doors from the interior hospital hallway open. Soon EC hospital administrator Miss Maxine Sanders came to the desk with two gentlemen dressed in street clothes. Morgan recognized one as the local chief of police. The other was a detective whom she had seen before but didn't know by name.

Morgan watched as Maxine stood very straight and commanding while waiting to be acknowledged by her underlings—and she considered everyone but the hospital president to be her inferior. Maxine was outlined by a muddy brown aura identical to bedpan contents. This was matched by her argumentative and contentious personality that made her so popular in the unit. Morgan reluctantly went to the desk to speak to Maxine and the lawmen.

"Well, Nurse Cutler, how nice of you to be the EC greeter today," Maxine sneered.

"Yes, Maxine, it's part of my job," Morgan said as she turned to the two men and added, "Chief Hill, what a pleasure." She beamed at the handsome detective.

"Hey, Morgan, it's always good to see you," Ed Hill answered. He was tall, mid-forties, with curly dark brown hair, warm brown eyes, and boyish charm. Morgan dated the detective two years ago and still had a soft spot in her heart for him. If he had been there without an audience they would have hugged and made plans for dinner later. Morgan sighed as she thought about how nice it would have been to have a meal with the man.

"I don't know if you've met our newest homicide detective, Adam Thornton. I told him to always get in touch with you for straight answers," Ed said to Morgan, turning his back on Maxine. His experiences with Maxine throughout the years had been unpleasant, as well.

Detective Thornton held out his hand to Morgan and she shook it. "It's a pleasure to meet you, Ms. Cutler."

"The pleasure is all mine," she answered and felt a twinge in her chest as Adam smiled with his mouth but not with his eyes. When she touched his hand, the image of a scene where he swore to another gentleman that Ed Hill was a dirty cop popped into her mind. Morgan stared at the man and said, "What did you say?"

"I said it was a pleasure to meet you," Thornton repeated.

Frightened by the vision, Morgan let go of his hand and took a step back. In an attempt to regain her composure, she looked at both men and asked, "What brings you guys here today? The female with the gunshot wound to the chest?"

Maxine was not pleased as she could see the conversation was going to be dominated by Morgan. She took in a sharp breath, turned on her heels, and stomped away to the exit.

Ed Hill leaned over to Morgan and whispered, "Do you remember the time Savvy threatened to throw water on Maxine to see if she'd melt? Maxine skittered away like vermin then, too."

"We're all pretty sure that when she's not here, she steals little Scottie dogs and rides a bike into tornadoes as a form of entertainment," Morgan said before continuing, "She happily does the dirty work for the administration like firing people or laying them off. She also saves the hospital a fortune every year with her heartless budget cuts. Truth is every hospital has a Maxine on the business end of things. I just wonder how long we'll have to put up with her."

"No one knows what her age is, and it's hard to guess, but Savvy says that evil is immortal and Maxine will never get older and she'll be here forever." Tiffany giggled. Ed and Morgan joined her with a laugh. "She's special," Ed said with a nod in the direction of Maxine's exit. "Anyway, Morgan, we are here about the gunshot wound lady like you thought. This victim was well known to everyone in the Bloomfield/Birmingham communities. Her name is Gloria Vanderveer or Mrs. Gordon Vanderveer. He's a bigwig at one of the auto companies and she's his stay-at-home socialite wife. They live in Bloomfield Hills, or she did until lunchtime today."

"What happened?" Morgan asked as she directed the two men over to the side of the hall away from the reporters who were not staying in their designated media space.

"This is barely the start of the investigation, but we think the husband is a person of interest. That's how it usually is in cases like this," Ed answered as he watched the TV reporter with the cameraman inching closer.

"I'll tell you what happened," Gloria Vanderveer shouted from the end of the desk. "They don't know anything. They have no clue what happened to me. Why do they say that stuff when they weren't even there?"

Morgan snapped her head to the right and saw a faint image of Gloria covered in blood as she stood leaning on the desk.

"Uh, this might not be the right time," Morgan hissed with her hand over her mouth.

"Well, okay, it can wait. Can you lead us to the body, though? We need to get to work on that since our crime techs should be here shortly," Ed whispered.

Morgan looked at him and back at Gloria.

"He can't see me. No one can see me but you, remember?" Gloria wailed. "He can only see my dead carcass on the cart, but he can't see me now."

"Oy," Morgan muttered and turned to Gloria. Over her shoulder, she said to the detectives, "You guys wait here and let me find the body. I don't know exactly where it is right now, but I promise I'll be back to get you in two minutes."

Morgan gently pushed Gloria with her shoulder and they walked together down the hall. "Where is your bed? You have to get back in it so I can show them your body. You really need to stay with it."

Gloria stopped halfway back to her bed and wailed, "Why? Why do I have to stay with it? I can't spend eternity like this, all covered in blood. This is no way to treat a $2,000 suit. I need fresh clothes. Can you help me with that?"

"I have no idea," Morgan whispered. "I've never had a dead woman ask me for a change of outfits before."

"Hey, Morgan, can you ask somebody where the body is? We need to get busy," Ed shouted because he could see her standing in the hall looking confused. "What?" Morgan looked back at Ed.

"You said you didn't know where the body was. Can you find somebody who does, so we can do our jobs," Ed repeated with his back to the media.

She held up two fingers and said, "I'll be back to get

you in two minutes. I think I know where the deceased is. At least, I know where she was." Morgan turned back to Gloria and hissed, "Get moving now. You have to stay with the body."

"Why? What difference does it make?"

"I have no idea. It just doesn't seem right that you've left it."

Morgan found the gurney and guided Gloria to the back hall.

"Will they touch me?" Gloria asked with eyes wide. "Please don't let them touch my body."

"I don't think they'll touch you. They may look at the wound, but they want the body to be intact for the medical examiner," Morgan answered. "Oh, go ahead and stand by the gurney, but don't leave your body or make a fuss. Got it? This is new to me, too."

"I don't want to watch. Are you crazy? *Why* do I have to be here for this? They don't need me to be able to examine the body, right?" Gloria asked as tears poured down her bloody face.

"I'm not clear about how these things work right now, okay? Just stay with your body while the police do what they have to do and leave. Then we can figure out what you can or can't do with or without your body. But don't leave it again until they're gone, since I don't have any idea what happens if you get separated for too long from it." Morgan raced back.

"C'mon with me, guys, I know where the body is," she said and hurried the detectives to the quiet back hall.

The three of them looked at the beautiful woman with a hole in her chest. The entrance wound missed the heavy diamond necklace; her mouth was open, and she stared dully with lifeless, green eyes.

"This obviously was not a robbery. That necklace is worth more than my house." Morgan looked at Chief Hill.

"Looks like a small-caliber wound at close range," said Adam Thornton. "We'll have her moved to the city morgue where they can confirm." He pulled a notebook out of his pocket and scribbled.

"I know what happened," Gloria said from behind Morgan, who jumped and turned to find herself face to face with the woman.

"I had brunch at the country club today with some of my friends. It was a charity event with all sorts of people there. The valet went to get my car, but he came back and said it had a flat tire, which he offered to fix once the rush was over. I didn't believe him and crossed the parking lot to see for myself. When I got to my car, it did have a flat tire. I didn't know what else to do, so I decided to go back to the valet and call for help."

Morgan stared with her mouth open as she listened to the woman recount the experience. She turned back to the detectives and coughed.

"Morgan, are you okay?" Ed asked.

Gloria stopped and glared at Ed. "Excuse me, officer, I was in the middle of my death story."

"Yes, I'm fine. Allergies. It's that time of year, you know, so hard to breathe." Morgan coughed into her arm and, without looking directly at Gloria, nodded quickly for her to continue.

"Well, I turned away from my car and another car pulled up and rolled down the window. I didn't recognize the car but assumed it was one of my friends. When I turned to face it, I felt a burn and pressure in my chest, like it was on fire. The car sped away and that was it. Just that fast, I died."

"You should—" Morgan realized the police could hear her, so she closed her mouth.

"We should what?" Detective Thornton asked.

"You should find out where her husband was at the time of murder," Morgan said as she shrugged slightly at Gloria.

In response, Gloria whispered, "It's okay, you had to say something."

"Yeah, we know that already. I believe the husband was picked up a few minutes ago, and we will ask him a few questions. There's always the possibility of a murder for hire in cases like this. A lot of folks with money don't get their own hands dirty." Ed turned away from the gurney.

"No one has been here to identify the body yet," Morgan spoke more to Gloria than the detectives.

"Yeah, and the husband is a flight risk. Had his passport right there in the office," Ed answered. "Her sister will be here later today to ID the body."

"Gordon didn't do it. He would never hurt me." Gloria cried again as she stepped closer to Morgan. "My sister? My sister will identify me? That bitch will make a play for Gordon now that I'm out of the way. Not that it stopped her before, but now *he* might be tempted. Damn it, I don't like this situation at all."

"Maybe it'll all work out and you'll find peace," Morgan covered her mouth and whispered to Gloria.

The detectives looked at her and then at each other. Ed frowned and shrugged as he motioned for them to leave. Adam walked ahead of him and Ed faced Morgan.

"Hey, I heard that you had a head injury a while back. Is that over with?" he asked as he touched Morgan's arm.

"I do have to say there are times when I question my sanity. There's a jumble of mixed real memories and pieces of television shows that get fused. I have to take it slow and be patient while all the wounds heal and the wires realign." Morgan smiled as she lied to the officer.

"You'll be back to your old self in no time." He elbowed her gently. "I really like the old Morgan."

"The old Morgan really likes you, too, Chief. I'm always glad to see you, regardless of the reason." Morgan smiled up at him and gently elbowed him back.

She escorted the police back to the EC entrance door. A light came on over room 9 and the phone in her pocket rang at the same time. There was another twinge in her chest as she watched the men cross the parking lot. She answered the phone, frowned, and rubbed her chest right above the heart before turning down the hall to answer the call light.

When she passed the desk, Dr. Lightfoot looked up from the computer. Ellen was there and looked from Dr. Lightfoot to Morgan. She decided to answer the call in room 9 and said, "I'm on it," as she left. Morgan put the phone back in her pocket.

"My guess is that this is not the best day you've had in a while," Dr. Lightfoot said, leaning back in the chair and looking right at home.

Morgan's heart did a little flip when she looked at him. He was certainly more than handsome, there was no doubt about that. He smiled at her, and she had the feeling he was laughing at her a little bit.

"I think you are very perceptive, but I've had worse days," Morgan replied as she leaned against the desk and rubbed her chest absently.

"You've lost two patients, the homicide squad visited, and you frequently drift off to another time or space," Caleb said, sitting up straight in the chair.

A bright red light followed his movements. His clear blue eyes locked on hers as he asked, "Are you having chest pain?"

"No, it's more of a superficial tic and not deep at all. Not a pain really, just a tickle that lasts for a second." She rapped her knuckles on the counter and turned away. After a few steps, Morgan looked back at him. The red glow ramped up and pulsed at a furious rate all around him even though he looked completely calm and collected. "Look, doctor, I always try to do my best even when everything seems to go wrong."

On impulse, she looked at her hands as she held them up to the light.

"Your aura is a bright yellow, almost gold," Caleb said softly.

"So, you know about these things?" She asked moving

closer.

"Sure, there are many different paranormal powers or abilities that frequently become more noticeable after a near-death-experience like you had. Your brain was traumatized and then healed with new bonds created by the network of nerves. Think of it as the ability to see or read energy. You agree that everyone has an energy field, right?

"Yes." She was back where she started and rested her arm on the counter.

"Then think of yourself as someone who can see and interpret that force."

"Okay, I can think about that, but how did you know about my near-death-experience?" she asked as her heart pounded. She looked closely at the sexy scar on his chin that curved like an arc and found herself aching to touch it.

Caleb smiled and answered, "People around here talk. I was told you had recently returned to work after having a brain aneurysm repaired." He then stood, reached across the counter, and placed his hand lightly on Morgan's arm. In a flash, her mind saw him in a hockey uniform right before he was hit in the chin by a puck. He didn't wear a facemask and the blood rushed down his face from the flesh that peeled away from the bone. As fast as the vision began, it was over.

Shocked and scared, Morgan looked him square in the eyes as he nodded.

"Who are you?" Morgan whispered.

"I'm the new guy, Caleb Lightfoot, and this is the first day of my tour of duty here at Good Sam. I still have a chest pain patient who needs evaluation by a cardiologist. Once his wife arrives, I will be introduced to the rest of the team, then go home, get some sleep, and come back and do this all over again tonight."

"Oh, so you're new here." Morgan cringed when she heard herself but Caleb smiled. "Has a cardiologist been down to see him yet?"

Caleb laughed before responding, "No, he needs to be evaluated by a cardiologist. His wife will also be here soon to take him home when the consult is finished. Separately. The cardiologist and the wife will not arrive together. Well, I guess I'd be pretty surprised if they did come together. I can only imagine what that would do to the patient's heart if he's surprised by it, as well. But no, they will be separate."

Morgan winced. Now she knew for sure he was laughing at her.

"I could take you into that closet and make you glad you came to work today," he said.

Morgan's eyes snapped open. "Excuse me, doctor, but what did you say?"

"Not one word out loud. I thought a few but said none of them."

She grabbed at the desk with both hands to steady herself, missed, and landed on the floor. "Do you greet all the new doctors this way? It's unusual, but somehow I like it," he said when he moved around closer and towered above her. He held his hand out to help her up, which she grabbed.

"Thank you, Dr. Lightfoot, and welcome to our team," Morgan said formally.

Still holding her hand, he tilted his head to the left. "You are in the midst of a challenge today as I suspected, right?"

"Yeah, I think that's a fair assessment. I will go now and check on my patients. Your patients, too. All patients. Yes, I will." Morgan wobbled down the hall. She turned to see if he had gone into an exam room, but he stood exactly where she left him. His back was against the counter and his arms crossed in front of him as he watched her walk away. "Damn that thick crust pizza I ate last night," Morgan muttered. She peeked in his direction again when she pretended to check the dirty laundry basket at the end of the hall. He was not standing there any longer.

Morgan checked on the patients in several rooms and forgot about Dr. Lightfoot. Everyone was stable, and she had time to stop in the hall and catch her breath.

Ellen came out of room 9, adjusted her lab coat, and started back to the nurses' station.

"Hey, Ellen. You having a good day?" Morgan could feel her own hands shaking in her pockets.

"I am, and I've been thinking about your problem. You know what you need? You need to get laid. That would cure all of your issues."

"Is that what you tell your patients?"

"Of course not, but you're not one of my patients. Listen, Morgan, you can't be alone forever. It'll bore you to death. Life is about passion and hot sex and the chance to be in bed on Sundays with a great man."

"Which is why you have four kids, and no, thank you. Not now. This is not a good time for me, and I can't deal with another heartbreak. Not now."

Ellen frowned at Morgan. "What heartbreak? Are you talking about Mr. Vegas? It's not my fault you got drunk and married the speaker at the convention. But, be honest, he did not break your heart. You couldn't even remember his name."

"No, I didn't care about that guy at all. He was an unfortunate incident who turned me off hairy backs forever. It's just that when I really care about a man, one way or another it never ends well. My little heart gets broken every time." Morgan stopped and looked at her friend.

"But it's been too long. You're a young woman, and Mr. Vegas was at least two years ago. It's time for you to get back out there."

Morgan shook her head and sighed. "I just can't, okay? There's enough going on while I adjust to the brain surgery and my short haircut that makes me look like a man."

"You're still a beautiful, shapely brunette, just with really short hair now. You can let it grow. Your face is the same. Your hot bod is fine. Don't let your love life wither away. But maybe you need time, so time you'll have. But when you're ready, I have several men lined up for you." Ellen put her arm around Morgan's shoulders and they walked together to the nurses' station.

Morgan sat at the computer away from Ellen, who was chatting with Tiffany. Her curiosity got the better of her, so she decided to search auras. Not that she didn't believe Dr. Lightfoot, but she wanted to check for herself.

All sorts of sites came up. She chose one and started reading. Apparently, a green aura meant a healer, a person committed to love. Savannah had a green light and would definitely be considered a healer and an excellent physician. Pink meant compassionate and romantic. There was no doubt about it that was the perfect description of Ellen. Maxine's brown aura indicated someone who allowed negative emotions to lead them through life. Not a psychopath, but definitely misguided. No surprise there, as Maxine looked for the worst in everyone. Dr. Lightfoot said her aura was gold and that meant an awakening of spiritual energy. She mumbled, "Well, that could explain a lot." Lastly, she typed "red aura." The text scrolled up on the screen. Red meant sexual, sensual, and confident.

"Yikes," Morgan muttered. "Triple threat. Who says this is right anyway? They could tell me that a green means you love lettuce, and I wouldn't know the difference."

She huffed at the screen and turned to see if anyone heard her talk to the computer. Relief settled in when she realized she was alone, but just as she turned back to the screen, Dr. Lightfoot appeared with two cups of coffee. He came around and sat next to her offering one of the coffees.

"No, thanks," she said. "I'm sorry, but I don't drink coffee. It was very nice of you to bring one for me, though."

Caleb smiled and sipped at his hot drink. When he finished the first, he drank the second cup silently. Morgan ignored him and wrote her status notes in the online charts.

After a few minutes of silence, all beepers went off at the same time. Everyone was paged to report to the nurses' station for an introduction to the new EC physician. When the staff arrived, Savannah cleared her throat and spoke as Caleb stepped off to her side.

"It's my pleasure to introduce Caleb Lightfoot, MD, to you," Savannah said.

"Savvy loves to play the hostess," mumbled Tiffany.

Morgan smiled and nodded. "Good thing. The rest of us have pagan sensibilities."

"We're very lucky to have someone like Dr. Lightfoot here on our team. He's Michigan-born and raised but managed to graduate from Harvard Medical School with honors …" Savannah droned.

When she finally finished, Dr. Lightfoot thanked her for the kind words.

"My thanks to everyone for your warm welcome to the team and the chance to spend some time here on your shift. I hope I can be half as good as all of you obviously are," he said. "I'd like to head home now and get some sleep. Thank you again."

The staff took turns shaking Caleb's hand and wishing him well. He smiled, laughed, and took time with each member of his team. He said their names and asked about the hours they worked. He promised a team meeting in two weeks to hear their suggestions and ideas. When everyone had left the desk and went back to work, Caleb leaned over the counter and said to Morgan, "Seems like a nice bunch of folks."

"We are a nice bunch of folks. Most of the time, anyway."

"How long have you been a nurse here?"

"More than twenty years. I was even born here and

trained here." Morgan picked up a cup of tea that steeped hours before. She sipped the cold fluid and shivered.

"Yuck." She turned to Caleb and added, "Tell me, Dr. Lightfoot, I'm very curious, did you get that scar on your chin from a hockey puck?"

"Yes. A hockey puck that damn near sliced my face in half. I'm lucky to have all of my teeth and just this little scar," he replied.

"What happened when you touched me? Why did I see the puck hit your face?" Morgan whispered. She pressed her fist against her stomach as it clenched.

Caleb whispered in return, "You don't understand the changes you've undergone, do you?"

"Why do I think that *you* do? You don't even know me."

"There's a lot involved in this, many layers. Would you like to have dinner sometime or go for a drink?"

"I'm just concerned about answers right now, not entertainment."

"I will only give you answers—right now."

Morgan nodded. "As enjoyable as this is, I don't have time to pull the information from you. If you can't explain the layers now, then it will have to be some other time. I have to get back to work before Dr. Holt gets on my case."

"I would guess that under all that silky, southern charm, Savannah has a nasty pair of brass balls." Caleb pulled on the jacket that he had left on the back of her chair.

"Yeah, Savvy is, at the least, formidable. She's also brilliant, and you're lucky to be here on her staff."

"None of this is an easy explanation, and we will talk later. I will answer all of your questions and give you exactly what you want." Caleb smiled and nodded once before he went out the main EC door.

Just as Morgan was regaining her composure, Tiffany leaned in and said, "You know, Morgan, he's your type."

"Yeah, yeah, and he smells fantastic. Whatever cologne he uses, it's expensive and subtle. You know, Tiffany, he's way too good to be true, which means, he's not what he seems." Morgan took a tissue from her pocket, wiped her chin for any evidence of drool, and hurried down the hall.

Tiffany smiled and whispered, "Oh, you're in trouble with that gorgeous man, Morgan. Big, deep trouble, and you don't even know it yet." Tiffany then grabbed the phone on the first ring.

CHAPTER 4

Morgan returned to the nurses' station and stood in the kitchen doorway. She watched her two best friends, Savvy and Ellen, as they grinned back at her. Savvy broke a powdered donut in two and handed half to her, which she bit into immediately.

"There were two pharmacy techs in the EC this morning. They had a conversation about some woman they worked with who just had a baby. The woman and her husband named the little bugger Berlin, because that's where the baby was conceived." Savvy talked and daintily chewed her half of the donut.

"Thank God that child was not conceived in the back seat of a Thunderbird someplace," Morgan said as she licked donut powder off her fingers between words. She also noticed that she had some on her shoes and knocked her clogs together to shake it off.

"Lucky for them it was a boy. I can't imagine a little girl called Berlin. I would expect that she would naturally have heavy thighs." Savvy turned and washed her hands in the small sink.

"How on earth did you come up with that logic?" Morgan laughed and blew powdered sugar all over the room as she walked to the sink to wash her hands, too.

Before Savannah could explain, Ellen said, "Wow, what if he had been conceived on a couch or in a broom closet?"

All three women giggled, but soon the laughter was not the only sound in the room. Morgan heard someone at the desk and peeked around to see one of the lab techs hovering with a basket of needles, bandages, and tubes for blood draws. Britney L. was the name on her ID tag.

Britney saw Morgan and said, "Yeah, hi, I just wanted to circle back and let you know that the patient—"

Savvy interrupted, "Circle back?" Do you have a wagon train to catch, Britney? You do know what year it is, am I correct?"

"Well, yes, Dr. Holt, I just meant—" the tech stammered as she turned to Morgan for support. Noticing the desperate look in Britney's eyes, Morgan placed her hand on Savvy's elbow to move her out of the way.

"Okay. Dr. Holt, before I leave the unit, it seemed important that one of you here should know that there's a dachshund eating a hot dog in the supply closet." Britney smiled and added, "At least, I hope it's a hot dog, and I'm out of here."

Savannah turned to Ellen and Morgan. "Now, one of you go get that damn dog and his wiener out of my EC. I don't care what you do with it, just get it the hell away before I see it."

Ellen, not wasting any time, raced down the hall while Morgan rubbed her forehead and said, "You're some piece of work, Dr. Holt."

"Now, what does that mean?" Savvy asked with narrowed eyes.

"I mean that you are clueless about how you earned the reputation for prickliness and orneriness, but right there was an example of why you terrify people." Morgan shook her head in dismay.

"Well, I'm sick of those phrases. Some new doctor on

staff asked if he could reach out to me the other day and Ellen had to explain that he wanted to call me. I thought he was a pervert of some sort. Why don't people say what they mean? I'm annoyed by all of it." Savannah sighed and asked, "Was I that bad, really? Maybe I broke a nasty habit for her. That would make me a good person, right?"

"Savvy, you are who you are, and we love you for it. But something besides proper English has you in a snit and you're blind to the effect you have on people."

"Does it matter?"

"I'm really not sure that it does anymore." Morgan tugged Savvy's sleeve to leave the desk area with her once she noticed Tiffany returning to her chair after a bathroom break.

Only a few minutes had passed when Ellen was back with the dog covered in a pillowcase. She said to Tiffany, "I'm not sure who to call, but this is Vanessa, and he needs a sitter until his owner is discharged."

"I'll call the Security Department and they'll have someone watch him," Tiffany answered as she punched buttons on the phone. She spoke to someone briefly before holding the phone receiver out to Ellen. "They want to talk to you."

Ellen took the phone and said a few words. Very quickly she disappeared through the hallway exit doors.

Morgan came back to the desk at the same time Ellen returned from the security office.

"They took Vanessa?" asked Morgan.

"Yes, they didn't want to, but they decided it was easier than an encounter with Savvy because she'd be all over them because they wouldn't help." Ellen looked around the desk area and said, "Let's get back to the topic of a man for you."

"Let's not, Ellen. Remember the whole Mr. Vegas cluster was your fault?"

"I suggested that you should have a few drinks and pick up a man, preferably one from the conference, so he would be reputable, of course," Ellen said. "I never told you to make a forever commitment to a total stranger."

"We had too much to drink, didn't gamble, got overly carried away, and woke up the next day confused and hungover. If I hadn't found the wine-stained marriage license in my purse a few days later, I wouldn't have believed it myself. He was a nice man, whatever his name was, but in the ugly light of day, I didn't appreciate how hairy he was. His back had as much hair as his front. When I asked him how he knew which way he faced, he took it as an unforgivable insult against his manhood, which remains forgettable to me, as well. It took me weeks to have a private detective track him down and all the proper paperwork processed to dissolve the hasty union. No, Ellen, I don't want your advice to the lovelorn."

"It wasn't my fault. You got carried away in the moment because you waited too long and you're bound to do it again." Ellen set her jaw and stuck her nose in the air defiantly.

Morgan rubbed her temples and watched Ellen go to the break room.

Ellen returned with a cup of coffee and said, "That new doc sure asked a lot of questions about you. I wondered if you were in some sort of trouble because he seemed like an undercover cop at first. Of course, the way you looked at him and the way he looked at you, I'd say you are in big trouble, but of a different sort." Ellen wiggled her eyebrows.

"He didn't ask me out. You are so wrong about that conversation. Totally wrong. It was not sexually charged, and I don't even know if he's married or not."

"I already checked for you and Savvy said he's single. I just hope he doesn't have an inappropriate amount of hair anywhere. You know, with your history and all."

Morgan put her forehead down on the desk. "You know that's a trigger for flashbacks of my unfortunate incident, Ellen. It's not funny. Truly, no one can ever unsee a man's hairy back." Morgan choked and tried to grasp her out-of-reach tea. Noticing the trouble Morgan was having, Tiffany pushed the cup within Morgan's reach, patted her on the head, and sat back down in front of the computer.

"It is inappropriate to discuss the physical attributes of the new Good Samaritan employee, as this discussion borders on sexual harassment. Besides, he looked Native American," Savannah said as she made her way back and sat down at the desk. "They don't have hairy backs, generally. The blue eyes threw me, though."

Morgan lifted her head, saw Savvy's grin, gave her a dirty look, and gagged again.

"Savvy, remember Mr. Vegas, Morgan's first husband? We discussed how that started this whole PTSD she has with hairy backs." Ellen giggled and wiggled her head from side to side.

"Please don't say those words," whispered Morgan.

"You need to be a better judge about men. Next time, you must pay attention to how he moves. I didn't get a chance to check the new guy out," Ellen whispered. "You know, to see if he'd be fantastic in bed."

"It's still sexual harassment, even if you whisper, Ellen," Savvy muttered.

Ignoring Savvy, Ellen continued, "You can always tell by the way a man moves. It has zero to do with the length of his feet or his fingers or any of the stuff our foremothers measured. Those myths are old wives' tales, and what did they know anyway? It's how he moves when he walks. If he looks comfortable in his skin, he'll be worth all the trouble he gives you. You can judge best when they're wearing jeans."

"I never once said Mr. Vegas wasn't good in bed." Morgan lifted her head and gulped air.

"Yeah, but if he made you gag that does take some of the fun out of it," Ellen replied.

Savvy grinned, then added, "That's true. I personally

don't like to sleep with men who make me vomit, but to each his own."

Ellen giggled again and Morgan frowned at both of her friends.

Savvy, in return, turned to Morgan and said, "I do believe that I picked up on an attraction between you and the new doctor though, Morgan. Be careful because it can appear to be harassment, and Maxine would love to come down here and reprimand you."

"It may start with a date for coffee, but I think you will have his children before it's over. Which is good for you since your biological clock ticks faster every day." Ellen pointed at Morgan as she spoke.

"He didn't even ask for my number. What is wrong with you two? Cart before the horse, my friends," Morgan replied between her fingers as she had her hands over her face. She put her hands down and realized that she could see auras on several of the nurses and aides who scurried from room to room. Morgan smiled at Tiffany who was on the phone at the other end of the desk. She had a baby pink light, exactly like Ellen's, and it vibrated all around her.

"I am surprised that she's so pink," Morgan said, quickly realizing the words were said out loud. She closed her mouth and looked away.

Savvy and Ellen turned at the same time to look at Morgan. Ellen asked, "Who's pink or what's pink?"

Morgan sucked in her lips and did not say a word.

After a few moments, Savvy said, "Morgan, I'll be the first to tell you that you haven't been yourself, so you must take things very slow for a while, here and at home." Savvy then wiped imaginary food stains from her perfect face. "I do mean the good doctor, by the way. Don't get into a relationship with someone you hardly know, although you have done that plenty in the past. The hospital encourages relationships between employees only because it saves them money on health insurance benefits when households merge, but I'm not sure about the line between good relationships and harassment these days. So, my responsibility is to encourage this, but not while on duty."

Ellen stood and frowned at Morgan. "You need some male attention. But what's pink?"

"A lot of things are pink, Ellen. I said part of a thought out loud, that's all. Also, I will not take romance advice from you, and please do not mention Mr. Vegas again," Morgan said. "I don't want to have another flashback today. It's bad luck."

Just as the conversation was wrapping up, Dr. Kelly arrived at the desk and said, "Hey."

Morgan glanced up and saw a turquoise glow all around him. His hair was thin, blond, and dull complemented by his pasty skin. Morgan had never noticed before how colorless he was.

"Look, I was rude earlier today. Let me make it up to you—how about dinner?" Ted offered.

"No thanks. I'm not hungry," answered Morgan as she stood to leave the nurses' station.

"I don't believe you," Ted snapped. The turquoise light now had brownish-red lightning bolts in it. Morgan backed away as the activity escalated all around his head and moved to his feet. There was one ugly bolt on top of another. "Morgan, stop being so mean, it hurts my feelings."

"Oh, Ted, you stop it. You would need a road map to find your feelings, if you ever had any besides pettiness to begin with." Morgan turned away from Dr. Kelly. "Please just leave me alone," she said as she hurried away from the desk.

The afternoon dragged when the patient volume slowed. Morgan checked the clock several times and knew her shift was not over for another forty minutes. She walked to the family waiting room and sat in front of the general-use PC. When she was sure no one was around, she searched Caleb Lightfoot. Pages and pages of results loaded on the screen. After she read for a few minutes, it was clear that Dr. Lightfoot did indeed get his medical degree from Harvard and completed his residency and fellowship in prestigious medical centers. He volunteered at inner-city clinics and frequently taught safety and first aid classes to high school students. The guy was too good to be true. She sighed and cleared the screen.

On the way out of the waiting room, another nurse asked her to check on a patient in room 3. Agreeing, Morgan walked to the room and went inside.

The gentleman in the bed was Raymond Stevens, fifty-five years old. He was in good health until a couple of hours before when he had chest pain and left arm numbness. Raymond was obese but otherwise healthy and had good color. Even though his dark curly hair was thin, he still had some of his boyish good looks. Raymond was hooked to a heart monitor and an IV. His wife sat in the corner of the room as she stared out the window and tore a tissue into small pieces. Her hair was light and pulled back into a stringy ponytail. Her jeans, T-shirt, and sandals fit her thin frame like a glove. She tapped her foot non-stop against the chair.

"Hello, Raymond, how are ya?" Raymond straightened in the bed when Morgan addressed him.

"I've been better. Scared mostly," he said.

Morgan tapped a button on the EKG monitor and checked the printout. She touched Raymond's arm and immediately turned her head away from him so he couldn't see her face. In her mind, a rapid succession of photographs flipped, one after another. She shook her head to concentrate on the EKG strip. The pictures were of Raymond from the night before.

"I don't know why this happened to me," Raymond said. "My wife keeps me on a strict diet."

With her chin tilted up, the wife nodded in agreement. Her bright red lipstick made her mouth look like a bloody gash across her face. Raymond sighed and looked back at

Morgan.

Morgan picked up the scent of garlic and salami before saying, "You know, Raymond, rather than a heart attack, this could just as easily be heartburn from the two Italian subs you ate and washed down with three beers before you went to bed last night." Morgan scribbled notes on her pad. "The leftover deep-fried mushrooms with cocktail sauce for breakfast this morning didn't help so much either."

"Beer," his wife screeched from the corner. "You swore you wouldn't drink anymore. It'll kill ya, Ray. You keep drinkin' your paycheck and me and the kids'll have to sleep on the streets to stay alive."

Raymond sighed and looked at Morgan with pain-filled eyes that quickly narrowed. "Hey, how did you know about the subs? I didn't tell nobody, so it ain't on the chart." He pointed his finger at Morgan.

"Aw, Ray, it was a lucky guess. I'll get the cardiology resident back in here to check out your test results, but you will likely get to go home soon," Morgan said as she backed out of the room.

"Who said I want to go home? What are you, a witch?"

"I'm just a lucky guesser." Morgan left the room and closed the door behind, charting the incident on the COW parked outside the room. Noticing Savvy coming in her direction, Morgan flinched.

"That sounded pleasant," said Savannah.

"Well, at least Raymond didn't die, so maybe I'm on a roll," Morgan answered before seeing Gloria walking through the EC as if she owned the place. She excused herself to Savvy and hurried to catch up to the beautiful redhead with the hole in her chest.

"Get back to your bed now," Morgan hissed.

"No, they took my body to the morgue, and I don't want to go there. You can't make me watch my own autopsy." Gloria smiled. "That may be the strangest sentence I've ever said."

"Aw, jeez, Gloria. What happened to you is tragic, no doubt. The problem now is I don't know what happens if you leave your body before the light comes for you. Or whatever comes for you. It might not be a good choice to ignore that possibility, no matter what your reason is. Have you seen a light that you're supposed to follow?"

"I saw a light, but I can't go if my husband is in trouble." Gloria inspected her nails. "How am I supposed to fix my nails now?"

"I don't know the answers to any of these existential questions. But fine, do it your way. Just don't get in anybody's way here." Morgan opened the door to the next exam room. "This is deep water to me."

"It's fairly deep to me, as well." Gloria flipped her hair over her shoulder and continued inspecting each room as she made her way down the hall. "I want to find a lab coat to hide all this blood."

"Don't worry about it, no one can see you, remember?"

Gloria waved as she moved along the corridor. She peered into every room and paused in front of some of them.

"There are others like me," Gloria turned and said to Morgan.

"I don't want to know," Morgan answered and went into another patient's room. Inside, an elderly gentleman sat on the exam table and dropped the case for his eyeglasses on the floor. She bent to retrieve it and handed it back to him. He smiled and patted her hand gently as he murmured his thanks.

When his hand touched Morgan, a clear video of the Peakes Funeral Home hearse pulling into a driveway and parking beneath a portico played in her head. Two attendants got out of the car as another attendant came from the pale pink brick structure. They opened the rear door and hoisted the body bag onto a gurney. All three men pushed the gurney inside.

The crystal-clear vision lasted for a few seconds. Morgan knew the sweet little man in front of her would die before the day was over.

She patted his hand and said, "God be with you. Can I call someone for you or stay with you for a while?"

"No, dear, but thank you," he said and stared down at his hands.

Morgan backed away quietly and saw Ellen in the doorway. When Morgan got close to the door to leave, she nodded to Ellen to move into the hall.

"Have we become a closet priest? I have never seen you bless a patient before, ever, Morgan Cutler. I'm way more comfortable with my image of you as a heretic and not a devotee of any particular religion."

"Very funny, Ellen. I'm not the anti-Christ and not without some religious conviction. I just have more of a problem with churches and their leaders than with the tenets. Besides, that is a dear, dear man, and I don't think he will make it through the day. I just wanted to give him some sort of comfort." The women walked together back to the desk.

Another light came on and Ellen abruptly turned into room 7 to answer it.

Morgan arrived at the desk and plopped into an empty chair. Savvy was there reading a chart from one of the emergency transportation services. "Do you want to meet me at the diner across the street and have a quick bite after work?"

Morgan nodded in response.

"Good. I'll head over there in a few minutes and get us a table. You can follow when you get off duty," said Savvy as her stomach growled.

Morgan looked at her and said, "I will."

"You've been pensive all day. More importantly, I've never seen you concentrate like that without a really good reason."

"I'm fine, Savvy. Just let me sort this all out in my own

way and my own time," Morgan answered. She pulled the notes out of her pocket and began to chart on the desktop.

When Morgan finished with charts, she searched for Gloria but couldn't find her. When the shift ended, she changed into the clothes from her locker, hurried to her car, and pulled out onto Woodward Avenue where she made a Michigan turn to get to the diner.

A Michigan turn is when you make a right, dart across all the lanes, and get into a turnaround lane in the median so you can make a left and be on the other side of the road and headed in the opposite direction of where you started. Crazy as it sounds, it works and is far more efficient than a left turn onto a very busy divided avenue with eight lanes.

The diner was a silver railroad car from the 1940s that had been turned into a restaurant during the war years. The diner also, incidentally, served the best breakfast in town. Morgan was convinced that some of the grease on the griddle had been around for seventy-five years, but there was no real proof. The clientele was mostly hospital employees before and after shifts because the price was right, it was close, and the service was fast. Nurses and doctors are discouraged from leaving the hospital campus during lunch or dinner in case of emergencies, making the diner popular since it was on the outermost edge of the campus. Plus, lunch and dinner were thirty-minute breaks and not nearly long enough to go very far to eat. The diner was convenient, charming, and rustic—complete with outside railroad lanterns and removable steps that the owner pulled up and tucked away every night when they closed.

The interior of the old rail car had dusty rose velour seats that were probably deep red velvet in their heyday. Each booth was divided by fold-down wooden tables with inlaid diamond patterns. Space was tight but comfortable as no more than fifty people could be seated at one time— that always seemed to be enough and no one had to wait long to be served.

Morgan parked and hurried up the steps. As she entered the diner, her senses were flooded with the sensation of the bygone era. She experienced a déjà vu moment complete with big band music, retro interior, and patrons dressed in the fashions from World War II. She squeezed her eyes shut for a few moments and listened. When she opened her eyes again, it was modern day and Savvy waved from the far back booth. Morgan walked slowly to the table as the smell of fine diner food made her nauseated.

When she reached the table, Savvy commented, "You look a little green. Stomach bothering you?"

"Yes," replied Morgan as she ordered a large Diet Coke with lemon from the waitress who hurried around to keep everyone served. Savvy sipped her iced tea and remained still. Morgan seemed lost in thought as soon as the waitress left the table.

"If you want some dinner, order it. I plan to eat." Savvy glanced at the menu one last time.

The waitress returned with a Coke and took Savvy's salad order. Morgan ordered a grilled cheese sandwich with extra pickles on the side. She looked at Savvy and braced herself for an attack.

"There's no sin if you need more time off," Savvy said, a concerned look in her eyes.

"I don't need it," Morgan replied, eyes closed. "I wish everybody would stop commenting about my health."

"You're not yourself."

"But I'm not someone else either and I'm not less of a nurse. I faced death, won, and it has left me somewhat changed. Can you accept that?" Morgan spoke very slowly without anger.

"Well, yes, I can. That makes sense to me. I hadn't thought about it in those terms. Thank you. I feel better." Savvy smiled before she took another drink of tea.

"Well, good, because that's what it's all about." After a beat, Morgan added, "So, tell me about the hunk you hired. How did you find him, and why did you keep it a secret?"

Just as Savvy was about to give the details, the waitress arrived with their orders. Before they could ask for refills, she was already on it, grabbing their glasses from the table and scurrying away to get their drinks.

Alone once again, Savvy continued where they had left off. "I should retire in the next few years and hospital admin wants me to train the next guy. Well, you met the next guy today and clearly gave him your stamp of approval."

"Wow, retirement. I just can't see you anywhere but the EC," Morgan said as her eyes filled with tears, feeling the impact of Savvy's words. "And what do you mean 'stamp of approval'?"

"Oh, I didn't hear anything negative from you about him, which can only mean that you completely approve. Besides, it'll be time for me to go in a few years and it's critical to train someone to the ins and outs in order to keep the quality and safety high for the patients and the hospital."

"That sounds like admin speak."

"It truly is. Why should my birth certificate be the sole factor of my employability? If I had a penis, they'd let me be president of the United States at eighty." Savvy was so loud, the patrons in the next booth were startled, and she looked at them for a long moment before they turned back to their meals.

"Who is this Lightfoot guy, though?"

"Am I supposed to believe that you haven't blown up the Internet doing searches on this man?"

"Well, I did look him up but I want your version."

"Fine. He's originally from northern Michigan and went East for his education. He's ready to come back home and chose Good Sam as his roost. I don't believe he's married but could have five ex-wives for all I know. I don't think he has any children. His education is solid, credentials are good, and he has a sense of humor. What more could you want?" Savvy smiled. "Just keep your hands off him until after work hours, and let him make the first move, Morgan."

"What is that supposed to mean? You think I will jump his bones in the laundry closet?" She clutched her chest in mock horror.

"Do I need to remind you about that male nurse who quit because you were 'too sexy to work near,'" Savvy said as she popped a tomato wedge in her mouth.

"It was not my fault that he couldn't handle himself. Besides, that was nearly twenty years ago and men today would never say that. And I'm not as hot as I was twenty years ago." Morgan played with her straw, avoiding eye contact.

"None of us are, child," Savvy said and licked her fork.

For the next few minutes, they ate in peace. Morgan sighed when she glanced at her watch and was just about to call it a night when a horn blared outside—a woman raced by in a vehicle while she texted and ignored the traffic.

The tires screeched followed by a loud *crunch* and a dull *thud*. People from the diner and others from the cars on the road that had moved curbside raced to the scene to help. In the midst of all the chaos, someone had the sense to call for an ambulance, which was there in less than five minutes, since the hospital was right across the street. The life support equipment available on the EMT wagon could mean survival for someone close to death, especially when seconds count.

For Morgan, the disturbance in the restaurant faded away to muffled background noise as she floated. The smells of burgers and pasta became stronger—she could identify every meal served at every booth. Transfixed in the smells, she barely even noticed someone tapping her shoulder, but when she turned around, no one was there.

Confused, Morgan looked around to find the culprit to

the shoulder tapping, but there was no time to waste on that when she noticed Savvy throwing a couple of twenties on the table and starting for the exit.

"Let's go help with triage in the middle of Woodward Avenue," Savvy said as she barreled to the door. "What a way to end the day, huh?" Triage is the process of determining severity of wounds when multiple patients are presented. Categories are assigned and the worst are helped first.

Morgan, following closely behind, went into action. She reached the door a few seconds after and saw Savvy talking to a cop outside before going to the driver's side of the first car and reaching in through the broken window. She checked for a pulse on the woman and shouted, "This one is gone," and moved on to the car that had been T-boned by the woman texting.

The texting woman looked at Morgan and asked, "Why did she say that this one is gone? What does that mean?"

Morgan stared at the woman and tried to think of some delicate way to explain that she was no longer alive. Tears fell from the woman's eyes.

"Oh no, this is all my fault, isn't it? I caused this accident, didn't I? Oh God, this is all my fault. I killed myself and hurt those people."

Morgan took a step back and watched a mist form over the woman who spoke to her, covering the body and twisting, disconnecting, and disappearing into thin air.

"Morgan, get over here," Savvy yelled, startling Morgan back into reality.

Morgan moved to stand at Savvy's side. The strong smell of gasoline and blood permeated the air while they triaged the four remaining people involved in the wreck.

"What is wrong with you?" Savvy was looking at Morgan and shouting while moving on to the next victim, "Get a tourniquet on that guy. Stat."

Morgan pulled a tourniquet from the EMT bag she found inside the ambulance. As soon as she finished, the patient was transported to the hospital with the other three passengers.

For the next two hours, Savvy, Morgan, and the afternoon staff of the EC worked non-stop to stabilize the patients. The woman who had spoken to Morgan was taken directly to the city morgue.

Morgan walked over to Savvy who stood near the captain of the rescue squad.

"Excuse me, Dr. Holt, but I think it's time for me to get home now. It's late and I hope my neighbor let Douglas out. If not, his little bladder will hurt and his belly will be empty," Morgan said, concern in her tone.

Savvy nodded and said, "I'm going to stay here at the EC for a while. Just in case."

"Call me if you need me," Morgan replied, turning in the direction of her car before stopping to address Savvy. "You know, I'm proud to be your friend, Dr. Holt."

"Yeah, whatever," Savvy said and blew a kiss in Morgan's direction.

Exhausted, Morgan got into her Jeep and pulled out on Woodward. There was a crew cleaning up the debris on the road caused by the accident. Morgan turned up the radio and sang along on her ten-minute drive home. Trying to decompress from the adrenaline high, she was too busy singing and didn't notice the holographic couple along for the ride in the back seat of her car.

CHAPTER 5

It was dark when Morgan pulled into her driveway. As she got out of the car, she noticed the lights blazed from the O'Hara house across the street, which was unusual at this time of day for the elderly couple. It didn't take long for the twinge in her chest to reappear.

Like most of the other houses on the street, the O'Hara home was a small bungalow in good repair, very close to its neighbors with only a driveway and slim strip of yard on each side to divide the lots. The bushes and shrubs in the yard were perfectly manicured and Morgan knew the elderly couple worked in the yard nearly every day, rain or shine, before the snows came.

Morgan crossed the street and walked up the sidewalk to the O'Hara house. Before she climbed the stairs to the porch, she could see through the glass front door where Mrs. O'Hara talked on the phone. A soft blue mist engulfed Mrs. O'Hara. As she moved, the blue mist moved with her until it surrounded her, turned to smoke, and suddenly jettisoned upward, right through the rooftop.

The ambulance came around the corner with lights on but no siren. It slowed and pulled into the O'Hara driveway. Patrick Burns, one of the paramedics with City

Service got out on the driver's side as his partner got out on the passenger side and hurried to the front door of the house.

"Hey, Patrick, what's up? Can I help?" Morgan asked from the sidewalk.

"Hey, how are you, Morgan? Long time no see outside of Good Sam." Patrick joined her and kissed her forehead.

"Good to see you, too, Pat. What's going on here?"

"We just got a call from the lady of the house. She said her husband passed away during a nap. She couldn't wake him," Patrick said as they stood on the sidewalk. Morgan could see his partner in the living room with Mrs. O'Hara. "We're here to get him out of there. I appreciate your offer, and it's good to see you out of your scrubs," he said and touched her cheek before he went up the porch steps, two at a time.

Patrick turned back, waved, and added, "Let's grab a coffee on my next run to Good Sam."

She waved back and nodded, turned, and crossed the street back to her own yard. Unable to move into her house, she watched the O'Hara home for a few moments. The stretcher with Mr. O'Hara's lifeless body was brought out. The guys put him in the back of the ambulance and helped Mrs. O'Hara into the passenger side of her car parked in front of the house. She sat very still as the ambulance drove away, again with lights and no siren. Morgan watched as the O'Haras' son sped up the street in his car, got out, rescued his mother, tucked her into his own car, and drove away.

With no other choice than to move along, Morgan opened the back door of the Jeep to get her stuff out. Mrs. Geneva Toland, her next-door-neighbor, who had lived in that house nearly forty years, came out to the driveway and stood at the edge of her yard.

"Hi, Morgan, how are you today?" Mrs. Toland asked with a slight smile. She was small, wiry, and had curly gray hair. She once admitted that she was in her eighties.

"Good, Mrs. Toland. Doug okay?" Morgan pulled her bag from the car and slammed the door.

"Dougie is fine. I did let him out a couple of hours ago and fed him. I had a hunch you might be late tonight." Mrs. Toland looked all around and wrung her hands. "Did you hear that Mr. O'Hara passed away at home?"

"Word gets around fast. Yes, I did hear." Morgan stopped and asked, "What else is wrong, Mrs. Toland?"

"I don't know, Morgan. That's the problem. Did you get a new timer on your lights in the house?"

"No, but I do have a night-light in the downstairs bath and one upstairs for Doug. Was there a problem with Doug?" Morgan inched toward her front porch.

"Well, I'm not sure, but the lights came on in your house today. I also heard a party, like a cocktail party, with laughter and big band music that got especially loud. I came over and looked in the windows, but not a hair was out of place." The elderly Mrs. Toland clasped and unclasped her hands.

"Oh, okay. But you didn't see any strangers around the house?" Morgan had her foot on the first step to her porch, eager to get inside and see if it was the same party she saw the night before.

"No, but I heard plenty." The woman shrugged and shook her head. "Morgan, I have to get back to my knitting right now. I didn't know how to tell you, but every word is the truth, so help me. I'm old, but I'm not crazy or stupid. I know what I heard."

"I don't doubt you for one second." Morgan's compassion for the woman won, and she knew she had a few minutes more to spare; she left the step and walked over to touch her neighbor's hand.

As soon as Morgan touched the woman, she jolted backward. Without fail, her mind flashed with a series of photographs. She saw Mrs. Toland balanced on a tiny stool as she peered into the living room windows, then fall off the stool and limp back to her own house. Just as quickly as it appeared, the vision was gone.

"Everything will be fine, Mrs. Toland. I probably left the television on or the radio. I forget sometimes," Morgan said, trying to comfort her neighbor before heading back to her porch.

As the neighbor walked away, Morgan noticed her limp. "Did you hurt your ankle when you fell?"

"Just a little, it'll be fine. It's not broken." Mrs. Toland walked back to her house. "How did you know I fell?"

"It was a good guess—falls are among the most common household accidents," Morgan lied and added, "Make sure to let me know if you need help."

Mrs. Toland waved over her shoulder and slowly walked up the two steps to her porch. Morgan wanted to make sure she got on okay, so she stayed and watched the woman go inside, lock her door, and turn off the lights.

Morgan glanced up and down her street. Most of the trees had not leafed out yet in her neighbors' yards, but the trees and flowers in her yard were thick and heavy with blooms.

"That fertilizer does wonders," Morgan said aloud. With keys in hand, she reached to unlock the front door, but before she could insert the key, the knob turned and the door popped wide open.

Morgan yelped and stared at the open door. Douglas would certainly bark if there was an intruder around. She sidled inside, closed and locked the door, and stood still as she listened.

The sound of her pounding heart filled her ears. She put her purse and keys on the hall table and called out to Douglas. He scampered from the living room to greet her, barking once, and shaking his stubby tail when he saw her.

Just as before, Morgan grabbed a baseball bat from the front closet and walked around the little house to confirm it was safe. She checked the back door and it was still locked. She returned to the front of the house and opened the basement door, turned on all the lights, and hurried down the steps. The basement was one large, nearly empty room. Morgan sighed in relief when she didn't notice anything out of the ordinary and went back up the stairs to the main floor. Douglas waited patiently at the top so she could scratch him and get welcome home kisses.

She stood in the entry hall and heard muted music coming from the library where a radio and retro record player were kept. Douglas barked and Morgan went to the kitchen to let him out the back door. When she entered the room, the light in the kitchen was already on. She counted to five, trying to remember if she had turned the light off before going to work. Leaning against the wall, she mumbled, "Have I totally lost my mind? This morning feels like a hundred years ago and I can't remember what I did."

She let Douglas out and watched him waddle down the steps to the backyard. Morgan could still hear the music mixed now with faint laughter and the sound of fine crystal glasses as they *clinked*. She was positive it was inside the house and left with no choice but to confirm her suspicion. Leaving the door open, she kept the baseball bat on her shoulder as she walked to the front hallway and stood between the living room and the library to listen. Gales of laughter and piano music swelled and faded over and over.

Douglas came back inside and barked for his cookie. She hurried to the kitchen, tossed his treat to him, and raced back to the outside of the living room. She heard distant voices and concentrated on listening.

She could have sworn a man whispered, "None of this is my fault."

Then a woman replied, "It's never your fault, is it, darling?"

Morgan remained still and focused on the conversation until she glanced around the first floor of her house. Doubting herself and desperately trying to explain faraway disembodied voices, Morgan decided to check the television to make sure it wasn't left on. With some relief, she propped the baseball bat against the stairs and opened the door to the living room only to face the dark television screen.

"How could it not be on?" She asked out loud, leaning against the cool plaster wall and staring at the dark television. Just then, an image passed across the screen. Instantly she felt her legs weaken. She put her hands on the wall to brace herself as the image passed in front of the screen again.

She hurried out of the room, got her baseball bat, and went back to the kitchen where the door was open and Douglas stood in the entry.

"Didn't I shut the door?" She put the bat on the counter then closed and locked the door. The dog danced from foot to foot as he looked her in the eyes.

"No more treats, Douglas. Go to bed." He raced off to his bed in the living room by the fireplace.

The distinctive *blip-blip* noise of the television remote filled the air. Morgan leaned on the counter as Douglas barked from his bed. Instinctively, she grabbed the bat and hurried to the living room where she found Douglas staring at the ceiling as he barked. His head went back and forth as if watching an invisible tennis match. Not knowing what to make of it, Morgan gulped in air and headed back to the kitchen.

She made one more security pass through the house and found no changes. She entered the front hall, looked in the living room again, and this time Douglas was snoring from his bed. The remote sat on top of the TV, where she left it the night before, and the television was dark. The library was quiet. Bathroom was empty. Dining room unoccupied. Back in the kitchen, Morgan filled the teakettle and placed it on the stove. With the bat balanced under her arm, she paced around the room until the kettle whistled. When she reached for it, she noticed a mug, saucer, and tea bag already on the counter and had no memory of placing them there. She poured the water, turned to put the pot back on the stove, looked back, and the saucer had been placed on top of the mug so the tea could steep.

Tears flowed down her cheeks as she clutched the baseball bat close to her chest and paced quickly back and forth across the room. She shouted all around the room, "What are you, and where are you?" No answer. She sat at the table and wiped her eyes and nose on the sleeve of her shirt.

"Whoever is here with me, show yourself, you *coward*. I can't live like this, and I don't understand any of it." She looked around the room for movement or light. Again, no response. The kitchen clock loudly ticked off each second.

She added milk to the mug of tea and carried it to the living room where she sat on the couch. Douglas wandered over to check on her, as if he sensed something wrong, so she hugged his head, letting him know everything would be okay.

"My little man. I've had a strange day. How was yours?" She snuggled him close to her chest and held tight.

It was 9:30 p.m. when Morgan turned out the lights and went upstairs to bed. In her bedroom, the little television on the dresser rapidly turned on and off and created a strobe light effect. A bitter smell filled the bedroom intermingled with a musty, wet cement basement floor odor. Douglas was wide awake, his head swiveled left to right. The curtains next to the bed billowed over the closed—and locked—window.

"Okay, that's it. Now, I'm pissed. I don't know who you are or what you are or what you want, but I've had it. I'm tired, scared, and have lost my sense of humor today. Get the hell out of here or make yourself known so we can work this out." Morgan's breath created bursts of icy fog as she shouted. The room became colder each second with bright orbs dancing midair. The brilliant dots flashed and reached a fever pitch, which excited the television in an accelerated frenzy to click on and off.

Two orbs hovered right in front of her face. Too bright to look at, she covered her eyes with her hand and when she opened them again, the orbs were gone. In a flash, the room was quiet. No orbs, no strobe light, and no cold. Still scared, Morgan did not bother to change her clothes and, instead, shot under the bedspread, curled into a ball with her head covered, and cried until she fell asleep.

The next morning, Morgan stayed in bed and thought about every incident of the past twenty-four hours. She listened for sounds that could indicate she was not alone in the house.

She got up, looked around the bedroom, and powered into the bathroom to shower.

She lathered herself and began to relax when an icy cold breeze washed over her. She tested the heat of the water on the back of her hand and it was fine. She rinsed as fast as she could, but not fast enough—a cold hand touched her neck causing her to stop. She jerked around. No one was in the shower with her, so she decided it was her imagination and proceeded to finish rinsing. Not even a minute passed before an icy finger traced her skin down to her backside. She stood very still. The cold digit again started at her neck and traced a line all the way to the top of her thighs in front, leaving a distinct trail in the soap. The hand was suddenly at the front of her neck and rubbed from side to side. She screamed and bolted out of the shower. Soap and water dripped everywhere. Morgan counted to three, hopped back in the shower, rinsed wildly, and scurried out. She dried her hair with the towel, ran a comb through it, dressed, and raced downstairs to the kitchen.

Her hands shook as she reached for the clean mug on the counter, but just as she was about to grab it, the mug glided away. She reached for it again, but it slid out across the counter farther than before. She clenched her jaw and positioned her left hand behind the mug, touching it with her right, and watching as it hit her left hand while scooting away from her. It was now trapped between her hands, so she picked it up, filled it with water, opened the microwave, put the mug in, and set the dial.

"If there is a ghost in that mug, he will be nuked." She looked around the room for some sort of reaction to her statement. Nothing happened.

While the microwave hummed, Morgan again heard music inside the house. It stopped for commercials, and she thought about the radio in her library. Douglas appeared and needed to go outside and since his wants and needs far outweighed her own, Morgan opened the door for him and without hesitation, he bolted into the fenced yard. She put a scoop of food into his bowl and watched him as he looked up at the sky, as though he could hear someone in the clouds. He wagged his tail at the unseen speaker and then darted around the yard as he did when he was happy to see her.

"This is great. Either my insanity or my hallucinations have rubbed off on the dog," Morgan mumbled as she rubbed her face with both hands. Douglas playfully crouched on the ground and jumped at something imaginary, which he returned to the invisible friend. He seemed to be playing fetch, which is unusual for a bulldog. He slowed down and came back to the patio exhausted. She let him in, grabbed a cookie from the jar, and placed the treat in his mouth. He then scampered away to the living room. "I am a well-trained bulldog owner," Morgan said to the ceiling.

She stood in the kitchen for a moment and then went to the refrigerator, which was often empty except for fresh milk for tea. The freezer represented possibilities but remained a disappointment most of the time.

She looked inside and found a blob that had once been cheese but qualified as a biomedical science experiment. She threw it in the garbage and walked over to the counter where she kept a small pad and pen.

She picked up the pen and whispered to herself, "I will buy cheese and some bread. That should last for a while."

Instead of "cheese," she wrote, *We are at the general's party.* Morgan frowned at her hand and the pen. She put pen to paper again and wrote: *We are dancing and dancing the night away.*

"I don't know any generals and, secondly, I would not dance a night away. There are many diversions that could entertain me overnight, however, dancing would not be one of them." She again looked at the ceiling as she spoke and wondered why she did that. For some reason, it seemed right. Frowning, she reached for the pad again. She held the pen tightly, but it was of no use as her hand slammed to the paper. She struggled to let go of the pen and push the paper away but to no avail. Before she knew it, she was writing again: *We are here to help.*

"Help who?"

You, darling. Morgan watched her own hand write the note.

"I'll take a leap here and assume you are not a family member who wants to communicate from the other side. My relatives never used the endearment 'darling' and probably only heard it on television." Morgan looked around for movement of any sort. There was no response to her comment.

"Just exactly who are you?" Her hand moved and dramatically poised itself over the paper.

Jonathan Henry Wilkerson. She wrote the complete name with a flourish like an autograph on the Declaration of Independence.

Morgan grabbed a kitchen chair and sat at the table. She put the pen and the pad on the table and held her head with both hands for a minute. She jumped up and raced to the bathroom to vomit.

After a few minutes, she composed herself and returned to the table. She picked up the pad and read what was written, studying the writing intently. She had watched as she wrote it, but the script itself appeared to be very masculine.

"Before, you said 'We. We are here to help.' Who is the other person? And help with what?" she asked aloud.

Elisabeth and Jonathan Henry Wilkerson, we're both here. She wrote in a very fluttery feminine script. At that moment, the room swirled and Morgan fainted.

When she awoke, dazed and confused, her first instinct was to mutter, "There is not only a trainload of crazy in my head, but it also carries passengers. You really are here with me, aren't you?"

There was no response.

She cried until it was too hard to breathe and texted Savannah at the EC to say she wouldn't be in for work. The cell phone rang immediately.

"What's wrong? Do you need me to send someone over?" Savvy asked her question as she gave orders to people around her.

"I'm so sorry, Savannah. I just don't have the energy to deal with work today."

"Morgan, did some delicious man spend the night in your bed and leave before you had a chance to say good-bye?"

"What? No, I worked late and went to bed alone. At least I think I did."

"Okay, then. Are you sick, sugar?"

"No, insane."

"Well, we can fix that. There are some wonderful drugs on the market. We just need to figure out what kind of crazy you are. I'll be over after my shift. Do you want me to stop and get supplies for you anywhere?"

"All I need is food and a drink. Right now, I'm headed back to bed."

"It's all gonna be all right—don't panic. We can figure this out and fix it."

"Savannah, you can cure almost any condition, but this might be more of a challenge than you've ever faced before. On the other hand, you're probably the only one who can help me." Morgan sighed and clicked off the phone.

"Okay, Wilkerson people. Who are you, and why are you in my house?" Morgan looked up at the ceiling with no response and no movement.

After a pause, Morgan went to the living room and curled into the corner of the couch. She grabbed the clicker, covered herself with an afghan, and turned on the television. There had to be a Cary Grant or Clark Gable movie someplace. A classic movie channel was the medicine of choice.

However, no matter how many times she pressed the power button on the remote, the television would not turn on. Frustrated, Morgan walked over to the set and felt around. She jerked her hand when a frozen blast of air came from the back of the TV. She sniffed the air and wrinkled her nose. It smelled like burned wood. It had been cool outside for several days, so she immediately thought maybe one of her neighbors had burned logs in their fireplace. She walked over to the picture window to see if there was chimney smoke nearby. Not seeing any smoke, she peered up and down the street and saw the old man, Rudy, three doors down and across the street. Rudy ran a tiny grocery that sold milk, bread, and very few other items. His father opened the shop before World War II and Rudy lived there above the store all his life. He often stared at Morgan's house from his upstairs bedroom window much like a creepy sentinel.

Rudy never bothered her, never waved, never approached, he just stared. He was very old and stayed in his little grocery all day until it was time to go up to his apartment at night. Everyone in the neighborhood stopped there a few times each week for some milk or a loaf of bread to keep him in business, but he didn't have much in his inventory anymore. He was crabby and chased the neighborhood kids away if he believed they lingered too long. His accent was Eastern European of some sort, but no one knew for sure because every conversation or exchange of pleasantries was brief.

Just then, Morgan's cell phone rang in her pocket and she jumped. She pulled it out and saw Ellen's phone number on the caller ID.

"Hello." She walked away from the window.

"Hi, Morgan. You okay? Savvy said you were sick," said Ellen.

"I had a rough morning and couldn't handle work, but I'm okay," Morgan said.

"Rough as in what?"

"Not being back to my old self yet. Nothing specific, okay?"

"Okay, I guess you'll tell me when you're ready."

"Or when you're ready."

"Yeah, when I'm ready. You sound very mysterious these days and that's not like you at all."

"I know. Some parts of my life need be sorted out right now. Give me some time and I'll explain all of it. Promise."

"Okay, my friend. I'll be here when you need me." Ellen hung up.

Morgan made rounds throughout the house and had the phone in her hand with one finger on the 911 key. She checked every door, window, and when finished, went back to the living room.

This time the TV turned on easily and she was able to find an old movie with a favorite actor. She was asleep on the couch almost immediately.

A couple of hours had passed when Morgan jumped awake. She looked around the living room and the television was still on the same channel as it was before. She thought she heard something and held her breath while straining to listen. A very soft voice said, "Wake up and make yourself presentable."

It was nearly four o'clock and Savvy would be there

soon, but who ordered her to wash? She went upstairs to the bathroom and took a good look at herself in the mirror. She had bags under her eyes along with dark circles that made her look as she did in the old days of heavy drinking and late-night parties. She covered her face with a steamy washcloth while counting to five. When she peeled the rag off, someone flitted by in the mirror, which caused her to cover her face again and then drop the rag quickly. A man's face was at the two o'clock position on the mirror. He was handsome with curly blond ringlets, a well-trimmed mustache, and brown eyes that twinkled with charm. He had a warm smile as he looked into Morgan's eyes. They stared at each other for a few seconds before the doorbell rang interrupting their connection. She turned toward the sound and quickly looked back into the mirror. The man was gone.

CHAPTER 6

Savannah stood at the door with a bottle of peppermint schnapps, carryout from a local deli, and ingredients to make hot cocoa. She was dressed in jeans and a long-sleeve polo. Her blonde hair was piled on top of her head, making her look positively regal.

"Savvy, you have a dignity that cannot be compromised even with jeans." Morgan sighed when she opened the door and stood aside to let Savvy come in.

"Hunh? Whatever are you talking about, Morgan?" Savannah entered the house and moved quickly to the kitchen. "You have the oddest expression on your face."

"I was wondering what it would be like to be you for a little while. Just a little while, you know." Morgan shrugged and added, "Busted. But if I looked like you for two weeks, I'd wear out all the parts."

Savannah put the food in the empty refrigerator and looked at Morgan.

"You are one of the smartest and quickest minds I have ever known, Morgan Cutler. Do not waste one second of your precious life with the desire to be someone else. It's a folly, and God doesn't want you to wish your life away. Besides, you get your share of everything you want and then some."

"I don't deny that, but you have such a monied, privileged forbearance. It's class, Savvy. Pure class that comes from generations of class. You can't buy it, and you can't fake it, but I'm envious."

Savannah frowned at Morgan, ignoring what she said. "I intend to make some cocoa for both of us with a touch of peppermint added to it. How does that sound?" Savvy searched high and low for a saucepan and lid.

"I saw your touch of peppermint and it's more than 100 proof," Morgan said as she slid into a chair at the kitchen table. "You southerners sure do know how to sugar-coat, don't you?"

"We do acknowledge and appreciate the genteel side of life, but don't be fooled. Every last one of us is made of steel. Still amazes me that we lost the war. My granny used to keep Confederate money because she was sure the South would rise again and she wanted to be ready to go out and shop when it did."

"Were you close to your granny?"

"Lord, no, Morgan. That woman descended from a proper family line that had very tight restrictions on how women could behave and who they could marry. The older I get, the easier it is to understand her frustrations. She had a terrible life and then reported to the gates of hell when she left this earth." Savannah sighed and batted her eyes as she smiled sadly at Morgan. "That woman was the mother of my mother, and by the time I knew her, she almost burst with anger. Her daddy fought in the Civil War for the Confederacy. Her husband's father, my great-grandfather fought for the North. Can you imagine what the holiday parties were like for their people? My grandparents were both born in the late 1800s, and the Civil War was still fought, albeit not officially. I would not have wanted their lives."

Savannah opened several more cabinet doors looking for a saucepan. "Okay, enough of that ancient history. Talk to me, Morgan. Tell me what's got you tied up in knots." Savvy found a pan and placed the milk, cream, and cocoa on the counter next to the stove.

"I will scrub this pan before I use it. You should be ashamed of the condition of your refrigerator, the utensils, and cabinets. I had no idea you were so disrespectful of the kitchen." Savannah searched for dish soap.

"Disrespectful? Of a room? Now you're being silly," said Morgan yawning and watching Savannah on her quest.

"Disrespectful of the process to provide sustenance for humans to consume. No wonder you never get sick; you're exposed to all kinds of germs in this room that will probably reinforce your resistance to nuclear attacks." Savvy sniffed when she found the dish soap in the pantry.

"Savannah, who cares? I rarely eat here since it's not a hobby or joy for me to cook and eat alone. Besides, I can eat peanut butter straight from the jar and skip the bread," mumbled Morgan.

"Remind me not to eat peanut butter here. I have known you for half of your life and have never seen you do more than boil water and make toast. Wait, actually, I take that back, you did make a bowl of cereal once."

"Cheerios are my favorite." Morgan perked up and smiled before adding, "I had to learn to cook to avoid starvation; however, sometimes I add white chocolate yogurt instead of milk. That's when I'm in a gourmet mood."

As Savannah dried her hands on a paper towel, Morgan couldn't help but notice Savvy's perfectly manicured nails. This prompted her to look at her own hands, causing her to shake her head and sigh at the awful sight.

"You trouble me, child," said Savvy.

"What if I have a tumor? What if the aneurysm is back? What if I'm crazy? What if I can't be fixed?" Morgan blurted out the words and froze as she waited for a response.

"Morgan, what? You don't make sense, sugar," Savvy

said as she finished measuring the ingredients and stirred the cocoa.

Unable to hold back, Morgan sobbed and Savvy turned off the burner and hurried to comfort her.

"You have to start over and explain to me what on earth you're so upset about. I'm mixed up here and don't quite understand what the problem is exactly," said Savvy as she let go of her friend.

Morgan stood, paced around the room, and recounted the details of her experiences, holding back nothing. Savvy listened patiently with a worried expression on her face. When Morgan finished, Savvy got two mugs from the upper cabinet, rinsed them out, and placed one in front of Morgan and one in front of herself. She reheated the cocoa and poured the mixture into both cups with an added generous splash of peppermint schnapps for medicinal effect.

"Say something, Savvy."

"Drink your cocoa."

Morgan sipped and said, "I have never given the afterlife much thought or credence. I've had issues with religion most of my life, but I do know that what I've seen and heard is real. I just don't know why—if it's because of spirits or ghosts or a humongous new tumor in my brain." She grabbed a tissue from the counter, wiped her eyes, and blew her nose.

Savvy cleared her throat and said, "Well, I'm worried about you, so the first step is to have your neurosurgeon order a CT with contrast or an MRI to rule out a recurrence of the aneurysm, new tumors, cysts, or whatever one could consider major distortions. Given that you do not suffer seizures, headaches, or other symptoms, I'm more inclined to believe that your experiences are not based on a recurrence or new growth of some sort. I believe they are more psychical."

"Great, just great. You think I'm nuts." Morgan slid off the chair and paced around the kitchen. "Great. Dandy.

The rest of my life is ruined."

"Morgan, I did not say psychotic, I said psy-chic-al, as in psy-chic. You may have psychic experiences that you acquired as a result of the accident. Let me remind you about how lucky you are that aneurysm blew while you were within the safety of the hospital's four walls. Not many folks ever live to tell about it."

"I'm grateful, but I want my life back. Pure and simple."

"We've been friends for twenty years, and I'm going to help you get through this—remember, you're not alone. Also, it's my training not to freak out, and I'm good at sorting bits of information." Savvy sipped her cocoa and continued, "Everything you've told me is likely caused by something fixable. That's what we're looking for here—fixable."

Morgan nodded and asked, "Do you believe in ghosts, Savannah?"

"I grew up in the South, and you know that we're a deeply religious people instilled with the fear of God. If you believe in an afterlife, you likely believe in spirits. I also know that my mother and her bug nuts mother were both of the psychic persuasion. Besides, when I came in here today, the hair on the back of my neck stood up and saluted. I sensed something afoot."

"At my house, religion was not that important unless it was Christmas, Easter, Palm Sunday, or Ash Wednesday. I'm out of my element here."

"This is not necessarily religion-based—it's more about quantum physics. If we believe theoretically that all of us are born with a sixth sense, then it makes perfect logic that scores of people enhance their psychic abilities after a head surgery or near-death-experience like you had. *Bang,* they survive like before—until one day the magic happens. They can see dead people like that little kid or hear conversations from the other side or smell food from a party. Some can even tell the future, which might come in handy for both of us, my friend, so please look for evidence of that. You need to keep a journal so you don't feel like such a victim—journaling is one way to do that."

"Oh yeah, well, how am I gonna keep a journal when the damn ghost or whatever it is uses my hand to write notes? Huh? Explain that to me, Dr. Holt." Morgan crossed her arms defensively.

"Morgan, you want control, and we need to determine if there are any trigger foods, drinks, or activities that prompt the appearance of your episodes. Is that all right with you? I will try to approach this as a scientist and not entirely as a friend."

"Oh fine, just fine. I'll do whatever the hell you want. Just help me, Savannah. I'm so tired and so scared and I don't know what to do." Morgan sat down heavily in the chair.

"Okay, that's good. Look, instead, let's go to the diner and get a couple of Coney dogs. I am not in the mood for the food that I brought. Does that sound good to you, Morgan?"

"I think you're a genius, Savannah. I think that sounds fantastic, but didn't you have them for lunch this week already?" Morgan asked as she picked up the mugs to place in the sink.

"Is there a limit on how many I can have?"

"No, but you usually contain your desire for hot dogs for some reason. Personally, I'd eat them every day if I had the time to get them." Once the mugs were placed in the sink, she turned back to Savvy and said, "Savannah, please don't tell Ellen about this, okay? I don't want her to think I've lost my mind."

"No one could drag this out of me, my friend," Savvy said as she crossed her heart.

"Let's go, I'll drive." Morgan grabbed her purse and keys.

Morgan locked the house, unlocked the car door for Savvy, and drove toward the diner across from the hospital.

"Morgan, you need to clean your car because it smells musty." Savannah looked around the interior. "I don't see anything repellent, but it's so strong, it has to be right in here."

"Are you a snob and think every car that isn't a Cadillac or a Mercedes has a certain stink?" Morgan smiled, then sniffed and said, "Hunh, it's almost musty or old moldy newspapers. That's odd because the seats are leather and not cloth. They never stay wet."

Savannah looked in the back seat. "I just know you've left a sandwich in here or some critter crawled in to die."

Morgan slammed on the brakes and shouted, "There's a woman in the back seat with light red-blonde hair in a French twist with soft curls on top of her head just like in the 1940s. She has a white blouse on and appears about forty-fifty years old." After a beat, she added, "She just disappeared."

"What on earth, Morgan. Don't shout, I can hear you. You scared me to death," Savannah muttered as she turned back in her seat. "I want to determine the source of your car's pungent offensive aroma and you made me think we were in for a head-on collision."

"Sorry, but did you hear me? Did you hear what I said, Savvy?" Morgan drove fast the remainder of the way and glanced constantly at the mirror. "The mirror fogged over, so I wiped it and there she was. There isn't enough humidity in the air to fog the mirror, not to mention the pungent smell of old, wet wool or dog."

Savannah glanced into the back seat and said, "Morgan, tell me again what you saw."

"A blondish reddish-haired woman in the back seat. It was only for a second, but I'm sure that I saw her." Morgan struggled to control the car and her tears.

She turned into the diner lot, parked the car, and jumped out. She opened the back door, desperately searching for any signs of the woman. Not finding what she was looking for, she opened the rear hatch door and looked inside, working her way all around the car as Savvy just stood and watched. After a few minutes, Savvy turned and went inside the diner. Morgan saw her leave and knowing there wasn't one shred of evidence to support what she saw in the car, she closed and locked the doors before going inside the diner, as well.

"I was afraid to tell you about the strange noises and activities at night in the house because you might judge me and think I'm hallucinating, and this is a perfect example of that. I saw what I saw," said Morgan angrily as she plopped down in the booth across from Savvy.

"Believe me, you're incapable of hallucinations without some help from big-time drugs, Morgan. You are aware that even though you didn't tell me the extent of these kinetic disruptions, it didn't lessen the experience," Savannah spoke in a calm and gentle manner.

Despite her demeanor, Morgan saw the yellow bolts all around Savvy's aura again.

"Are you frightened or are you angry?"

Before Savvy could answer, the waitress appeared at the table and asked for their order. "We'll both have loaded Coneys and chili fries on the side. Please also bring Diet Cokes for us," Savvy told the waitress. She looked across the table and Morgan nodded her agreement to the order.

"Do you think I'm incapable of fear?" snapped Savvy as soon as the waitress left.

"No, but I've never seen it on you before. It does, indeed, prove that you are no more than a mere mortal like everybody else. That alone is hard for me to digest."

After a few minutes, the waitress served their drinks and the hot, steamy food. Morgan broke the silence by commenting, "For such a genteel southern lady, you can really suck down food with lightning speed. I've had two bites and you're almost finished."

"I am clearly more focused than you are," drawled

Savannah.

"Savvy, don't be mad at me. Who else can I talk to about these changes and weird noises?"

"I know, Morgan, but I'm tired and worried about you. Lately, I've been feeling every day of my age and that makes me angry. Please take your time and enjoy your meal, however, I want to step outside and get some fresh air." Savannah stood and dropped three twenties on the table. She walked to the front of the diner and said something to the man at the register while pointing back to the booth. Morgan assumed she told him that the money for the tab and tip was already left on the table.

Morgan finished eating and walked to the diner exit. When she stood next to the counter with the cash register, she noticed dozens of black and white snapshots of customers and waitresses in the years around World War II pinned to a corkboard. Posed with and without food, inside the diner and out, everyone in the photos looked as though they enjoyed themselves.

She stared at the photos thinking that the people were familiar, yet she knew these pictures were taken long before she was even born. It was a strange déjà vu moment. One couple grinned at the camera—she with beautiful strawberry-blonde hair and he with curly blond. Backstories raced through her head about some of them. Suddenly her heart stopped as she realized the woman looked like the lady she saw in the back seat of her car an hour ago. Morgan grabbed the edge of the counter and steadied herself.

The cashier touched her arm and shouted, "Miss, are you all right? Do you want me to go get your friend for you?"

Morgan let go of the counter, shook her head, and smiled at the man. She glanced outside and saw Savvy leaning against the Jeep waiting. Morgan thanked the man and went out the door.

"Thank you for dinner, Savannah. I hoped we could

stay for a little while and talk," Morgan said as she neared the car.

"We need to have a 'come to Jesus talk' in private without any other eyes or ears. I know you're upset because you did not make one comment about the large tip that I left," Savvy said. "I have thought it all through, and I do sincerely believe you have a ghost and psychic phenomenon at play in your house and in your noggin. You may not believe in the psychic existence, and that's fine, however, I believe it's real, and you're living an experience. You know perfectly well that I am not a crazy person, but that doesn't mean I can't accept concepts that are outside the box or beyond the so-called norm."

Savannah was really wound up and put her hands on her hips as she continued, "Did I ever tell you about the time when my own daddy died? Let me tell you, when my poor old father passed away, my marriage was in a shambles, and I was a nervous wreck. Throughout the wake, at the funeral and for a couple of days after that, I felt someone's arm around me. Either he held me or a guardian angel held me if you can fathom such a notion. Mind you, my father never once held me in my entire life, yet there were arms around me from the moment he crossed over throughout the next three or four days.

"Whatever it was, I felt it, and it was real. It was invisible, but it was there and held me up throughout the entire ordeal. When I got back home, in my own house, it was gone. When I was back on my turf, safe and sound, 'it' wasn't needed anymore. The sensation was totally absent from that moment on and never came back. Does that make me a lunatic? I don't think so. There are a ton of people on television who talk to the other side and no one waits at the curb to take them to a mental hospital."

"I don't know what to think anymore," whispered Morgan. "I do honestly appreciate that you listened to me and didn't laugh."

"Me? I'm no laugher. No way. I like this stuff when it

comes from a reputable source. I think I like it, anyway. It gives me hope that there's a future after the bitter end. Besides, a ghost is better than a tumor, I think." Savvy giggled and said, "C'mon let's get you home; you're probably exhausted."

KATE MACINNIS

CHAPTER 7

While driving back home, Morgan sagged as she realized how deeply bone-tired she was. The past few days had been a frightening and emotional roller coaster, which was every bit as physically depleting as hard manual labor.

She pulled into the driveway at her house and parked. Savannah got out first, walked to the front sidewalk, and glanced up and down the street. She then stretched and asked, "Morgan, have you noticed that the flowers in your yard are bigger and better than the ones at every other house in your neighborhood?"

"Do you suppose there's a radioactive leak around my house?"

"Well, there's energy here of some sort, but I doubt that it's radioactive." Savvy laughed. At that moment, a breeze ruffled the evergreen trees. Morgan watched the branches as they swayed yet the trees right next door in the direct line of the wind were motionless.

Morgan stood there transfixed when two teenage boys on bikes stopped in front of the yard to see what had her attention. After a few seconds, they moved on, but one of them said the house was haunted.

"I'm not altogether sure that those boys are wrong,"

whispered Savvy as she followed Morgan into the house.

Unlocking the front door, Morgan went inside, dropping her purse on the table in the hall. She promptly went to the kitchen where she stopped short, pointing at the table. Savvy was right behind her and looked to see two clean mugs with napkins already set out. Savvy glanced at the stove and saw a clean pan on the burner.

Confused, Savvy asked, "Neither one of us cleaned up before we left, isn't that correct?"

"Correct, we left the dirty dishes in the sink," Morgan answered and moved to fill the kettle with cold water and placed it on the stove. She retrieved more mugs and tea bags out of the cupboard.

"I don't know what to say about this right now, in fact, I have to ponder this situation," Savvy added, "I'm confused and need to think it through." She opened the fridge to get milk for hot tea.

After a few minutes of quiet, Savvy commented, "Well, none of this really seems like a tumor, however, it could be a pervert with a camera mounted in your downstairs while he lives in your attic. I saw that in a movie or read it someplace—some crazy guy lived in a vacant house until new people moved in—then he lived in the attic and came down at night when the family was asleep. Was this house vacant very long before you moved in?"

Morgan rubbed her forehead and croaked, "Good grief, woman, I don't think someone is living in the attic— at least, I hadn't given that possibility a thought."

"Well, you're probably right, but I like to rule out everything before settling on a diagnosis."

"I would hope that Douglas would bark at a stranger living in the house—maybe he would anyway. Wait, he would unless they bribed him with cookies."

"Bulldogs are useless protectors."

Douglas entered the room at that moment glaring at Savvy as he crossed the room to his owner. Right then the kettle whistled and as she poured the hot water into mugs, she laughed, "You do realize that Douglas thinks you don't appreciate him for the star he is."

Savannah ignored the comment as well as the dog and asked, "Do you think you've had seizures of any sort?"

"No, I don't believe that I have." Morgan rubbed her eyes.

"Okay, if we rule out a vagrant in the attic, I don't believe that you have a new physical problem—I do believe that there are supernatural powers at work here."

"So, what do I do?"

"Well, I think we need to talk to a professional psychic, and I happen to know one who's very reputable—more than ninety percent accurate."

"Oh, maybe this is all stress-induced since I don't sleep well. That could certainly happen—we see sick people every day because they're over-stressed. I could try to sell the house but the law requires that you report if a house is haunted and that would cause the price to plunge. I could be forced to walk away and lose all that I have in it." Morgan sighed and continued, "If the neighboring kids think it's haunted, everybody else will, too."

"Wait, think about it—a ghost could be sort of hip and fashionable." Savannah laughed and added, "Some handsome dead guy feels you up and, for all you know, he figured out how to have wild passionate sex with no strings attached. It could be a big plus for the next young, single, female buyer."

The lights in the kitchen blinked on and off, stopping both women from speaking.

After a minute, Savvy said, "Oh, I bet that's your grabber from the shower communicating his approval. I'll just bet he likes the idea of wild passionate sex with no strings."

"I don't think I ever believed in ghosts before the accident," said Morgan. "Now, I'm a convert. That's a weird coincidence, don't you think? I mean, you mention sex with a ghost and the lights flash. Great, I have a ghost with a sense of humor."

"Well, better than cranky. In a way, I'm excited about this. Really, don't you think it's a comfort to know that it doesn't all end and there's more on the other side of death? We are such complicated creatures physically, mentally, and emotionally—how can this be all there is? You get seventy-five years or so on this planet and then it's over? Just over? An afterlife is a fantastic proposition. Somebody survives death and comes back to play slap and tickle with you in the shower. What if he's an old boyfriend, or better yet, some secret admirer? Listen, have you ever heard about those rooms at the hospital that are supposed to be haunted?"

"No way. Haunted? I've never heard such nonsense," Morgan answered as the lights again blinked on and off. "But I think you're onto something, and he agrees." The lights blinked faster.

"Wait a minute, you work in a hospital that has haunted areas and the nurses talk about it in the cafeteria all the time, yet you've never heard about it? Some pretty weird science goes on up on the floors, and I find it hard to believe that you know nothing about it. I thought you had the pulse on all the action at Good Sam."

"Clearly, I know nothing about Good Sam," Morgan answered with her nose scrunched at Savvy. "Where are these haunted rooms?"

"There are two rooms on seven south that the hospital won't admit patients to because everybody thinks they're haunted."

"If they're not positive, why wouldn't they still use the rooms? Hospitals make money wherever they can. I cannot believe they would purposely lose money on empty rooms."

"I've heard that the plan was to convert them to offices, but no one wanted to work in those spaces. After these two executive patients came in for their annual physicals and had the snot scared out of them, the word spread all over town. The hospital checked it out several times and there was never any proof of the place being haunted, but people heard the rumors and believed. Administration had no choice but to leave the place as is, since it wasn't a good public relations move to use rooms that could scare people to death. It's also not good for business to cause patients to have heart attacks and these two men had irregular electrocardiograms during their visit. We're healers, remember, not murderers. Anyway, the VIP patients swore the ghosts sat on the beds and created a big stir in the room. The doors and windows opened and closed repeatedly—they heard voices laughing, crying, and singing. One guy saw his mom touching his head and crooning a lullaby while he tried to sleep. The other insisted he could smell his grandmother's best chocolate cake baking in the room. Of course, this was a few years ago but the rooms haven't been used for patients since." Savannah smiled and added, "Look, these guys were high-powered big shots with no reason to make up stories like that. You had to believe it, and you know darn well that they repeated the experiences to everyone who would listen to them."

"Maybe a whole world exists between flesh and spirit. You know, it could be that someone hasn't invented the right microscope yet to see the other side or dimension," Morgan said. "Nonetheless, how did I miss all that dirt about seven south?"

"You partied pretty hard in those days. No one wanted to mention potential hallucinations to you in case of a sensitivity."

Morgan frowned at Savvy and watched her walk over and pick up the pad and pencil from the counter.

"Let's try an experiment," said Savvy as she handed the items to Morgan. "Let's see if you can do the automatic handwriting in front of me. I'll be your witness, and we'll see if this is a talent you have only when you're alone or if it can be done in front of someone. I knew a young woman back home who used to go into a self-hypnotic trance so she could do automatic handwriting. She divorced her husband and became very religious in her later years."

Morgan looked at Savvy and rolled her eyes as she reached for the pad and pen. She took the items and sat down at the kitchen table, fussing with the tablet until she found an angle she liked. She then poised her hand over the pad.

"I know you are not of the religious ilk, but I do suggest that you bless yourself right at this moment. Call me superstitious or call me cautious—but I ask that you please do that," Savannah sighed.

Morgan blessed herself and waited. "Savannah, I just wanna say that you're pretty bold to witness this. I don't have any idea what it's gonna be like for you." Morgan rubbed her hand and stretched her neck like a boxer. She held the pen steady against the first sheet of paper, the same as she had when she made a grocery list.

"Well, I'm curious. It's also totally off the wall, which appeals to me. I will watch you, Morgan, don't be afraid, I'm here."

Immediately after Savvy uttered the last comment Morgan no longer had control of her hand. *I am dancing at the general's party. Dancing and dancing.*

Savannah leaned forward in her chair to see what was written on the paper. "What party? What general? Morgan, can you hear me?"

Morgan was awake yet super-focused and stared at the page without answering. She wrote: *General Washington's party. He is a marvelous host. All have such a pleasurable time.*

"Whoa, Morgan. Can you hear me? Your dancer just answered my question. Morgan, can you hear me at all? Give me a sign if you can."

Savvy shivered and realized the room felt colder. Knowing it could be a case of nerves, she spotted the thermostat across the room and went over to check the temperature. The digital readout indicated it was seventy-two.

Coming back to the table, Savvy spoke in a very calm, reassuring manner, "Morgan, your dancer answered my last question. Who is your dancer?"

Morgan wrote: *Excuse me but I am not her dancer. I am her friend. Morgan is awake, but she is very frightened and cannot speak. You are also her friend and may converse with her gently.*

Savannah nodded, and while looking at the notepad she asked, "All right then, if you're not her dancer, who are you?"

Morgan wrote: *I am Jonathan Henry Wilkerson, young lady. I am dancing and dancing.*

"Yeah, well, I'm frozen and covered in sweat at the same time," Savannah mumbled as she stood and paced around the room. "Young lady? I haven't been called that in quite a few years. I see that your name is Wilkerson, but I want to know *who* you are."

Morgan wrote: *An actor and professor of the arts. Alas, you probably haven't heard of my work.*

Savannah smiled and asked, "Excuse me, sir, but with whom are you dancing?"

Morgan wrote: *I am dancing with my lovely wife. This is a most pleasant experience.*

"Sir, you are dancing with your wife and in touch with me through Morgan at the same time? Quite the multitasker." Savvy paused and added, "How do I know you are who you say you are and you're not just her subconscious? I mean, can you prove to me that you're a ghost or whatever?"

As Savannah waited for a response, Morgan held the pen to paper, but she did not write. The compact disc player mounted under the kitchen cabinet abruptly blasted big band music from the 1940s loud enough to startle Savvy, and she snapped her neck in the direction of the sound. She moved quickly over to the shelf to turn the player down and the power light was already off. She touched the power button and jerked her hand away from the heat.

"Why is this so hot?" Savannah asked aloud as she turned to face Morgan and the notepad. The music continued. Savannah opened the player and found an empty CD tray. "How can this play with no disc?" she mumbled. Trying to think of something different to make it stop, she pulled her shirt over a finger for protection, pressed the power button, and held it steady. Nothing changed. Again, Savannah opened the player and the very same song continued.

She backed away from the CD player and said, "Okay, that's good, that's good proof. Un-huh. Yessir, that worked." She walked back to the table and stood by her friend.

Morgan wrote a signature with great flourish: *Jonathan Henry Wilkerson.* Under the autograph was written: *See, I told you—I am real. I wrote a great many plays that were staged at the university.*

Savannah answered, "Fine, okay. Where are you now?"

Morgan wrote: *I'm dancing and dancing in the general's ballroom.*

"What ballroom. What house? What planet? This doesn't make any damn sense to me at all. I will listen and keep an open mind, but so far you wanted to scare me and, now, sir, you've pissed me off." Savannah stared at the notebook and added, "Is this house possessed? Or Morgan? Or the notebook? Or me? There isn't any ballroom here."

Morgan wrote: *Such a shame. It is a wonderful party.*

"Mr. Wilkerson, Professor Wilkerson, excuse me for this impertinence, but are you dead?"

Morgan wrote: *Hmmm. Perhaps to you I am not of the flesh, but I am still very lively. To me, you are the one who is on the other side.*

"I'm on the other side? Hmmm," Savannah mumbled as she circled the room. "Anyone else there with you?

Anybody I would know?"

Morgan wrote: *Mr. Lincoln is expected to be present this evening. Also, a few stately critics of mine are here. No one to impress you, I'm sure.*

"Lincoln at Washington's party? That sounds like a stretch or a very impressive guest list. You don't sound like someone who fraternizes with dead rock stars and actors, but I had to ask. No harm, am I right, sir? My instincts tell me that it would not be prudent for me to make you angry." Savannah stood very close to read the response.

This time, no words were written. After a few moments, Savvy grew impatient and asked, "Well, sir, do you have a message or a request for Morgan? If not, I do have one more question if you don't mind."

With a flourish, Morgan wrote: *Proceed.*

"Thank you. Here's my question: 'Why have you done this anyway? What's the point?'"

Savannah moved closer to read the reply. *That was two questions, but I forgive. Tell Morgan that she and I were once close and that this was my house at another time. I shared this home with my beautiful wife and family. We have many wonderful, warm memories here.*

"Why now … why must you reach her now? Will the world cease to exist?" Savannah asked excitedly.

Morgan wrote in very large letters: *DON'T BE SO MELODRAMATIC. The world will not end. We can share her life in a most helpful way if she desires. Unfortunately, she is trying to block us and not listen. She will not acknowledge our signs.*

"*Our* signs? Is there more than one of you?" Savvy asked.

Madame, you do not pay attention. We would most like to communicate with Morgan.

With that, the pen fell out of Morgan's hand and onto the floor. Savannah bent to pick it up but dropped it immediately when blisters started forming on her palm. She stared at the burn and blinked several times. Not knowing what else to do and having so many more questions, she chose to sit in the chair and wait quietly while gathering herself. She blew on her hand to stop the pain.

After a few moments, Morgan asked softly, "Wrote again, didn't I?" She rubbed her hands together and shook her arms.

"Oh, yes, you certainly did. With many thanks to Jonathan Henry Wilkerson, you did write. Are you fully awake now, Morgan?" Savannah spoke as she inspected the blisters that had spread to her fingers.

"Yes, I'm awake." Morgan tilted her head and asked, "Are you okay?"

"I'm not sure what really happened here. You zoned out, and I'm not sure where you went. It's pretty clear, though, that Jonathan Henry Wilkerson is the reason for your stress. He's your ghost and old friend from another life. He was a writer and professor at the university, as well. Ever hear the name before?" Savannah asked as she indicated the notebook with a nod.

"Only when he wrote his name the other day." Morgan shrugged and added, "It could have been on some of the paperwork when I bought the house, but he lived here years before I was born."

"Look at what you wrote, Morgan. You do feel okay to handle this, don't you?" Savannah picked up the notebook and held it out for her friend to take. "I have to get some ice for my hand."

"What's wrong with your hand?" Morgan asked as Savannah held it up to show her the burns.

"Did I do that to you? Oh my God, I felt like I was asleep—I might even have overheard some of your conversation but had no idea you were hurt." Morgan stood and looked closer at Savvy's hand.

Savvy moved to the refrigerator, opened the freezer, and got some ice cubes. She put them in a plastic sandwich bag from the cupboard with one hand as she grabbed the dish towel with the other. She went back to the table and sat down across from Morgan while she cradled her burned hand.

"If this happened to somebody else, it would be so cool," Morgan said as she thumbed through the pages of the notebook. After she read a few pages, she looked at Savannah. "Do you think it's just my subconscious behind this?"

"Not unless your subconscious can also freeze the room and boil the pen while you're in an apparent fugue state. It's warm in here now, but believe me, it was like a freezer while your buddy visited." Savannah rushed to the CD player, punched buttons, and played with the on/off switch. "Well, I'll be damned."

Morgan watched and asked, "Why are you concerned with the CD player? You suddenly want some music?"

"No, when this all started the CD player was blasting big band music. It was too loud, and I tried to turn it off, but the button didn't work. I also tried to take the CD out of the changer, but there wasn't a CD in there." Savannah faced Morgan and continued, "I'm serious—I didn't imagine this at all. I can't believe it happened, but it's fine now. It's fine. The damn player is fine. How did he do that?" She turned the player on and off and it worked perfectly. She opened the deck and saw a CD, which she removed and showed to Morgan.

"The ghost? I don't have a clue. He is a ghost, right?" Morgan asked as she chewed on her lip.

"The human body can display ideomotor effects or responses—that's when someone performs an action unconsciously." Savvy paced as she spoke. "Here's how it works—you're sound asleep and cry out from sadness because your unconscious mind dreamed about a disaster or the death of someone close. It did not happen at all in real life. With that in mind, some people say that the ability to automatically write or cause one of those triangular pledgets on a board game to move is the very same theory of ideomotor effect. There are also those who say that these same examples are a sign that your unconscious mind is in command and not the result of an outside influence, presence, or being. In other words, it's all in your imagination."

"I understand, but if I become a bag lady because I can't work, please help me find a really nice, upscale neighborhood to do it in," mumbled Morgan as she rubbed her head.

Savvy frowned at Morgan's words and said, "But you *don't* understand. How could it all be in your imagination when I have blisters on my fingers, the room froze, and I had a conversation with a man who claimed to be dancing at General Washington's party—where Lincoln was a guest, by the way?"

Savannah paced again, put water in the teakettle, and turned on the burner. "Morgan, I can *almost* justify the handwriting in my mind as an unconscious exercise, but I absolutely cannot reconcile the cold and heat aspects as being part of your unconscious events."

"So, I'm not crazy? Back to my question—is he a ghost?" Morgan looked at Savannah through her hands held up to her face.

"No, I don't believe you're crazy, and yes, I think he's a ghost. He indicated that he and his wife once owned this house and they were quite happy here. That's solid information that we can research and verify. I asked if he were dead or alive and he said that he's not of the flesh as we know it and that to him, we're the ones on the other side. That makes sense to me. He does want to get in touch with you because he claims that he and his wife *can help you*, whatever that means. He seems to be using the writing as a vehicle to communicate."

Morgan dropped her hands from her face and said, "Why, because a video would be too creepy? I say we check him out—we have his signature and might be able to verify that online. He claimed to be a writer, so let's search for his works. Maybe we can get one of his books and quiz him. Or perhaps the university has archives of his materials. We can also find out the history of my house and who the previous owners were. If we can double-check a few facts, we'll know if it's for real or a dream that stars a dead writer-professor."

Savannah gently stroked her blistered hand and said, "We'll figure this out—don't panic yet. I don't think you're a lunatic, and I suspect that before this is over, you'll be convinced that you're one of the sanest people on earth."

"Why are you so sure that we can contact him again?" Morgan asked as she got up to make the tea.

"I guess because he's so sure that they can help you in some way. Maybe because of your brain surgery, he thinks you need their help. Maybe they *can* help with something, who knows? Of course, they are the bulk of the problem haunting your house, right, so what can they possibly help?"

Morgan shivered as she served tea. "Yeah, I guess there's some danger contacting dead spirits, but what can they really do? Do you think it's like the horror movies? I just had another thought—yuck, does he fondle me with his wife around?"

Savvy shrugged and said, "Even though he's still a man, I can't believe he'd behave like such a dog with his wife around. She wasn't in the shower when he grabbed you, correct?"

"Correct."

"Okay, then I believe we have to contact him again because there must be some logical explanation for this intrusion. They are going to a lot of effort to secure your attention, and although I'm not sure about this, we'll find out. In our conversation he may have hinted about reincarnation, and why not? Many religions embrace the concept of reincarnation, and why do we, in the Western world, insist that they're wrong?" Savvy sipped her tea and sighed before adding, "Look, he was here but he wasn't seen. He's out there, but where's out there? He got in touch, but he's also apparently dead. Let's go surf the Internet."

Morgan picked up the mugs to put in the sink. She glanced through the window to look at the stars and full moon that lit the sky. A man's face appeared high on the kitchen window and stayed for a fraction of a second. It was a familiar man's head with curly blond hair and mustache. She dropped the mugs, breaking one in the sink. She grabbed a paper towel to pick up the pieces and throw them away.

"I wonder how many times my heart can stop before it gives out forever?" Morgan asked out loud. She put the pieces in the garbage, ran the water for a few seconds, and hurried to catch up with Savvy.

"I just saw the blond guy with curls way up in the corner of the window. It could easily have been Mr. Wilkerson again." Morgan looked washed out and tired.

"Oh my," Savvy replied. "Well, I don't know what to say. It's easy to assume it's him, but unless we find a photo that identifies him, we won't know for sure. Let's get started digging, so to speak."

CHAPTER 8

Savannah went into the living room where the computer was kept and Morgan followed behind—noticing the TV remote was not in its usual place on top of the TV. She glanced around and spotted it on an end table. Tired of dealing with this, she picked it up and put it where it belonged. Soon after, a shadow passed in front of the television. Not *on* the TV but between the set and where she stood.

"Savannah, do you feel anyone else in the room with us?" whispered Morgan as she moved around the room waving both arms in search of temperature changes.

"Well, when your professor was here before, the room felt below freezing, and I don't feel that now at all. Also, why on earth did you whisper, Morgan? He can hear you no matter what volume you use to speak. Besides, why do you even ask—what happened?"

"I saw someone cross in front of the television. No mistake. They walked right in front of me and made a shadow on the TV." Morgan continued her search, poking at the empty air.

"Maybe you're a little bit nervous. Why don't we call it a night? You work the weekend, don't you? We can pick up where we left off on Monday. I'll head home now, and since I'm off and don't really have any plans for the weekend, I can do some research on my own from my house. How does that sound?" asked Savannah as she stood up and stretched.

"Okay, Savvy."

"Will you be all right?"

"Sure, a little jumpy, but I'm okay. How about yourself, doctor?"

"I'm intrigued and think this has to be weird for you, even though it's a cool and unusual experience. We'll get it figured out. Who knows, it could turn out to be a fantastic voyage."

"Yeah, Savvy, that's possible, I guess. I'm hoping it isn't an elaborate attempt by my imagination to entertain me—you know, lonely single looks for excitement, that sort of situation." Morgan walked with her friend to the front door.

Savannah opened the door and stood there with her hand on the knob. Morgan peeked around and saw that the trees were heavy with leaves to the extent that they rustled in the night air. Hours before, the trees had a few buds.

"Why doesn't everyone use fertilizer?" Morgan shrugged.

"I'm sure that they do, however, with this kind of growth in such a short time, you very likely have other influences that make your little garden grow." Savannah hugged her good-bye. They stood on the porch together for a few moments and let the breeze wash over them.

As Savvy went down the steps, she said, "You know, Morgan, since my divorce I get lonely, but I don't believe either one of us is capable of being bored enough to invent this whole scenario. We saw evidence of something that is very likely paranormal, so let's have some fun and investigate to see what we find, see where it takes us." Savvy turned as she crossed the lawn and added, "Besides,

I know that in the past, when you truly got desperate enough for male attention, you relied on Ted Kelly. You have never resorted to making up stories to get someone to notice you. So, please keep that in mind if you doubt your sanity."

"Thank you, Savvy. Fingers crossed that I don't have to fall back on Ted again, figuratively or literally. He's such a bore and soooo needy. Surely there's someone at that hospital who would like to take him as a husband. He's a doctor with a good income and job security. I only went out with him because he was a desperate measure for a desperate time. I've made him into a tool to be used on occasion and that's all. It's not fair to him and not fair to me to be exposed to him. So to speak." Morgan stared at the porch floor.

"Sometimes, you know, it's not the sex that I miss, although I do miss that a fair amount. Really, it's the conversations. I miss the sweet compliments, kind words, and gentle laughter," said Savannah. "Of course, after all I've seen in the EC over the years, I don't have a clue what I want or need in a relationship anymore." Savvy sighed and walked over to her car.

"If you are convinced this psychic-ghost encounter makes sense, then I have to believe it, as well. You are a scientist and healer first and foremost. We were in contact with some nutty professor and possibly his wife from the past who party now with two former presidents and a bunch of people who dress in black and white. It's not entirely in my head because you, my most cynical and trusted friend, experienced parts of it, as well. You also don't think I'm dangerous or totally insane. You are one helluva friend, Savannah Holt. Thank you."

"You tell me, what does it feel like to be involved in this? It's either psychic, supernatural, or ordinary garden-variety schizophrenic. What's your guess, Morgan?"

"I'm terrified right to my bones, Savvy. But oddly fascinated at the same time."

"That's why you're not crazy, my friend. I'll be in touch soon, but for now, take two aspirin and get some sleep. Oh, and as you race around and lock the doors and windows, remember the ghosts are inside with you. You can't lock them out."

Morgan put her hand over her mouth and watched Savvy laugh as she got in her car, wave, and pull away from the house.

"Sleep, sure. Thanks, Dr. Holt. Like I'll ever sleep again in this lifetime. Maybe zombies are real just because they can't get a good night's sleep. They start out like us, then they don't quite sleep enough nights in a row and there you go. Bad clothes, bad breath, and bad luck with love. All from lack of sleep," Morgan muttered and looked around her street to see if anyone heard her. No one seemed to be out. She glanced at Rudy's little store and saw the creepy sentinel in the upstairs window staring in her direction.

She shivered, went back inside the house, and locked the door. Morgan looked around at her pride and joy, her home with the shiny, dark wooden floors throughout and the beautiful French doors that made the entry warm and friendly. Her taste ran a little more to the frilly and girly than she would want anyone to know about—only a chosen few from work had been invited to her sanctuary because of that fact. The house was small but comfortable and the neighborhood had a few larger homes for big families. She loved this community because it was diverse and comprised of people on their way up and down.

Morgan had one foot on the bottom of the stairs when she heard the television. Hesitantly, she went to the living room where her flat-screen had turned now into a black and white model from the 1960s. It was a portable television that sat on a spindly, fake brass TV stand of some sort. There was something black and white playing on the screen—she went inside the room to see what it was. She sat on the couch hard when she realized it was an episode of "What's My Line?" complete with John Charles Daly, Bennett Cerf, Arlene Francis, and Dorothy Kilgallen on the screen. She used the remote to turn up the volume. The show was just exactly as she imagined a Manhattan cocktail party would be and they were the upper-crust guests. So many inside jokes and such a clique. The secret guest was a very young Debbie Reynolds who entertained her heart out. Morgan marveled at how British all the New Yorkers sounded.

While watching, the cushion next to her shifted and an indentation formed. She waved her hand over the spot to check for cold or heat but felt neither. She looked back at the television and it was gone—replaced by her high-def, flat-screen that she had purchased with her own hard-earned cash.

There was an odd smell in the room she hadn't noticed before, like a hair dryer left on too long. She walked around the entire room but did not pick up any signals. Morgan shook her head, said "goodnight" to the room, and went upstairs.

In the master bathroom she turned on the water in the old clawfoot tub. Douglas followed and insisted that he had to go outside one more time. She turned the water off and went back downstairs to let him out and decided to sit on the top porch step to watch him. She leaned against the banister and wondered why she didn't keep an emergency cigarette in the house. She didn't have an inclination or desire to smoke on a regular basis again, but damn, one cigarette right at that moment would have been lovely.

Douglas finished his business and scurried back to the porch with a sloppy kiss for Morgan. When he was a little guy, he ate most of the woodwork in her hallway, but other than that he had been a good companion. With spring in the air, she took in a deep breath through her nose and stood to go inside. She looked up at the stars and whispered, "Whatever this is, we will get through it." A shooting star crossed the sky. She looked around and added, "That's a sign of some sort but I'll be damned if I know the details." She turned and followed Douglas as he hurried ahead of her to go upstairs.

The second floor of the home originally had three bedrooms and she chose to have a wall knocked out to give her a very large master suite with attached bathroom. Her bedroom was rosy pink and white with lots of ruffles and frills that prompted Savannah to declare any man who set foot in there would be drained of testosterone before he could even remove his pants. Savvy also said it looked like Laura Ashley exploded in there but Morgan loved every inch of the room.

She restarted the water in the tub and placed a clean bath sheet on the closed toilet so it would be easy to grab. She picked an album by The Eagles from her playlist and climbed into the tub. She looked around the room as goosebumps broke out all over her and the twinge in her chest started again. The baseball bat was propped within reach of the tub. She shivered from the uncomfortable vibe she sensed and decided that hugging her knees and putting her head on her arms would provide some comfort. Morgan said aloud, "You will not scare me away. *This is my house.*"

The twinge in her chest eased and her eyes were closed when she heard the bathroom door swing wide open. She stared as no one came in and the door closed. She sat bolt upright and rigid in the warm water.

"I can't believe what you've done to the place," whispered the male voice in her ear.

Morgan gasped to get air into her lungs, scrambling to stand up and get out of the tub. She grabbed her towel and wrapped it around herself. Water was dripping on the floor as she stood frozen in the center of the room. Once again, the bathroom door opened but this time it didn't close. She heard faint footsteps in the hall.

Terrified that the entity would return, Morgan let the water out of the tub and put on her robe. She grabbed the baseball bat and moved to the doorway to see the hall more directly. She didn't see anyone but heard the tense, hushed whispers of an argument as her parents used to do when she was little. She dropped the bat to her side and listened to the couple in her second bedroom.

"Shush, Elisabeth, I think she can hear us," the man said.

"I don't care if she does hear us. You have to stop your voyeuristic ways, Jon," the woman replied. Morgan assumed the lady was very likely the missus of the pervert.

"Jon, must you continue to be a scamp even now after all these years," continued the woman.

Morgan made a *hummphhh* sound outside the door and the voices stopped immediately. She put her head down and hurried back to her room. There she sat on the bed, kept the bat on her lap, and rocked back and forth while holding her head with both hands. Suddenly she could hear big band music from her bathroom. It was the same song that played in her car.

"This is the most bizarre déjà vue experience ever," Morgan said aloud and then realized her phone was in the bathroom. She hurried in there, grabbed the phone, and turned it off. The music continued to play.

Exhausted and scared out of her wits, Morgan choked and began to cry. This was a no-win situation. At that moment, someone's gentle arm went around her shoulders and held her close. It was a kind touch and Morgan leaned into it without thinking. As quickly as she leaned in, she stiffened—remembering no one else was in the room.

"Please don't be afraid," said the female voice.

"How could anyone in their right mind not be petrified?" Morgan sniffed as she looked for the source of the voice.

"We don't mean you any harm." The disembodied male voice spoke from somewhere above the bedroom door.

"Great, that's what they say in movies about aliens who

invade the earth, and here I hadn't even considered that possibility," Morgan said as she looked around the room.

"We are here to help you, Morgan," the woman's voice said a little louder this time.

"Help me with what? I don't need help. You're the problem, lady. You and your deviated husband," Morgan stammered. "I want my life back. Without you two in it."

As if disappointed by Morgan's words, the woman removed her arm from Morgan's shoulders. After a few minutes of silence, Morgan didn't bother to remove her robe and crawled into bed. Within seconds she fell into a deep sleep.

At 3:26 a.m., she awoke soaked in sweat and shivering from a recurrent dream about an elegant, dressy ball. She listened for music or noises of some sort. Frustrated, she looked at the clock again and turned over to get more sleep before it was time to get up for work. Maybe Savvy and everybody else was right—she did go back to work too soon after the surgery. She tried to make sense of the last few hours just as there was movement to her right and the edge of the mattress formed a slight indentation.

She waved her hand gently back and forth but felt nothing. A faint form materialized— the outline was barely visible as she reached to touch it. The sensation was liquid and as it gained form, it morphed into the arm and shoulder of a woman wearing a white silk blouse.

"Why don't you feel cold?" Morgan asked moving her hand back and forth in the air.

"I don't know," the woman whispered. "I believe it's your perception. To someone else, I might be hot as coal."

"Who are you?" asked Morgan as she sat up in the bed.

"Elisabeth Wilkerson," the voice said softly as she materialized.

"The professor's wife?"

"Yes, the professor's wife." She laughed at this, appearing more real.

"Why do you whisper, you know I'm here alone?"

"I need to practice in order to get better at speaking. Much like building muscle—it takes time." Elisabeth looked around the room, touched the frilly bedspread, and rubbed her hand across the silky sheets. She added, "I've missed this, the smooth, feminine materials."

"What do you want, Mrs. Wilkerson?"

"We want to help you," she said tilting her head to look directly at Morgan.

"Help me what?"

"Deal with your new abilities. Your new powers can be abused by those on both sides. You've developed a skill that appeals to all of us who move through your dimension and ours. Using your energy conserves our energy. Do you understand?"

"I'm not sure. I've heard a lot about physics lately, and I'm not an expert, Mrs. Wilkerson. Aren't there thousands of people out there with this ability?"

"Oh, yes and every one of them experiences some communication from this world. You're a good soul, Morgan, and we feel protective of you. You need to know that there are evil spirits that would love to intercept your powers, overtake you, and use you for their own gain."

"Are you talking about possession of my soul?" Morgan drew the covers closer to her.

"Yes, I am."

"To what end? Why would a spirit on your side want to possess me?"

"To have the flesh and blood experiences once again. To have the pleasures that come with being alive and warm-bodied. There are also those who starve for revenge with evil intent and deeds. They could do more damage if they have a human body to control," Elisabeth explained as she touched her hair. "We have close relationships with loved ones but intimacy is not the same as it is on your side.

"Were you here before my accident and I just didn't know it?" Morgan asked as she reached to touch the woman.

"Yes. Did you know that we lived in this house when we were first married? We are all forever joined by circumstance." Elisabeth laughed and her face became even more beautiful.

"Are you guardian angels?"

"No, we aren't angels—we were once alive just like you. Now we are your defenders."

"Are these evil spirits around all the time?" Morgan glanced around the room as she asked the question.

"No, not generally, but enough to be a nuisance. Once is too much if they get into your head." Elisabeth glanced at her hands and turned her wedding ring around on her finger.

"Did your husband come into the bathroom a while ago when I was in the tub?"

"Yes, Jon can be a little precocious, and he doesn't like to miss an opportunity to see a beautiful, naked woman." Elisabeth laughed and turned her ring again. "He was like that when he was alive, so I can't really fault him for it now."

With all the strength Morgan could muster, she turned on the bedside lamp. She could not see her in entirety, but she touched Elisabeth gently and it felt as if she were alive. That's when someone got on the bed behind her and placed a hand on her shoulder. She turned her head slightly and no one was there. The heavy hand remained on her shoulder.

"Is that you, professor?" Morgan looked over her shoulder.

"Yes, it is," Jonathan replied.

"Why don't you two go into the light as they do in the movies?"

"We did and returned by choice. Now that you have developed powers, we can use you to connect more often with this dimension," Jonathan explained as he reached for his wife.

120

"We're going to leave you now so you can ready for work in peace. Come, Jon."

Morgan heard a *pop* followed by silence. She sat on the side of the bed overwhelmed by the encounter with the Wilkersons. Her heart pounded and shivers covered her entire body. She laid down and sleep came immediately as if she had just finished a marathon. When the clock went off, she hit the snooze, and her first thought was that Savvy was the only person on earth who would ever believe this story. She got up, quickly showered, dressed for work, and walked out the door at 5:30 a.m., just like most mornings for her early shift at the hospital. She opened the car door and it dawned on her that the ghosts had used her energy for the conversation—that's why she was still exhausted. On the upside, maybe she could lose a few pounds.

She glanced across the street and spotted an ambulance and police car parked in front of Rudy's little grocery store. Numerous neighbors were gathered on the corner. Without concern about the time, she crossed to see what happened.

"Is Rudy okay?" Morgan asked a familiar man who nodded to her.

"Rudy didn't open the store this morning for the delivery man, so he called the police. They found him inside, dead in his bed upstairs in the apartment," the man answered.

"Oh, I'm so sorry. So, there wasn't any foul play?"

"Naw, they said it looked like natural causes, but I don't know what's natural about death." The man sniffed and tightened the belt on his bathrobe.

"Death is part of living, sir. It's perfectly natural."

"Hey, you're that nurse, ain't ya?"

"Yes, I am." She nodded—then turned to go back to her driveway.

"You probably see this all the time and it's not a big deal to you. But the older you get, the bigger a deal it is."

KATE MACINNIS

"I've seen enough of it, yes," she mumbled as she crossed the street to reach her driveway.

"See you later, miss," the man shouted to her. She waved back at him and went to work.

It was an uneventful Saturday in the EC with the usual gallbladder attacks, dog bites, and weekend warrior injuries. Around two o'clock, Dr. Caleb Lightfoot called and changed Morgan's entire outlook.

His name appeared on her cell phone and she immediately ducked into a closet to speak with him.

"Would you like to go with me to a huge flea market next Saturday?" Caleb added, "I thought that I could pick you up, drive there together, have some lunch, and then see how the day goes."

"I'm flattered, Dr. Lightfoot, but I truly don't want to start a relationship with anyone right now. If I did, I swear you'd be at the top of the list, but this is not a good time for me."

"Morgan, it's just a flea market. Two new friends out for the day. Maybe I could teach you some stuff."

"Oh, I don't doubt that for a minute, but I don't have the energy right now. You do intrigue me though with your ability to see auras."

"I'd be happy to discuss it with you."

"Should I agree to go, so I can learn more?"

"Depends on how many times you want to discuss it with me. It also depends on whether or not you really want me to leave you alone."

"Fine. What time do you want to pick me up?"

"If I didn't mention it before, this is a special flea market up north. It has antiques only, so I hope you like that. I'm a sucker for antiques, and it doesn't matter if it's cars, magazines, or old junk around the house. I love all that. Can you be ready by seven-thirty in the morning a week from today?"

"Sounds great; let me give you my address."

"Look, I'm a co-worker and have your address on the

call sheet." He laughed and added, "Let's not even share with anybody that we have plans. Keep my number in your phone just in case you have to work or need to call me. I don't want you to get in trouble since I'm the new guy." With that, he hung up.

Morgan steadied herself against a dirty laundry cart and stared at the phone. She felt the twinge in her chest, but this time it was very faint. She left the closet and grinned all the way back to the desk.

Once the shift finally ended, she hurried home, retrieved her mail from the box, and entered the house. Douglas was there to greet her in his usual form, which was a mix of excitement, hunger, and desire to go outside immediately. They walked to the kitchen together so she could let him out in the backyard.

While he was out, she did the usual—got him some food and fresh water and put on a pot of water to boil for tea. Then she sat down at the kitchen counter to take a look at the mail. Douglas ran up the steps, came into the house, and barked. She smiled at him as the loud music started. The sound was from a full-blown party underway inside the house. Morgan looked around and thought the sounds came from the first floor, but as she made a loop through all the rooms, there was no party. She started up the stairs and the higher she got, the louder the party became.

As music played, the laughter and crowd noise filled the house. The smell of fresh rolls, shrimp with cocktail sauce, and grilled meat permeated the upstairs. Morgan changed from her scrubs into a T-shirt and jeans while Douglas watched his usual imaginary friends. On a closer look, she also saw tiny dots of light darting all over her bedroom and bouncing from wall to wall, to the floor, over to the window, back to the door, and onto the bed.

Morgan grabbed her cell phone from the bed and took two or three pictures of the orbs before they suddenly stopped. She put the phone in her back pocket and looked around.

The orbs hung in the air for a few seconds. With a flash, they continued to bounce all around the room and Douglas looked thoroughly entertained and amused. Morgan thought he must be getting used to the company.

The curtains in the bedroom parted and the bottom half of the window lifted and opened as she stood very still. Douglas felt the breeze and moved so it would rush over his body. Morgan blinked several times as she watched the window close by itself. She backed out of the room, and before she got to the stairs, the window locked itself. She raced down the stairs with Douglas close behind. The only sound on the first floor was the loud retro kitchen clock and the whistling of the tea kettle.

Morgan wobbled on unsteady legs into the kitchen. Douglas stayed close and she patted his back. Douglas repaid the attention with a sloppy kiss on her leg. When the pounding of her heart subsided, she poured herself a mug of hot tea.

The kitchen landline rang causing Morgan to jump. It was an old-fashioned, yellow dial phone mounted on the wall since the '60s. For a fleeting moment she wondered if the Wilkersons had that phone installed. No one had called the line in months and she delayed disconnection just in case somebody from the old days tried to reach her. She answered and expected Ellen or someone else from the hospital to be on the line. Instead she heard static on the other end. After shouting "hello" a few times without an answer, she hung up.

The phone rang again, and even though she contemplated ignoring it, she picked up the receiver. This time the static was still there but had lessened and now had a hollow quality much like a tunnel. A faint voice spoke from far away.

"Morgan, I need to speak with you—you have to trust us," someone said.

She wasn't sure if it was a man or woman on the other

end of the line. She listened intently as the caller repeated the message somewhat louder.

"I'm sorry, I can't hear you," she shouted. Her hands were clammy and stuck to the phone, but she managed to hang it up. This time it didn't ring again.

"Damned old phones anyway." Morgan sank to the floor as the room swirled. She rubbed her hands and struggled to breathe before she gagged and raced to the bathroom. When she returned to the kitchen, Douglas sniffed her hand. She rubbed his face and patted his head before she decided to pick up the receiver delicately and listen. She heard only dead, hollow air. Giving up, she hung the phone back in its base.

"C'mon Douglas, let's go sit in the other room," Morgan said. She was suddenly on a mission and decided to write about this experience before she forgot. She grabbed the notebook from the counter and Douglas followed her.

As they entered the hall from the kitchen, Morgan heard the remote going crazy in the living room—the channels changing every split second with a *blip-blip*. She opened the door and seeing no one, she shouted, "Jonathan? Elisabeth? Do one of you have the remote?" She looked at the ceiling as she turned around in the room.

Hearing no response, she went back into the hall where she heard the distinct sound of a chair dragging across the tiled kitchen floor along with the dinging noise made by a microwave.

She hurried back to the kitchen and found a chair tipped against the counter, the microwave ajar, and back door wide open. She put everything in its place as it should be and returned to the front of the house. The library was across the entry hall from the living room and had floor to ceiling bookcases. No television in this room but a radio was kept on the shelf. Also, a retro-style phonograph with a built-in CD player was located in this room.

She got comfortable on the couch with Douglas right

next to her and opened the notebook to write the date and time. Instead, she wrote: *Hello, Morgan, I've been waiting for you.*

She watched as her hand moved gently across the page with a penmanship that was much fancier than her own. She found herself crossing and dotting the letters with a grand flourish. When a page was full, she turned to the next page and stopped occasionally to shake her arm and invigorate her circulation. Her fingers, hand, and arm buzzed with intense pins and needles.

When she finally stopped, she rubbed her cold hands together. The clock read 10:30 p.m. and it was dark outside. She placed the notebook on the coffee table in front of the couch and rubbed her face as she grumbled, "Okay, Morgan, get a grip. You wrote for almost three hours. You are not crazy, or maybe you are. No, Savvy said you're not."

She took a drink of tea and shivered as the cold bitter fluid slipped down her throat. She picked up the notebook and read:

My daughter Elisabeth and her husband Jonathan were the original owners of your home. They had happy years and six children while in that house.

Morgan glanced through the notebook and counted that she had written nearly twenty pages in large script about Elisabeth, Jonathan, and their children. Nothing out of the ordinary and certainly not personal, but the recount seemed to be pride in their daughter and her husband. She took the notebook out to her work bag by the hall table to show Savvy. She went back to the kitchen and filled the kettle for tea. While it heated, she stared at the wall. By the time it boiled, Douglas wanted outside and she opened the back door for him. She poured her tea and went to the open door and leaned against the doorframe. She crossed her arms on her chest as a light breeze tickled her face. She smiled as she gazed at the night sky. She thought about the changes in her life, discovery of ghosts in her home, and the ability to write automatically for those on the other side.

"Listen, whoever you are, we are going to figure out how to make this work on my terms. There's room here for all of us, but no more scaring me. Do we understand each other?"

"Certainly, we can consider your offer, young lady, but that also means you have to stop carrying that wretched baseball bat around. Really, what good is it anyway? It just makes you look silly," the male voice said.

"Well, Mr. Wilkerson, you have a point. I'll put the bat away and you'll leave me alone in the bathroom. Always."

"We shall take it under advisement and you may call me Jonathan," said the voice.

Morgan looked around and saw a faint mist hovering over the banister of her porch. It disappeared after a few seconds. She shook her head and went inside. "I'm buying a new lock for the door even if he swears that he won't scare me anyone. I know it makes no sense overall, but I'll feel better and that's what matters most," she mumbled as she turned out the lights and went upstairs.

CHAPTER 9

At work, bright and early on Friday morning, Gloria Vanderveer visited Morgan at the kitchen behind the nurses' station. Morgan still had her coffee shop chai tea in her hand. She put it on the table and sat so she could watch for anyone coming into the room.

"They arrested my husband for my murder," Gloria said with worry written all over her face. "He didn't do it, I tell you."

"What do you want me to do?" Morgan asked softly.

"I want you to call that handsome and clearly very nice police chief and tell him that there's been a terrible mistake. A terrible mistake. But I do think I know who did it."

"Who?"

"My no-good sister. She wanted my life, my husband, my position in the community, but she wouldn't work for it. With me out of the way, she can just slip right into my closet and Gordon's bed."

"Your husband would go along with that?"

"Sure, she's my twin. She's pretty, available, all my clothes and shoes will fit. Besides, she'll please him in ways I wouldn't even consider. As if." Gloria sniffed and tossed her hair over her shoulder.

"Then why defend him? Sounds like a dog to me." Morgan again looked around for any staff who might overhear. Tiffany was busy at the desk, but she couldn't see anyone else.

"Because he's a guy and doesn't have a clue about how manipulative she is. He can just go back into his routine and pretend she's me. He really did love me, but she'll have him twisted around her finger before he knows what happened. I can't let it be that easy for her."

"Look, do you have any evidence to show her guilt that I could give to the police?" As a precaution, Morgan placed her hand over her mouth as she talked.

Gloria sat in one of the chairs across from Morgan— pulling it close to the desk so she could rest her elbows on it. Almost immediately another nurse came into the room and chose that particular chair to sit on.

"Oh no," Morgan whispered.

"Did you say something to me?" Nurse Betsy asked as she pulled on the chair.

"Hey, Betsy, how are you? No, I just thought about a conversation I need to have with my neighbor," Morgan lied. "She keeps an eye on Douglas when I'm at work."

Betsy nodded and tried to pull the chair out from under the desk, but Gloria hung on to the desk with all her strength.

"What in the heck is wrong with this chair?" Betsy said as she yanked on it again and again. "I've never seen this happen before."

"Who knows? All this furniture is so old—that chair was probably recently glued together and now it's stuck to the floor."

"Oh, well, I don't have enough time to sit anyway. I just wanted to chat with you for a second to catch up and grab one last cup of coffee before getting started. It's good to see you back at work, Morgan." Betsy looked under the desk again trying to figure out why the chair was stuck.

Gloria raised her hand to smack Betsy in the back of the head. Morgan stood up and moved closer to the kitchen while Betsy focused under the table. She pointed a finger at Gloria while she mouthed "no." Gloria lowered her hand and turned her head to look in the opposite direction.

"I don't see a problem, but it's weird to be stuck," Betsy commented.

Morgan went into the kitchen and got Betsy a cup of coffee.

"Hey, thanks, Morgan." Betsy took the cup and left the room.

When she was gone, Morgan turned back to Gloria.

"What is wrong with you?"

"I'm dead. What's wrong with you? Why won't you help?"

"I need evidence. Real evidence."

"Well, try this. When my sister Geneva came to identify my body, she whispered to me that I got exactly what I deserved. Then she said, 'Thanks for the new car, new husband, and rich life, sis.' That sounds pretty darn guilty to me."

"Yes, it does. But how will it sound to Chief Hill and that Thornton guy if I tell them that the late great Gloria Vanderveer told me that her evil twin sister killed her and confessed the crime to the dead body in the morgue? They're seasoned cops—I don't think they'll buy it."

Gloria flipped her hair over her shoulder and said, "You've got a point. I have to think about this some more. But if I come up with an answer, will you help?"

"Yes, I'll try to help you."

"Oh, you're so sweet. Let me think about it." Gloria stood to leave.

"Gloria, even in death, and despite the hole from the gunshot wound, you are a striking beauty. Did you ever model?"

"Why yes, I did, all the way through college. That's

how I paid my tuition."

"Some women have it all." Morgan smiled and shook her head.

"Yeah, I had it all. Now, not so much." Gloria smiled and added, "Thanks, Morgan."

Gloria left the desk and walked by the rack that held breakfast trays for the patients who had spent the night in the EC for observation. A nurse aide delivered the trays as fast as she could to hungry patients allowed to eat. Gloria reached onto one of the trays and took a slice of bacon. Looking back, she smiled and waved as she continued down the hall, glancing in every examination room on her way.

Morgan was sure that the bacon disappeared the moment Gloria touched it. She made a mental note to ask Gloria how this worked. She looked around the nurses' station again to make sure there were no witnesses to her conversation with Gloria. Tiffany was the only one at the desk. Morgan suspected the desk clerk heard some portions of the exchange with the ghost, so Morgan walked over and stood next to her.

"I didn't hear a word," Tiffany said before Morgan could ask. She did not look up from the keyboard and focused on entering the information into the computer for the stack of lab orders so they'd be distributed electronically to the correct charts.

"What did you hear?" Morgan asked with some concern.

"I don't really know, and I won't ask." Tiffany looked up to Morgan. "See, you're one of the people around here that I honestly trust. You give good advice, have excellent judgment, except about men, and you stick up for the little guy when administrators like Maxine sniff around. I don't know what happened to you recently, but it doesn't matter. When, and if, you need my help, please know you have it. I'm here on-call for you. Whatever it is and whenever it is, I'm here. Any conversations you have with new ghosts in your life, time loops, or even yourself, don't matter to me. I have your back."

Morgan's eyes filled with tears as she whispered, "Wow, I had no idea."

"Yeah, well, that's how I feel, and now you know. I will never talk about what I witness here at work unless you tell me to. I can play dumb when needed. Deal?"

"Deal. You're okay, Tiff, and I'm in your corner. Always," Morgan said.

"I know." Tiffany nodded and continued typing.

"Could you see or hear who I was talking to?" Morgan asked.

"No, but I heard a wee bit of your side of the conversation and heard you call her by name. Besides, we've only had one murdered female patient in the last couple of days."

Morgan went around the end of the desk as Tiffany cleared her throat.

"It's none of my business, but you might tell Gloria that if she has the capability, she ought to follow her sister herself and find out exactly what she's up to. You know since nobody can see her anyway." Tiffany shrugged, still keeping her eyes glued to the computer screen.

"You're right. She can do her own investigation. That is a great idea, thank you." Morgan walked away from the desk following the path Gloria had taken a few minutes before.

She checked in the closets and exam rooms walking around the entire EC but did not find Gloria. She went outside the EC and into the employee garage and then back inside. She made her way to the inside hallway that connected the EC to the hospital and that's when she finally caught a brief glimpse of Gloria—who seemed to be on her way to the cafeteria.

Morgan hurried to catch her, but Gloria moved at a fast pace with the hungry crowd on their way to breakfast.

Like any cafeteria, the huge open area was noisy with a

lot of people walking around. There were microwaves lining one wall next to water and ice dispensers. Floor to ceiling windows overlooking the courtyard were on three of the cafeteria walls. In the summer, extra tables with umbrellas were set up in the courtyard for diners.

When she got to the front of the cafeteria, Gloria was standing there with her arms outstretched as she breathed deeply through her nose.

"How do you do that?" Morgan asked in a low voice while moving her lips as little as possible.

"Do what?" Gloria swayed side to side with her eyes closed.

"Inhale without an exhale." Morgan looked all around to see if anyone was watching.

"It's not an inhale. Watch me because my chest doesn't move, but my nose fills with the most beautiful scents. It's bacon, glorious bacon. And eggs, oh look at those eggs. I love breakfast, and this aroma is to die for, as they say," said Gloria. She opened her eyes and grinned as she walked around the food stations.

"Are you hungry?" Morgan turned away from the people lined up for food.

"I'm not hungry, still, I ate that bacon from the tray in the EC, and it disappeared. I don't know where it went, since most of my stomach is gone, but there you have it. My nose still works, too. You know, when alive, I never ate bacon, because it's supposed to be so bad for you and look where that got me. I wish I'd eaten a pound of it a day. Anyway, I thought it might be nice to hang here for a while. Smells better here than everywhere else, certainly better than the EC, and I like the idea of food with unrestricted calories." Gloria checked the tray of each person in line to pay the cashier.

"I need to talk to you at some point. Not here, though. I don't want anyone to see me." Morgan covered her mouth with one hand and waved to a few people who called out her name.

"I'll check in when I return to the EC. Seriously, I need to get out of there for a while—it's not a fun place, and I'm bored, but I promise I will find you." Gloria abruptly followed a man to a nearby table. He was carrying a tray containing a double order of eggs, bacon, and toast that made Gloria drool over his food choices. She waved at Morgan, sat down across from the man, and got comfortable to watch him eat.

"He won't notice if a little bit of it disappears, right? He looks like a nervous eater to me, not the kind of guy who keeps track of how much food he bought."

When the gentleman answered a call on his phone, Gloria stole two strips of bacon from his plate. As before, the moment Gloria touched the food, it disappeared. The man put his phone back in his pocket, stared at his plate for a moment, shrugged, and continued eating.

Gloria giggled and applauded. She looked up at the ceiling and whispered, "Jackpot."

Morgan laughed and left the cafeteria. Once back in the EC, she checked the whiteboard and saw the usual asthma attacks, kidney stones, respiratory cases, flu, and potential heart attacks. She glanced at the list of patients in observation and noted that a Rosemary Garrett had been there overnight. The computers at the desk were in use, so Morgan left the nurses' station and went to a COW parked near the waiting room. She fired up the computer and read the report.

Rosemary Garrett was an attractive, thirty-five-year-old X-ray technician who worked at Good Sam. Morgan knew her well and they had shared a few laughs and conversations while on duty. From the EC record on the chart, Rosemary suffered severe bites, bruises to her eyes and lips, and a bump on the head when she fell on a glass coffee table while at a party with a friend. Morgan frowned as she read the chart and thought that Rosemary was lucky there weren't any serious injuries. She rubbed her neck as she continued reading and then felt that same twinge in her chest creep back.

Apparently, the patient denied any wrongdoing, but her story was off and didn't add up. In the history, Rosemary claimed that the bites were from what is now her ex-boyfriend and were received several nights ago—but the marks looked fresh to the resident who examined her and dictated the report. It also appeared that she was brought in by another Good Sam technician, Patsy Brigham, who attested to Rosemary's story.

Wanting to look for herself, Morgan entered Rosemary's room to get vital signs before discharge. The tall, willowy patient was on her side with her back to the door—a red aura with daggers of white-hot lights bounced around in time to her heartbeat.

Walking closer to the bed, she said, "Rosemary, it's me, Morgan. I have to take your blood pressure and temperature one last time so you can go home."

Rosemary stirred, turned over, and opened her eyes as best she could. The damage to her face was not extensive, but her eyes were swollen shut. The bruises were dark, her skin was cut in several places and held together with butterfly bandages, and her bottom lip was split.

"What happened?" Morgan asked as she touched Rosemary's shoulder. Immediately, in her mind's eye, there was a very muscular and completely nude man with long, blond hair who repeatedly bit the naked and exposed Rosemary. He teased her more each time she cried out in pain. He was far too rough, and Rosemary begged him to stop. Another woman was in the same room watching and, after a flash, Morgan recognized Patsy and noticed that she was nude, as well. Patsy was smoking a joint and popping a pill as she watched the man get on top of Rosemary, pinning her arms over her head, forcing himself on her.

Morgan realized the scene playing before her was from Rosemary's point of view—she was seeing the man through Rosemary's eyes.

"None of this seemed like a bad idea two hours ago,"

Patsy said to Rosemary in the vision.

"Get him off me," Rosemary cried.

"I can't," Patsy said helplessly.

Morgan saw the fist in her face as the blond man punched Rosemary hard. The lights went out and the room was black.

"You all right?" asked Rosemary.

"Yeah, I'm sorry, I drifted off for a few seconds there, which has become a habit for me since my surgery," Morgan lied.

"Well, do what you gotta do, Morgan. I just want to go home."

"Are you absolutely sure you don't want us to do a rape kit and call a counselor?"

"No way. I told the people here last night that it wasn't rape. It just got a little bit out of hand," Rosemary said as tears fell from her swollen eyes.

"It was a good idea two hours before it happened, though, right?"

Rosemary stared at Morgan. "What makes you say that?"

"I don't know, it just came to me," Morgan answered and held the woman's gaze.

"Well, let it go. It's over. I'm fine. Rosemary clenched her teeth and lifted her chin.

"Your friend Patsy is fine, as well?"

"Now who said Patsy had anything to do with this?" Rosemary sat up and propped her weight on her elbow in the direction of Morgan's voice. "I want to know what people say about us."

"Nobody said a word. It's just me. Was Patsy involved since she brought you in here?" Morgan pressed the button on the monitor for a last readout of the vital signs.

"Patsy's my friend. I called her when I got hurt."

Morgan sighed and said, "He gave her a hypnotic drug—she couldn't help you. *Oh my gosh*, she *couldn't* help you, Rosemary. It's not that she didn't, she *couldn't*."

Rosemary's nostrils flared. "I told you that Patsy wasn't there."

"And I say it wasn't totally Patsy's fault that she didn't help you. He gave her the hypnotic and she was unable to move. What did he do to her when he was finished with you? Listen, they will let you go home with a prescription for antibiotics and some discharge instructions that you should follow. Maybe Patsy needs them, too. Please, please, Rosemary, don't hesitate to come back if you need to. And think about the felony charges—you don't have to let him get away with this." Morgan walked toward the door ready to open it but stopped in hopes that Rosemary would change her mind.

"He drugged her?" Rosemary asked weakly.

"Yes, and I doubt if she even knows it. Rosemary, don't be angry with her. And please come back if you need us."

Ignoring Morgan's last comment, Rosemary rubbed her forehead as she asked, "How do you know this?"

"I don't know. Since my head exploded and was rewired, I know a lot," Morgan answered truthfully. "So far I'm pretty accurate."

"Maybe you can get some guaranteed lottery numbers," Rosemary said as she sat up on the side of the bed.

"That sounds great, but I don't think it works that way. Someone will be in to help you get dressed."

Out in the hall, Morgan shuddered and blew out a breath. She stood up straight, shook it off and said, "Okay, onward nurse. No time for emotions."

"I'm really sorry to hear that," Caleb said.

"Dr. Lightfoot. You need a bell on you if you plan to sneak around these halls like some sort of ninja." Morgan laughed, pleased to see him.

"Whatever turns you on." Caleb grinned and went the other direction.

Morgan blushed as she stood alone in the hall. She glanced around, smiled, and went on about her duties.

When she made her way back to the empty nurses' station, she sat in front of the computer and entered the data from Rosemary's visit. Morgan typed the time of discharge on the chart and before she knew it, next to that she was keying: *You did not lose your mind. You did not lose your mind.*

She was typing at a feverish pace with sweat breaking out on her forehead. It wasn't until the page was full that her hands fell to her sides. Morgan stood up and went to the kitchen for a cup of cocoa. She paced the tiny room as she sipped her drink and stared at the computer. She went back to the desk, held down the delete key, and watched the letters disappear.

She spotted Ellen walking down the hall, put her drink down, and hurried to her friend.

"What's up?" Ellen asked.

"I'm very hungry, in fact, I thought you could be talked into a fast ham and egg sandwich for lunch," coaxed Morgan. Ellen nodded and followed. Morgan pulled her cell phone out of her pocket and called Tiffany to let her know they were going to get a quick sandwich. Tiffany agreed to call if they were needed.

The cafeteria hummed with hundreds of people who ate, laughed, and cried, but Morgan was too focused searching all around the noisy room for signs of Gloria. It didn't take long to spot the redhead moving from table to table, stealing food from the plates of innocent diners. Morgan smiled and ordered two sandwiches while Ellen found seats at a table filled with nurses from other units in the hospital. By the time Morgan joined them, the ham from one of her sandwiches was gone. She scanned the room hoping to see Gloria.

They sat with Jenna, Katrina, and Daniel from the pediatric unit. The fourth nurse in their group, Rebecca, was in her thirty-ninth week of her first pregnancy and complained that she was tired and wanted to go into labor. Her friends shared ideas of how to get labor started.

"Sex always worked for me," Ellen said. "I've had four babies and each time I made love like a rabbit and delivered the next day. Of course, I was pretty close to my due dates at that point anyway."

Daniel laughed and said, "That's also how you started your pregnancies."

"Seriously, there's supposed to be oxytocin in the sperm that triggers labor to begin," Ellen insisted. "My mother saw that on the "Phil Donahue Show" years ago, and that's how she delivered me the next day. Ellen Burstyn was one of his guests that episode, and that's where she got my name."

"Look, I'm so miserable, I don't want my husband near me. I can barely get in and out of the car," Rebecca moaned.

"I've heard that champagne works," Daniel said. "I'm not sure exactly what you do with it, but I assume that you drink some of it and maybe douche with it."

"That's crazy," said Jenna. "Nobody douches anymore. And, Ellen, if there was oxytocin in sperm, then every baby would be delivered early."

"The apple doesn't fall until it's ripe or some idea like that," Morgan said. "You know, it could be how it's absorbed, so maybe that's why some women miscarry so often. I believe Ellen."

"Thank you, Morgan. I've always known you to be a wise and wonderful woman," Ellen replied.

"I've had two kids—each was overdue two weeks and had to be induced. Of course, I didn't try sex or champagne. Maybe that was my problem," Katrina said.

After a few minutes of debate, they said good-bye to the peds nurses and hurried back to the EC. Just as they entered through the pneumatic doors, a motor vehicle accident victim was brought in. Hit head-on by a truck, the teen was not expected to survive.

Morgan and Ellen assisted the doctors as they worked to save his life. They started IVs, monitored vital signs, and ordered X-rays. At one point, Morgan placed her hand on the boy's shoulder and knew instantly that he would be fine. The video in her mind revealed the accident and she knew he was distracted behind the wheel. In her vision, there was also an older version of the teen as he played soccer with a slight limp. He had a scar from the tracheotomy tube that had not yet been inserted and which she noticed added character to his handsome features.

When the boy was taken to the operating room, Morgan went to the EC waiting area to tell the parents that their son was on his way to surgery.

"Mr. and Mrs. Brewer?" she asked the couple she guessed to be his family. They sat close together with their hands intertwined and stood immediately when she said their names. The husband was clearly scared—with the muscles of his jaw visible as they grinded, and there were noticeable sweat stains on his shirt. The wife was tearful and bit her lower lip as it quivered.

"Your son was taken to surgery for multiple repairs. One of the doctors will speak to you up there and give you details. Please be assured that you have the best trauma surgeons in the region available to work on him," reported Morgan.

"Will he make it?" Mr. Brewer asked.

It was impossible to state that their son would survive when so many variables were at play in the operating room. Blood loss, prior health, drugs, and alcohol are critical factors to the outcome. Morgan saw the boy as an adult in her vision but was still unsure about the accuracy and didn't trust that her instincts were always right.

"He has the best possible chance to make it, Mr. Brewer," she said and walked them to the elevators closest to the surgical center. The elevator arrived and they got on—thanking her several times.

She turned her back on the elevators as a tingle started at the top of her head, traveled through her entire body, and exited through the bottom of her feet. She had no idea why she knew, but she whispered, "He will be fine." She knew it was truth. She smiled and returned to the nurses' desk.

Morgan pulled her cell out of her pocket and pressed buttons while she stood at the front of the desk. Savannah was home and answered on the second ring.

"Are you gonna be busy in a few hours?" Morgan asked.

"Depends on what you want," Savvy drawled. "I'm knee-deep in closets right now."

"I love it when you clean your closets. Do you have a new wardrobe for me in there?" Asked Morgan since Savannah often gave her clothes with the price tags still on them.

"Actually, I have a pair of faded jeans with lots of studs that might fit your long-legged frame. I bought them from some worthy charity and never planned to wear them. I think they'd be nice on you."

"I didn't know you would have jeans with studs in your house. Frankly, I'm stunned."

"Like I said, Morgan, they were purchased from a charity, and I had no plan to wear them, *ever*. I do wear jeans frequently but not those faded by some chemical means or decorated with shiny accessories. Now, what do you want besides my questionably tasteful garments?"

"I need you to come over after work and protect me while I share a complicated but fabulous story."

"I don't believe that I have eaten today, so on my journey to your neck of the woods, I'll pick up some of my favorite foods and appetizers so that we may dine elegantly while you tell me your story. I'll see you later." Savannah made kissy noises as she hung up.

Morgan smiled and put the phone back in her pocket. She heard a loud rustle coming from the table area at the back of the nurses' station. She followed the sound and stopped when she realized administrator Maxine had the random lab results and notes left there by the night shift in

142

her claw-like hands. She hadn't seen the woman since the detectives stopped by about Gloria.

"What exactly are you up to?"

Maxine nearly jumped out of her skin. "Oh, I thought Dr. Holt would be here."

"She isn't in that stack of paperwork."

"Don't be silly; I know that." Maxine dropped the papers on the desk.

"Then please leave the paperwork alone. You've violated a ton of privacy laws and someone could turn you in. Excuse me, Maxine, I have a call to make to the legal department, oh yeah, and security."

"Well, we'll see about that. Dr. Holt will be held responsible for confidential information left exposed where just anyone can read it. She's the one in violation of privacy laws." Maxine's face contorted into what could have been an evil smile. "Besides, who's going to believe you. Ever since your surgery, everyone working with you thinks you've lost it and you're crazy."

"I swear, Maxine, you are worse than a drive-by colonoscopy," snapped Morgan as she clenched her fists and glared at the woman.

"Oh, you think you're so smart and so special. We'll see about that." Maxine stared back with her cold, beady eyes. Her mouth was so pinched up and uneven, Morgan chuckled wondering if that also could have been a reptilian smile of some sort.

Satisfied that she remained queen of pointless remarks, Maxine skittered away from the conference room and back down the hall. Morgan watched her and had a brief pang of sympathy for the woman who had no friends and many enemies.

Morgan stood next to Tiffany's chair and said, "I wish that woman would stay away from here. I'd feel sorry for her if she weren't so damn black-hearted."

"She is the pencil-pusher for our area, boss. You know we have to deal with her whether we like it or not. Why does everyone dislike her so much?" Tiffany asked while clearing computer screens containing chart pages.

"Oh, child, many years ago some opioids went missing from the drug cart. Savvy found the shortage and notified Maxine, which is protocol. Maxine then unjustly accused Savannah of stealing the pills. It all blew up and got very ugly."

"Who did take them? Only the doctors carry keys."

"After three weeks of investigations, nasty words, and bad feelings, it turned out that the pharmacy had signed out the drugs and forgot to put them in the cart. They were later found as an overage on their inventory. The thing that really set Savvy off was the lack of loyalty from Maxine who was trying to use the situation to promote herself as an ace administrator. Truthfully, I'm surprised she's still working here, but I don't make the rules."

"I've never trusted her. She doesn't even acknowledge that I'm here and I keep my distance," Tiffany declared and added, "Maybe I'll hang some garlic here around the desk."

Morgan chuckled but quickly stopped as she felt the twinge in her chest, which made her wrinkle her nose. "I know something bad is going to happen, and I sure do hope that Maxine is not involved, but damnit, I know she will be somehow." She was rubbing her chest as she walked toward her office muttering. "I can feel it. It's so close I can almost smell it. Damn that woman."

CHAPTER 10

On the way home an odd smell permeated Morgan's car again. It was the burnt wire smell that was becoming familiar to her, so she kept one eye on the mirror and the other on the road. Once she caught a red light, she took the opportunity to look directly into the back seat, but there was nothing there. Confused, she sat back in place and glanced at the car in the lane to her right. Rudy, her newly deceased neighbor, was the driver. He looked at her, nodded once, and looked straight ahead again. When the light changed, he made an immediate right turn. Morgan sat dazed, unable to move until the car behind her blew their horn. She peeled away from the light and drove like a bat out of hell to her house.

By the time she pulled up to her house, Savvy's SUV was already there. Looking over the top of the newspaper in her hands and noticing Morgan, Savannah grinned. She sat on the top step of the porch and waited.

"Good afternoon, I've reported for duty as ordered. I also have assorted bagels, cream cheese, and chai tea." Savvy put the paper down and lifted all the bags at once. "I would have brought some chocolate, as well, but feared that would become a highly orgasmic experience.

Nonetheless, these foods cure most illnesses." Savannah paused and added, "You're as white as a ghost. Oh, sorry, poor choice of words, but what happened to upset you?"

"Well, I had a pretty darn creepy day. Come on in, my friend, because do I have a story for you." Morgan's hands shook as she tried to insert her key to unlock the front door. She added, "I can't swear that I believe it all myself."

As she finished speaking, the door popped, creaked, and opened wide before Morgan got the key in the lock. The aroma of freshly baked bread greeted the women.

"I thought you worked today. If I didn't know better, I'd think my grandmother had been here since sunrise. You don't bake do you, Morgan?"

Morgan looked at her friend and muttered, "You know very well that I can't bake—I can barely find a bakery with a map."

"I didn't think you knew your way around a kitchen. That skill set requires using pans and that square oven appliance that you use for storage," replied Savannah as she walked into the kitchen and placed her hand on the oven's glass door.

"No heat." Savvy turned to Morgan.

"I don't know what to tell you. I smell the fresh bread in here as much as you do, and I don't have a clue what it's all about—I was at work." Morgan looked around the room.

Savannah looked around, as well. "Well, besides gardening, my guess is that your ghostly roommates also bake. By the way, did you notice that the roses in your back yard are much taller and fuller than they were a couple of days ago? The colors are also far more vivid."

"Well, no, I didn't notice the flowers. I guess the Wilkersons could be gardening, cooking, and baking. I'm gonna have to pay more attention to what's going on around me I guess."

"So, what's new from the cosmos and in your little bungalow?" Savvy tipped the bag of bagels to peer inside.

"I think I might have positive proof that ghosts do exist."

"Well, I think I'd like to hear about that." Savannah smiled as she selected a garlic bagel and sawed it in two. "I really should have bought a couple of the decadent brownies they had at the bagel shop. It would have rounded out this meal with dessert and we wouldn't miss any of the food groups—chocolate being its own food group, as you know."

"Before you overdose on food, let me explain what happened to me in the last twenty-four hours," Morgan said as she smeared cream cheese on her bagel choice. "I'm not sure where to begin, but here it goes." She took a big drink of chai.

Morgan was factual, unemotional, and very precise as she recounted what she saw and experienced in the last couple of days. The writing, Rudy's ghost, the young man from the motor vehicle accident, and her multiple conversations with Gloria. When she finished, Savannah nodded and pursed her lips.

"This is just a bit more than I expected," Savvy said in between sips of her drink.

Morgan hesitated for a moment and then said, "That's not all—now I hear sounds and voices day and night. I used to be able to clean the house or read or whatever to stay busy and ignore it but gradually, it became so involved, it felt like I was part of it and not an observer anymore. I hear voices all over this house. I know the Wilkersons but there are many other voices and they're not in my head. I hear them from other rooms, and when I follow the sound, no one is there. I've told you about the recurrent party dreams and the sound of fine china and crystal. Savvy, there's a party here in this house, and I'm not invited."

Morgan shared her experiences with faces in the car and bathroom visits in detail. She stopped and took another drink of tea.

"I'm still with you," Savannah said as she nibbled at her bagel and drank the tea. "This is certainly a lot more than I expected, but I'm still listening."

"It's a lot to take in. Are you scared yet?"

"No, not yet. Keep on." Savannah made the sign of the cross over her heart and smiled.

"There have been several more unusual experiences at work than I told you at first. It seems I can predict which patients will die and which ones won't. I also saw a sexual attack from the victim's perspective." Morgan pinched her lower lip and watched for Savvy's response.

"You saw the attacker?" Savannah tilted her head to one side. "Did you call the police?"

"Yes, I saw the attacker, and no, I didn't call the police, because the victim refused to press charges. She apparently knew the guy, and the victim was Rosemary from Radiology, you know her. She and her little twisted friend Patsy got into some nasty sex, and Rosemary was injured and attacked. Bites, scratches, bruises, and tears. I don't know what he did to Patsy except for the hypnotic drug."

Savannah sat very straight and nodded. "I do know Rosemary. Please continue."

"Rosemary said it was consensual and that it got out of hand." Morgan tossed the remainder of her bagel onto the plate. "I suppose you haven't looked at the journal that I kept as you suggested?"

Savvy shook her head. "I'm sorry, I didn't look at it."

"Well, there was an old notebook around here and had quite a few clean pages left in it. I wrote about a woman who walked around Detroit. I don't have a clue who she was other than Elisabeth Wilkerson's mom. She knew me, though."

Morgan continued, "When I snapped out of it a few hours later there were pages and pages of notes written in the notebook. Savannah, it wasn't the handwriting from before—none of it." After a pause, she added, "Do you believe everything I'm telling you?"

"Don't be silly, of course I believe you. We've seen the results of automatic handwriting, but this time it was Elisabeth's mother. Correct?"

"Yes, that was new. Elisabeth's mother turned around and spoke to me as if I were part of her audience. You know how actors on TV turn and talk directly to the camera? That's what she did, and she called me by name and said I would feel better soon. This gives me the creeps." Morgan wrapped her arms around herself.

"Do you want to write now?"

"Not really, but I'll do it if you want."

"I want you to, but bless yourself, child. Can you stay awake while we do this?"

"Look, it seriously drains my energy. If we don't spend a lot of time, I can stay awake. If it goes on for a while, I'm gone and running on fumes."

With the pen and notebook still on the counter, Morgan picked them up and sat at the table. She held the pen and hovered her hand over the notebook. Her hand did not move.

"Write your name or start a grocery list or pretend it's a letter to someone," Savannah suggested.

"Who?"

"I don't think it matters, Morgan, just put pen to paper and see what happens."

"Oh, okay, well, this is a grocery list and the word 'bananas' should appear on the paper directly from my pen." However, the pen wrote *Kirk Chester*.

"That's an odd way to spell bananas," Savannah drawled.

"No joke." Morgan watched the pen in her hand write: *He lives in Patsy's complex, on the second floor. Patsy knows him well and trusts him not.*

Morgan relaxed and stopped for a few seconds but not for long. Suddenly the pen popped up again and she continued to write: *Police want him.*

"I bet that's the guy who hurt Rosemary," said Morgan

aloud. Again, she wrote: *He is wanted by all police, not just one policeman. Patsy is her friend.*

"Pardon me, but just exactly who are you?" Savannah directed her question to the piece of paper.

Morgan wrote: *We are Elisabeth and Jonathan Wilkerson.*

"Why have you chosen now to become involved in the life of Morgan Cutler?" Savvy paced the room as she spoke.

As we've already told you, she needs us, and we can help.

"Are you two some kind of ghostly crime stoppers? I'm not so sure that either of you realize what harm you've caused our fine friend here." Savannah pointed to Morgan who was crouched over the paper.

Morgan looked up and said, "Savannah, don't be so rude to them. Hey, this pen is too hot to hold." She tried to drop it, but it was stuck to her hand. She pulled on her fingers one at a time—still couldn't let go.

Savannah got the ice out of the freezer and plopped the cubes into a freezer bag that she took to Morgan.

"Our friend Morgan here is used to a life alone and does not appreciate contact with someone from your world," said Savannah as she tossed the bag of ice to Morgan who was still busy pulling on her fingers to let go of the pen. Morgan caught the bag with her left hand and placed the ice over her right fist.

"Obviously, you mean no harm, but we must come to some sort of compromise so that everyone is peaceful in this house," Savvy said.

"The heat from the pen stopped," shouted Morgan. "I can let go. Thank you."

"So, are we in agreement?" Savannah said to the room.

Morgan wrote: *Yes.*

"Good, now let's recap so everyone understands the rules. Number one, no more Mr. Grabby-Touchy with Morgan when she's naked in the shower, in the bed, or in the arms of another man. Is that clear, Professor Wilkerson?"

Yes, madam, was written on the notepad.

"Excellent. However, it is doctor and not madam. Next, you are to respect Morgan's privacy overall in terms of gentlemen callers, as well. No giggles, no ears against the doors, no invisible peeps. Is that clear to both of you?"

Morgan wrote: *Yes, doctor.*

"Good, then let's go on and celebrate this new union. Morgan, turn on some of your big band CDs for your guests."

Instantly, Morgan released the pen and wiggled her fingers before she went to the CD player in the library where the music was kept. She loaded the CD, turned up the volume, and started back to the kitchen. Savannah was in the hall waiting for her.

Savannah asked, "Do you smell wet dog? Where is Douglas?"

"He's sound asleep. This isn't his time of day to be social." Morgan sniffed and tried to follow the source.

The lights got brighter and dimmed.

"Do you see what I see?" Savannah inched along the wall to the kitchen.

"I think so." Morgan crept along the other side of the hall.

The two women went into the kitchen and stood by the sink while they watched a very elegant couple, probably in their forties, gliding and dancing in the middle of the kitchen floor, into the dining room, and back to the kitchen. The tall, graceful couple was equally beautiful as they kept time with the music. He had blond ringlets and she had strawberry blonde hair piled high on her head. They looked so in love with each other as they dipped, laughed, and moved fluidly around the room.

"Savvy, can you see through them?"

Without taking her eyes from the couple, Savvy replied, "Oh, yes. You know, I've never had this happen before. I've heard of it but never had it happen to me."

"Then they're not flesh and blood?" Morgan whispered

and strained to see the dancers move into the dining room.

"No, it's more of a hologram." Savvy turned away from the dancers and added, "I think my work here is done."

"Your ass it's done. You are not going to leave me here alone with them while they dance in the kitchen. You summoned them—you make them leave, Savvy. I mean it," Morgan hissed.

"Don't they look like Ken and Barbie from another time? I swear they are the most stunning couple I've ever seen."

"Ever *seen through*, you mean. Let's not overlook that tiny little detail. Savannah, I do appreciate that you have acted as a mediator, but honestly, rather than reach a compromise, I would like these visitors to go away back to their dimension. They can find another house to haunt and leave me and my dog alone."

"These people are delightful. Let them cut a rug for a while."

"Savvy, you've handled this quite well—you've been in control and quite friendly, which is generally beyond your patience and tolerance. What's the truth? Have you interacted with ghosts before?"

"I have never in my life seen a connection such as this between our world and theirs. Never." Savannah walked over to the table and took the last bite of bagel off her plate and popped it in her mouth. She sipped some tea and dabbed her lips with a paper napkin before announcing, "I think it's time for me to go." She then walked quickly to the front door.

Morgan caught up to her and they watched the couple dancing, dipping, and twirling in the kitchen, dining room, and hall.

"See, they don't even know that you're gone." Savannah was smiling and picked up her purse and keys and turned back to Morgan.

"Be nice to your guests. This is an exceptional situation, besides, they've chosen you to protect and communicate with."

"And you. Don't forget they acknowledge you, as well. I'm not alone in this, right?" Morgan crossed her arms and stood toe to toe with Savvy as she continued, "As long as there aren't any grabs or peeps, I might be able to handle this situation. They aren't as scary once you see them as people. It's confusing because last time they seemed solid to me and this hologram appearance doesn't totally make sense. Besides, how could I get them out of here anyway? It was their house first, technically. Maybe it is the energy at work here. New batteries work better than old ones, right? Hmmm, I could be onto something."

Savvy cleared her throat and said softly, "Morgan, I've told you before that my mother has the gift and her mother before her had the gift. Some believe that I have a little of the gift. I've never seriously tested it before, but who knows if any of that is true? The point is—you and I clearly see and hear what others cannot. Let's just enjoy it for what it is, okay?"

"*I knew it*. Why didn't you ever tell me that you're psychic? You have an ability to plug-in to the other side, and not once in twenty years did you share that with me? Don't you trust me?"

Savvy looked away and whispered, "I thought you'd assume that I was lonely, insane, or a combination. I also didn't want you to race to a shelter and buy me a dozen cats so I wouldn't be by myself."

Not saying another word, Morgan hugged Savvy and walked with her to the SUV. Savannah started the engine and waved as she backed out and drove down the street.

Turning to the house after watching Savvy drive away, Morgan noticed the front door was still open—making it easy to see all the way through to the rear of the house and the back door was now wide open. She tensed as she hurried to the kitchen.

The music was playing but the Wilkersons were nowhere in sight. Morgan went to the front of the house and checked the living room, library, dining room, and small bath. She stood in the foyer and shouted, "Where did you people go? If you left this house, tell me so I don't keep searching."

Douglas barked from the kitchen and she raced to his side. She glanced through the open door and saw the Wilkersons dancing in front of God and the entire neighborhood in the backyard. The top half of their torsos looked like a professional dance team while their bottom halves were invisible. Morgan grabbed a dish towel, raced outside, stopped, went back to the library to turn off the music, and ran outside again.

The Wilkersons danced so closely together, they looked melded into one. She swung her dish towel at them.

"Go back in the house, you two. What if someone sees you?" Morgan hissed as she slapped at the couple with the dish towel.

"Morgan, calm down," Elisabeth said. "No one else can see us."

"Your neighbors are far more likely to react to the sight of a deranged, open-mouthed, but quite lovely, brunette intent on attacking thin air with a skimpy dish towel, young lady," Jonathan spoke as he elegantly dipped Elisabeth.

"Just get back in the house. This is not part of the deal. I don't want the neighbors to say this house is haunted. It's really bad for the neighborhood," she shouted as she followed them around the yard.

"Woman, again, no one can see us, but they can see you. Is it part of your plan to tell everyone you have taken up some ancient art of folk dance? You look ridiculous with that rag in your hand." Jonathan faced her with his arms visible only to the elbows. She guessed that his hands were likely on his hips as he admonished her, but since his hips were invisible, it was difficult for her to say for sure.

Morgan and Jonathan were in a standoff prompting Elisabeth to pull Jonathan alongside to return to the house. He glared at her as Elisabeth guided him to the back porch and into the house—out of view of neighbors. Morgan leaned an arm against a tree waiting for her heart rate to slow and giggled as she thought about the new cardio workout she had invented. It would be called the aerobic ghost dance.

She approached the house and could see the Wilkersons in the kitchen. They waved at her through the open door and disappeared in an instant. Morgan entered, shut the door, and set the deadbolt remembering what Savvy said about not being able to lock them out. She began to laugh and cry at the same time. When she couldn't cry anymore, she wiped her nose on her sleeve and looked around the room.

"I will go to my bedroom now," Morgan said aloud as she got up on her knees. The kitchen light blinked twice. She now understood that the Wilkersons blinked the lights when they agreed or approved of her comments or actions. She continued, "There will be a gentleman here in the morning for an informal first date and you promised that you'd behave." The kitchen light blinked several times. "You know, guys, we have a long way to go, but this just might work out."

CHAPTER 11

The next morning, Morgan dressed in her favorite jeans and bright red Henley T-shirt. She was in the kitchen fixing a travel cup with tea and one with coffee when the doorbell rang. Glancing around the room she saw the overhead light flash several times. She smiled and said in a hushed voice, "Please, don't mess this up for me." The light stopped.

When she opened the front door, Caleb was standing there looking absolutely gorgeous. He wore a white oxford shirt with the sleeves rolled up to show off perfect arms with exactly the correct amount of hair and muscle. His faded jeans were tight in the right places. His shoulders were broad, legs long, and good muscle tone everywhere.

"No one like you has ever been at my door before." Morgan grinned as she stepped aside to let the man enter.

He smiled and held his arms out to his sides. "There's more to me than the package, you know."

"Who cares?" Morgan replied on her way back to the kitchen for the drinks.

"Let's go soon. I want to get to the flea market early because good items sell out fast." He grinned as he saw the two cups in her hands.

Morgan handed the coffee to him, grabbed her jacket from the table, and hurried him out to the porch. She was locking the door when she heard a very soft voice say "yum." She wasn't sure if she heard it or had said it herself. Looking at Caleb waiting on the sidewalk undisturbed, she decided it must have been Elisabeth. God forbid it was Jonathan.

Caleb opened the door to his SUV as Morgan threw herself inside the vehicle. She turned to speak to him before he went around to the other side.

"I can't pretend to be dainty when I get into a full-size SUV, since I don't know where my feet should go or how to leap without looking like a clod. Regardless, I'm comfortably seated now and the leather feels like butter and so cushy." He closed the door and went around to the driver's side. She grinned at him when he opened that door and slid into the seat.

Caleb smiled and said, "Obviously, I can take you anywhere as long as I do it early."

"What does that mean?"

"You haven't spilled any food on yourself yet."

"How do you know about my reputation with stains?"

"There are medical residents who know the cafeteria menu based on the color of the stains on your scrubs."

"Ah, now I get it. Well, the day is young, my friend. I could be a rainbow of hues by the time we return to this little abode." She motioned for him to get the car in gear.

After a few minutes of silence, Morgan asked, "So why do women find you so cold and detached?" She put her hand over her mouth and added, "I am so sorry, I have no idea why I blurted that out, since it's none of my business anyway. I guess I'm nervous—you make me nervous."

"It's okay. Women do find me aloof. I'm used to it. I also make a lot of women nervous."

"Oh, you're one of those men. You like the quick women, not to be mistaken with the fast girls who also have a purpose, but you're more entertained with the quick verbal ones. If they don't challenge you or stimulate your mind—it's all quiet on the western front, right?"

He kept his eyes straight ahead on the road, but she thought he smiled a tiny bit.

"Hmmm, no comment. Smart man. Okay, I have another question for you," Morgan spoke as she turned in her seat toward him.

When Caleb nodded for her to continue, she asked, "Okay, when did the accident with the puck happen?"

"Just about twenty-five years ago, when I was only seventeen."

"Ah, we're about the same age."

"That's good to know. Anyway, I was out cold for a long time after the accident. The puck hit me so hard, I flew back and cracked my head on the rink wall and then again on the ice. By the time the ambulance got there I was losing a lot of blood internally and from my face." Caleb absently stroked the scar on his chin as he spoke. "I was in a daze for another day or so. When I finally did wake up my world had changed and I've been gifted ever since." He paused and added, "In my mind it's just a heightened awareness, you know, like superior eyesight or hearing."

"I came back to work less than two weeks ago and still don't understand the activity in my head. I hear people moan, see wisps of smoke, smell burnt paper and cords, and a new talent—the ability to see auras. Can you explain that to me?"

"You know, you could talk to a psychic or a neurologist or you could even have a cleansing of the Emergency Center, if the hospital would approve it. That won't stop the auras but the smells, sounds, and sights could disappear."

"No way to have a cleansing if I want to keep my job there. They are not tolerant of supernatural or paranormal issues. Strange, isn't it that we're in the business of health, life, and death but we don't recognize the spiritual aspect? We're supposed to be the ones with all the answers—not more questions." Morgan straightened in her seat and looked out the side window.

"You can always go home every night and do research on the Internet, and when you're more comfortable, I'll take you to a couple of lectures at the university. They can give you the scientific basis for what has happened to you. In the meantime, find a psychic."

"I think I have already." Morgan grinned at him.

"Not really. You need a real psychic, not someone who's just gifted. There's a big, big difference. You need to understand that there are talented people who can paint, sing, or play the piano in such a way that it lifts your spirit—these people are sensitives. Then there are people who can use their minds the same way a fine carpenter uses his hands to create a masterpiece that moves your soul—that true artist would be a psychic. You need help from a real psychic, not someone like me." He glanced at her and continued, "I'm more of a sensitive because I see auras, sense vibes, and pick up on electrical changes."

"So, you have never seen a ghost?"

"I think maybe in my dreams, which is more of a visitation than a sighting."

"Do you believe some people can honestly see ghosts and communicate with them?"

"Of course."

"Why can't everyone see them?"

"Same reason one guy walks into the EC with a point-blank gunshot wound to the head, or a small woman pulls a car door off its hinges to rescue her baby and only has a bruise to show for it. These are both examples of extraordinary situations where they both survive despite the expected outcome and scientific logic. Why does this happen? Miracles? Okay, maybe we see several miracles a week at work. Truth is, it doesn't matter why it happens, but as humans, we desperately want explanations and closure for everything we see and hear. If we see ghosts, the general population wants clarification and definition of exactly what it is. It also generates such fear and trepidation to most of us, very few are willing to share their experiences with this phenomenon for fear of being thought insane or silly. I think that's from the lack of control in the situation and the scary movies and books. I do have a theory, though, if you want to hear it."

"I would love to hear your theory."

"Okay, we live in a three-dimensional world, right? We understand the spatial science of a straight line having no depth whatsoever. Think of that straight line drawn on a piece of paper. Now you want to make it two-dimensional. So, you take your straight line, draw three additional lines, and create a square. That square is two-dimensional because it has width and height, but still no depth. Well, you want depth, so you add even more lines to turn this picture into a cube with six sides. What started as a straight line is now a cube with front, back, top, bottom, and sides. It is now three-dimensional by virtue of width, height, and depth. Are you still with me?"

"So far, but it sounds like math and I could check out any time."

Caleb laughed and continued, "What if there is a fourth dimension? What if that fourth dimension is heaven, hell, or where spirits go when we die? The human mind can comprehend just three dimensions, therefore, if the fourth dimension exists, only some of us, who are highly gifted, or wired differently can see it."

"Oh, so when someone goes 'into the light,' it's the light from the fourth dimension?"

"Yes, I think so. Maybe spirits go to the light and choose to stay there, or they come back to earth in the third dimension and claim to have had a near-death experience. If they choose to stay there, they still have the option of going back and forth, if they wish, for unfinished business, or whatever. Because the light is different there and vibrations are different, they appear to us as ghosts anywhere from holograms to three-dimensional figures, depending on their electrical strength. Also, while they're visiting here in this dimension, if they don't have a great deal of energy of their own, they take ours. I've heard psychics on television talk about being exhausted after a day's work communicating with the other side. I'm sure the entities are using power from this side."

"Makes sense, but what if a ghost on this side picks something up, like a coffee cup, or some food? Why don't we see those things floating around a room?"

"I would think that as soon as they touch it, the item becomes part of the fourth dimension because they are part of the fourth dimension and just passing through here. We can no longer see the object once they have it."

"Caleb, are you saying the fourth dimension is all around?"

"I think it has to be an infinite space that exists everywhere around us. We are surrounded by the fourth dimension. I refuse to believe that with the intricacies of the human body and the brilliance of the human mind, that this existence is all there is."

Morgan remained quiet while she thought about what he said. Caleb glanced at her often and finally asked, "Do you think I'm out there in space? Totally nuts?"

"No, it's actually good logic. Who's to say? Maybe I need to do more research." She smiled warmly at Caleb and looked out the window as the twinge started deep in her chest.

"If you get really good at this psychic power, it'll be more difficult to surprise you," Caleb said and patted her hand. She could feel the heat that poured from him making her heart flutter.

"Where are we off to?" Morgan asked as she moved her hand away from his reach.

"A little town with the most fantastic flea market you've ever seen," Caleb said as he put his hand back on the steering wheel.

They drove along for a while before he pulled into a

restaurant. "How about another coffee, oh wait, you don't drink coffee," he said. "How about the best tea on earth?"

"No arguments from me."

"It won't match your shirt very well."

"I know, but the shirt is meant to match the ketchup, salsa, or sauce that will be on my fries, tacos, pizza, or spaghetti. I weighed all the options, and red won as the safest color."

"That's why I like you—you think ahead." Caleb went inside to order and returned to the SUV a few minutes later with tea, donuts, and a bagel split in half. He gave her half of the bagel, and when she finished, she worked on the donuts.

"Where did you grow up?" Morgan brushed crumbs from her shirt as she spoke.

"A small town in northern Michigan, close to Traverse City. I'm the middle kid of five, so overachiever from an early age. What about you?"

"I grew up in Pontiac, so pretty much a city girl. I had a sister who died years ago. My parents are gone now and it's just me. I'm all that's left." She sighed.

Caleb glanced at her and then looked back at the road.

"Lightfoot sounds like a Native American name. Is it?"

"No, it's Anglo-Saxon. The name comes from Olde English, but as luck would have it, I am half Chippewa on my mom's side. Dad's side is all English."

"Lightfoot is English? It sounds like a supreme hunter who can sneak up on animals or enemies."

"Or it sounds like Gordon Lightfoot, popular Canadian singer of English descent," Caleb said and smiled. "He's not my father but I'm sure they're related. And I can't sing, so don't ask."

"Okay, okay. Moving on. How do you know about this little town with the flea market?"

"My parents didn't have a lot of money when I was a kid so we used to do one or two tank trips around the state instead of major vacations. You know, drive one long day

KATE MACINNIS

on the road without spending their hard-earned cash on camping or a motel. We found the flea market on one of those trips and it sort of became a habit to visit. It's one of my favorite places. I also started a free clinic there on Saturdays to help the locals when they lost their health insurance. The factory where luxury boats were built bellied up years ago and left them all without work."

Morgan nodded and looked away. She had heard that story so many times when the auto industry downsized ten years ago causing all related manufacturers to suffer, too. No extra money meant no extra purchases. Businesses evaporated left and right, leaving unemployment in their wake.

They rode along in silence until a sign indicated the flea market was ahead. At the crest of the hill overlooking the area, Morgan saw tent after tent that stretched along roughly twenty-five acres of property.

"This looks as big as the Ann Arbor Art Fair." Morgan was impressed and inspected all around. The aroma of the food trucks, popcorn, and fresh air made her smile.

"Not quite the art fair yet but someday they'd like to be that big. I know a lot of people who run some of the tents. I'll introduce you." Caleb began searching for a place to park the SUV. He finally found a spot and they got out to walk to the tents. The tents were in rows with wide aisles in between. Everyone knew Caleb, and he took the time to speak to each person who got his attention. He shook hands, hugged, and bumped fists with two dozen people in the first half-hour. While he was busy with old friends, she wandered around the aisles looking at merchandise. He had introduced her to a couple of his friends as "a good friend and co-worker from his new job." It made her feel less important, even though it was the honest truth.

"What do you think of the place?" Caleb asked when he found her at a tent with old magazines.

"This place has stellar quality and variety. I'm shocked that I've never heard of it before. Oh, by the way, I got a few dirty looks from some young ladies who are, no doubt, enamored with you." Morgan shrugged and added, "If I were one of them, I'd give me a dirty look, too."

Caleb shook his head and pointed her to the main aisle of the tents. For hours, they browsed, ate popcorn, Cajun French fries, buffalo French fries with hot sauce and bleu cheese, deep-fried Snickers, deep-fried pickles, and funnel cakes. When Morgan's red T-shirt was covered in too many drips, Caleb bought her a black one with a map of the Michigan mitten and a large finger that pointed to their location in the famous Michigan thumb.

"I like this shirt. The graphic adds a certain cachet to my ensemble," said Morgan. "Thank you, Caleb."

Caleb squeezed her hand as he directed her to a booth with antique electronics. He spotted an old tabletop radio and walked over to it.

"My dad had one of these Zenith radios when I was little. He used to listen to the hockey games from Canada every Saturday night. He said the announcers were better on the radio and the games always looked better than on television." Caleb grinned as he touched the radio and moved the dial.

"My dad had one of those, too," Morgan said. "He listened to hockey, baseball, and football games on it. Same reason, he thought the announcers were better on radio than TV."

"This is a 1949 Zenith Bakelite and it looks like it's in great condition." Caleb picked up the radio and asked, "Hey, Jack, how are you today?" A very large man turned around to face Caleb and Morgan.

The burly man with kind eyes smiled and answered, "Hey, doc, how are ya? Did ya fall in love with my granddad's radio?"

"I think I might have. How much?"

Jack leaned around Caleb and looked at Morgan. "Well, who are you, honey? Are you a new friend of the doc? We sure do keep an eye on him here, ya know. He's one of our special people, even when he's away in the big city. He's a small-town lad at heart. Plenty of ladies around here are still after this guy." Jack winked and indicated Caleb with a nod.

She held out her hand to Jack, "Oh, I'm Morgan Cutler. Your doc found me at the hospital in Oakland County—we work together."

"Oh, I see, city girl. Well, lucky you. You'll have to be careful, though, there are plenty of ladies who won't take kindly to strangers who have his attention." Jack grinned.

"Not that many, Jack. You make me sound like the town stud, and I'm far from it. Besides, you have a woman who loves you the way you are, so why worry about me?"

"I hate to see you alone, Cal. If I'm happy, I want everybody to be happy," Jack answered as he sipped a cup of coffee.

"Yeah, yeah. Now, back to the radio. What do you want for it?" Caleb asked as he tinkered with the dials.

"How about twenty bucks?" Jack put the coffee down and crossed his arms.

"Wait a minute, does it work?" Caleb held the radio up and tilted his head as he spoke to Jack.

"Of course, it works. Hang on a second and I'll plug it in and show you." Jack looked around on the ground, found a surge protector, and took the radio from Caleb.

"You don't have to do that, I believe you," Caleb said as he handed the radio to Jack's outstretched hands.

"No, I want to show you just how good it is." Jack plugged it in and the radio popped, whistled, and cracked. In seconds, WJR from Detroit, more than seventy-five miles away, blared out of the speakers as if the radio were brand new.

"See, I told you it worked." Jack beamed as he nodded to Caleb and Morgan.

"I didn't doubt it. How about twenty-five dollars instead? I want you to get what it's worth." Caleb stuck his hand out to shake with Jack.

"Deal, it's yours. I'll get a box for you," Jack spoke as he went behind a screen to search for a box to fit the radio.

"I own an old radio now." Caleb grinned at Morgan.

"That you do. Now the thrills will never stop." Morgan touched the radio gently.

"I think this purchase is special, Morgan."

"Well, I don't know what your dad's radio was like, *Cal*, but my dad's radio was not special. In fact, it buzzed and hummed and had a plan of its own when it played."

Caleb grinned and said, "I am really excited about this purchase."

"Far be it from me to ruin your good mood." Morgan touched his arm and jerked her hand away as his heat shot through her hand and up to her shoulder. She felt herself blush and looked up to see Caleb grinning.

"Whoa, fella. We don't know each other that well."

"Oh, I'm excited … about the radio."

"We still don't know each other that well. Slow down, mister."

Jack returned with the box, packed the radio, and added some Styrofoam peanuts. "You're all set." He handed the box to Caleb.

Morgan saw a pink aura appear all around Jack, indicating he was a compassionate helper just like Ellen and Tiffany. They said their good-byes and moved away from the tent. On their walk back to the SUV, Caleb glanced at his watch and said, "You won't believe this, but it's almost 5:30 p.m. Would you like to go to a local place and have an early dinner? We've eaten so much junk today, I genuinely need some solid food to balance all the bad. How does that sound?"

"Well, I think I could use a meal, too. We did eat a lot of sugar, but I assumed that we walked it all off, so dinner is a bonus and we don't have to worry about the calories at all."

"You don't have to worry about calories anyway,

Morgan. You're perfect and luscious in all the right places."

"Yowza," Morgan said as her legs turned to rubber. "Yeah, well, thanks, that's nice. Yikes. Let's go to a restaurant soon, okay."

When they got to the SUV, Caleb pulled his cell phone out of his pocket, checked his voice mail, and scowled. "I have to make a call. My sister says it's urgent. This won't take long." He got out and walked far enough that Morgan couldn't hear his conversation.

Morgan watched him as he paced or stood with one gorgeous long leg propped on a metal bench. Caleb clicked off his cell phone, put it back in his pocket, and returned.

"What's wrong?"

"A baby was kidnapped near Houghton Lake, which is way north of here," he said as he slid behind the wheel. "Caroline, my sister, said that her best friend's baby was snatched from a cart at a local grocery store when the mom turned away for a second. That is so cold to take a baby from its mom."

"Ohmigod, that's awful." Morgan put a hand on Caleb's arm and asked, "What can we do?"

"There's an Amber alert and the state police and Feds are involved. All of us should be on the lookout. She called me because you never know if a kidnapped child will show up in an emergency room and she assumed I was at work. Maybe I should call the EC. She didn't say if it was a statewide alert or not." Caleb took the phone out of his pocket and tapped the EC number. He gave the details to the doctor on duty and put the phone away. Morgan watched him as she chewed on her lip and thought about the baby and the parents.

Caleb said, "Let's get on the road and go to Sadie's Diner and have a decent meal." He put the car in gear and pulled out of the park.

Five minutes later they were parked in front of a little restaurant that looked like a time warp from the 1930s. It was a one-story rectangle made of cement blocks painted barn red. Small windows were cut into the stone and each was decorated with a window box on the outside and Priscilla curtains on the inside. There were metal advertisements attached for various brands of pop and cigarettes that were no longer around. Michiganders call soda "pop" because of the sound it makes when the cap is removed. Soda in Michigan is something else entirely and associated with alcohol or ice cream. On the front porch were old-fashioned rocking chairs and a little pot-bellied stove for cold days.

"If one of the Waltons poked their head out of this place to say goodnight, I wouldn't be surprised," Morgan said, watching for Caleb's reaction.

"They still dine here. The whole family comes down off the mountain just to eat here at Sadie's." He smiled at her and Morgan laughed. Again, the twinge in her chest itched.

They got out of the SUV and walked into the diner's interior that was pure knotty pine. The place exuded warmth, garlic, and the smell of fresh coffee. The cash register was near the door and sat perched on top of a glass counter filled with candies Morgan hadn't seen since she was a child.

The place was busy and noisy. There were red and white checked oilcloths on every table with a small vase of fresh flowers in the center. A television was mounted in the upper corner of the room and set on TV Land. "Leave it to Beaver" was on the air.

The woman behind the counter obviously knew Caleb and waved for them to take a table at the front of the restaurant. There was an elderly couple on one side of the empty table and a couple with a fussy baby on the other, but Morgan's eyes were fixed on the television show.

"I watched the reruns of this when I was a kid," she whispered to Caleb. He smiled and picked up the menus standing on the table—handing one to her and keeping one for himself.

The menu reminded her of an older time. The selections and prices were typed onto the page in two columns. She was surprised to see the diner had an eclectic list of foods given the place looked like a Depression-era restaurant with the requisite blue willow dishes on every table. Morgan would never have expected choices to include meatball subs and spaghetti carbonara, but they did.

The woman behind the counter had cashed out a few customers and hurried over to the table the first chance she had. She carried an order pad with pencil and looked to be in her mid-sixties with a hard platinum color to her hair. Her eyes matched Caleb's, although hers were more tired and wary. Morgan noticed there was affection in the woman's expression when she looked directly at Caleb.

"How are you, Aunt Sadie?" Caleb stood and hugged the woman.

"I'm okay, Cal, how're you, your mom, and dad?" Sadie patted him on the head as he sat down.

"I'm good. They're good. They haven't been down this way in a while, though, have they?"

"Aw, they're always busy, just like everybody else. We all should make more time for each other," Sadie responded, ruffling Caleb's hair. She pointed to Morgan with her thumb and asked, "So, who is this girl?"

"Aunt Sadie, this is my good friend and co-worker Morgan Cutler. Morgan, this is my dad's little sister, Sadie Lightfoot."

"I'm pleased to meet you," Morgan said, standing to shake hands with Sadie.

"Same here," Sadie replied. "Ready to order, kids?"

Caleb ordered a large turkey club sandwich and Morgan opted for the spaghetti with sweet bell peppers and Italian sausage.

Sadie took the order and went back to the kitchen. Morgan stood and searched around for the restrooms, which she spied in the very back and said, "Excuse me while I go to the ladies' room."

Caleb nodded and stretched his legs out to watch television. Morgan glanced back at the table before going into the restroom and noticed that Sadie was sitting at the table with Caleb. Morgan decided to slow her visit to the bathroom so Sadie and Caleb could have some alone time together.

The bathroom was knotty pine and looked original from the '30s. The room was very small and had an ornate, antique sink and porcelain faucets. The commode was next to the sink with no room between. She could barely move around and there was nowhere to put her purse.

After she finished her business, Morgan washed her hands and glanced up into the gilded mirror. A face that didn't belong to her stared back—the face of a younger woman with light brown hair whose eyes were swollen and face was wet with tears. She looked directly in Morgan's eyes and said that her baby was taken. Morgan stood frozen in place watching the woman until someone knocked on the door. She glanced to the door for a second before returning her attention to the mirror—the other face was gone.

"Excuse me, Morgan, are you all right," Sadie said from the other side of the door. "Caleb is concerned."

Morgan shook her head to clear it and dried her hands before opening the door saying, "I'm so sorry. I was trying to get some of the stains off my shirt before they set and I didn't pay attention to the time."

Sadie nodded and smiled. "You were in there nearly fifteen minutes. Caleb is a good guy and he sent me to check on you."

Morgan looked at her watch and said, "No joke? Oh my gosh, I had no idea. I was trying to make a good impression and didn't pay attention to the time."

"No harm, we can reheat your food if it's too cold," Sadie said.

Morgan hurried past Sadie and rushed to the table. When she got close enough to touch Caleb's shoulder, the baby from the table next to them reached out and grabbed Morgan's shirttail. She laughed, touched the little hand, and immediately took a step back. Images flashed through her head so rapidly, she couldn't speak. She freed her shirt from the baby's grip and sat down across from Caleb. Morgan touched Caleb's hand and he smiled in return but then frowned as he sensed something was wrong. He started to say something but Morgan shook her head once so he wouldn't speak. He remained quiet.

The young woman at the next table stood up and went to the bathroom with the baby who was crying. Morgan looked at the husband and saw a horrible brown aura throb all around him. He looked around the diner twice and out the window once as he twisted several paper napkins into long strips. He followed his wife to the restroom.

"Caleb, that isn't their baby," Morgan whispered as she watched the man leave to check on his wife.

"What? How do you know?" Caleb turned in his seat to see where the couple was.

"Shhh, be quiet. I just know. I touched the baby and she doesn't belong to them. She doesn't even know them." Morgan pretended to look for something in her purse. "They both went to the bathroom and there's only one bathroom, so somebody is on the outside of it right now."

"How sure are you? Do you think it's the Amber alert baby?" asked Caleb.

"I'm positive, and yes, I think it's her or one heck of a coincidence. Do you have any description of her?" Morgan asked.

"Yes, my sister said she was wearing a yellow onesie."

"That's the baby. Go call the police."

"I'm going outside to make the call. You stay here and act like the world is fine."

He went outside and paced back and forth on the

porch. He was speaking intently into the cell phone when he stepped into the street and looked at the cars parked there. He paid the most attention to an old Ford Taurus once he realized it was parked away from the other vehicles.

The couple came back from the restroom and sat down at the table. The woman looked around and asked Morgan in a flat voice, "Where did your husband go?" She was dressed in old jeans with a dirty blouse and cheap leather jacket. Her mousy brown hair looked as if it hadn't been washed in a week or more.

"Oh, he wants to close a deal on a new car and the dealer is being difficult. With the poor sales around here, wouldn't you think those guys would want to sell a car? Oh no, they just want the few little guys who can afford to buy one to pay through the nose. Yep, he's out there right now negotiating to get what he wants," Morgan chattered as the woman stared at her.

The man was equally dirty. His long nails were filthy and his jeans and shirt were just as grubby as the wife's. His expression seemed to be locked in a sneer. The man stood and threw a twenty-dollar bill on the table. He tipped his head to indicate toward the door and the wife obediently stood and followed him.

"Your baby is very beautiful," Morgan stammered as she reached to touch the child one more time to stall a little longer. "She seems a little fussy today."

When she touched the baby, Morgan could feel the infant's confusion. The baby wanted her mommy and daddy.

"She's a good baby most of the time." The woman turned to prevent Morgan from reaching the infant so easily.

"What's her name?" Morgan asked. She had no idea why Caleb was still outside, but she didn't want the couple to confront him.

"Jennifer," the man said and placed his hand on his

wife's back to push her along. At the exact same moment, the woman said, "Angela." Realizing their mistake, she gave her husband a dirty look then blinked several times at Morgan.

"Isn't it unusual for two brown-eyed parents to have a blue-eyed baby?" asked Morgan. "I mean, it's none of my business but that has to be rare."

The other diners in the restaurant put down their knives and forks and paid attention.

"Excuse us," the man said, pushing his wife along again. The couple went outside and walked to the parked Taurus. The man opened the door and the woman sat in the front seat with the baby on her lap. The man got in on the driver's side and started the car.

Morgan went out and saw Caleb in the corner of the porch.

"There's no car seat for the baby," Caleb whispered. "Let's follow them till the police get here."

"Are you out of your mind? We can't do police work. The kidnappers already think that you're suspicious. I have to add that they're not in love with me, either," Morgan was saying as she opened the SUV door, climbed in, and clicked her seatbelt. "I'm 100 percent against this, but we better get going before we lose them."

Caleb got in and followed the Taurus from a safe distance. There weren't any other cars on the road in either direction.

"The entrance ramp to the expressway is a quarter-mile on the right," Caleb said as he glanced in the rearview mirror.

As the Taurus veered to the right, three state police cars came from behind with their sirens blasting. They passed Caleb and Morgan and caught up to the Taurus. One of the state cars pulled in front of the Taurus to slow it down. At that moment, Caleb slowed and pulled over to the side of the road. All six of the troopers got out of their cars with guns pulled. They yanked the man from the driver's side and threw him against the car where he was cuffed and moved to the trooper's car. The woman screamed as she got out on the passenger side, clutching the baby in her arms. She decided to run and two of the officers chased her and took the child. Caleb got out and had a conversation with the remaining officers. A few minutes later, one of the officers handed the crying baby to Caleb.

Caleb cooed to the little girl and she seemed to relax. A police officer approached and stood off to the side to give him time to examine the baby for any obvious injuries. An ambulance arrived and the EMT got out and spoke to the officer and then turned to Caleb and said, "Dr. Lightfoot, we're going to take the child to the hospital where she can have a complete check. Her parents will be notified to meet us there." Caleb nodded and handed the baby to the EMT.

Caleb got back in the SUV, turned to Morgan, and said, "Wow." He added, "we have to go back to the restaurant—I didn't pay the bill. I hope Sadie kept my sandwich."

"I don't think I'm hungry anymore," Morgan answered and cringed.

"I'm even hungrier," said Caleb.

"You are one cool customer, I'll give you that. I've never had such an unusual first-time friend-date with anybody," Morgan said as she ran her fingers through her hair.

"You won't call it a regular date, will you?" Caleb glanced at her.

"No, I won't. Too soon."

"Let's go back to Sadie's."

"Sure, why not."

They drove back to the diner and went inside. There was a round of applause from every patron, including Sadie, who stood behind the counter. The cooks banged on pots from the kitchen while Caleb nodded at each person who cheered or shook his hand as he weaved his way to the table where their food had been. All the while he held Morgan's hand behind his back.

"I knew you'd come back," Sadie said as she dried her hands on her apron. "I've never seen you leave a bite of food behind, much less almost a whole meal."

Morgan sat at the table while Caleb remained standing. When he got the chance, he asked Sadie, "How did you guys hear about it already?"

"Chris, one of my cooks, is married to one of the troopers. He called her a couple of minutes ago," Sadie said. "That was the little Starr baby girl, wasn't it?"

"Yes, ma'am, it was," Caleb answered.

He stood behind his chair and tilted his head at Morgan. "You still have a chunk of sausage on your chin and spaghetti sauce on your upper lip."

Morgan groaned and grabbed the napkin to clean herself.

Caleb looked at his watch and said, "I had no idea how late it was." He turned to the kitchen and shouted, "Aunt Sadie, will you wrap up our food? We need to go."

"You betcha," Sadie shouted from the kitchen.

Sadie brought the food in a bag, handing it to Morgan. She turned and hugged her nephew and kissed him on the cheek before saying, "Thank you for stopping by."

Caleb kissed her and went to the counter to pay the bill. Sadie waved him away and the diner erupted in cheers and applause as the couple left.

"Will you eat as you drive?" Morgan asked as she peeked into the bag. "We have silverware and a ton of napkins."

"Yes, I can and not spill a drop." Caleb started the vehicle.

Morgan got his sandwich out of the bag and said, "I am more impressed with you every minute. I can't eat anything on a flat surface without debris all over. And you can do that and steer. Impressive."

"I know. You're gonna love some of my other tricks."

Sweat broke out on Morgan's upper lip at his words, so she turned her head to look out the side window, hoping he hadn't seen her reaction.

Caleb smiled, nodded, and concentrated on his sandwich as he drove. After he finished it, he said, "I'll call my sister and tell her what happened."

Morgan listened as he explained. He also told his sister not to tell the baby's mom until the police contacted her for the return of the infant. He clicked off his phone and smiled at Morgan.

"Let's stop at a rest area and buy a Coke to wash the food down."

Morgan glanced at his shirt and all around his clothes. "Dr. Lightfoot, I can barely drive and drink a cup of tea on the way to work without spillage. Your dexterity has to be its own reward in several situations."

Caleb smiled and said, "Well, thank you, and I hope you ponder the possibilities on the remainder of the drive."

Morgan laughed at him and shook her head slowly as she thought, *Oh, doctor, I think I'm in trouble here. You are just too good to be true.*

KATE MACINNIS

CHAPTER 12

They arrived at Morgan's house a couple of hours later and Caleb walked her to the door. He looked at her for a very long time before hugging her.

"Do you want a nightcap?" Morgan pulled away from him and fumbled with her purse as she searched for her key.

"I have to work at four a.m. tomorrow," Caleb answered, touching her face with his index finger.

"Can't you take five minutes and come in?"

"I should go home and get some sleep, but okay, five minutes."

Smiling, Morgan unlocked the front door and turned on the lights with Caleb following behind. Not thinking it through, she realized the Wilkersons could be just about anywhere, so she stopped and scanned every room to check their location. No one was there except Douglas, waiting at the back door and barking to go out. She walked to the kitchen, opened the kitchen door, and he scurried to the grass. The house seemed safe—and there wasn't any visible evidence of ghosts.

"Remember you promised to give me privacy," Morgan whispered to the empty room. The lights in the kitchen flashed signaling their agreement. Douglas hurried back in and she closed and locked the door behind him. She was startled to see Caleb standing in the kitchen doorway since she had left him in the foyer.

"Who were you talking to?"

"Douglas, of course. He's particular about strangers. What would you like to drink? Beer, coffee, or pop?"

"A quick beer sounds good."

"You want that in a glass?"

He shook his head and walked around the house looking in the rooms. He gestured to Morgan that he was going to see every room and she nodded her approval as she opened his beer. When he got back to the front door, he went outside and returned with the radio box tucked under his arm.

"You okay?" Morgan asked as she handed him the beer and took a sip of her Diet Coke.

"You were very cool today. I mean that, very cool." He tipped his can at her in a salute.

"You weren't so bad yourself." Morgan tipped her Coke can back at him. "What's the plan with the radio?"

"I'm sure there's a perfect room for it here. I think it belongs in your house. Besides, I want to share it with you."

"So, I get custody first?"

"I have a hunch that we'll be here more than at my place, so it makes sense to have it here," Caleb said, walking down the hall and looking at the library and living room again to make his final decision.

Morgan shivered as she followed him. "Look, this doesn't mean there's any kind of commitment involved. This is moving too fast."

"This will move at the speed it should—don't worry. Oh, I know the perfect place for the radio. It would look great in your library, well, I think it's your library. The room where the fireplace is and all of your books are, so it seems like a library."

"That sounds pretentious. It's the room with my books. We can put it on the mantle in there since there's even an outlet hidden among the bricks," Morgan said as she took the box and opened the doors to the room. Caleb followed her into the library, looking around appreciatively before saying, "I like this room a lot and I'm comfortable in here."

Morgan set the box on the end table, opened it, and took the old radio out very carefully. She unplugged the modern radio she had on the shelf and put it in the old box.

"I hope the drive didn't jiggle the wires apart," she said while Caleb placed the antique radio right where he thought it should go and easily plugged it in. She stood behind him as he turned the power dial and said, "Let's fire this up, make sure there's no damage."

The light came on and the radio popped, cracked, sizzled, and emitted a dusty antique smell. He turned the dial slowly and soon a song from the 1940s came out of the speaker. He moved the dial both left and right but the same music played on every channel. He looked at Morgan with his eyebrows raised and confusion all over his face.

"I knew this was a special radio," he said as he took her hands and put them around his neck. "The radio wants us to dance."

They danced for a minute or two before Caleb stopped. He held her chin as he kissed her gently and slowly on the lips, then traced her cheekbones and nose with his finger. He took his hand away and looked her straight in the eye.

"The bedroom is upstairs," Morgan whispered, holding his gaze.

"We need to make this last. The newness and excitement don't come along all that often anymore in our lives. We won't hurry. Intimacy and sex are physical pleasures that God designed very well and very deliberately. I'm not a particularly religious man, but let's show our respect to what He created."

Caleb kissed the top of her head before letting her go. "There is very little that I would like better than to take you upstairs and make love for hours. But not tonight."

"If this is a major rejection, you're good at it," whispered Morgan.

"This is most definitely not a rejection, just a postponement. I want this to be right, and I can't concentrate on you tonight. I want to get some sleep. It's been a hectic first week at the hospital."

They walked arm-in-arm to the front door before he kissed her forehead. "I don't have a plan for a one-night stand, Morgan. We need to work together at the hospital, and it would be such a waste to mess this up, so let's do it right. Agree?"

"Believe me, I don't want to, but I do agree," said Morgan as Caleb touched her cheek. She released her arm from his and followed him onto the porch.

Caleb got in his SUV and waved as he pulled from the driveway. She returned his wave and leaned her head back against the door and thought about her dating past. She truly loved no strings or demands with the boys she dated, but this was a man, and any involvement with him would be part of a grown-up relationship. "I don't have the energy to ponder this tonight," she said aloud upon entering the house. The lights in the foyer blinked twice.

"Good night, Jonathan. Good night, Elisabeth," said Morgan, waving as she climbed the stairs. The house was quiet all night. No nightmares, no visits from ghosts, no orbs flying around the room, no camera taking pictures. Finally, having been able to get some uninterrupted sleep, Morgan woke up early and in a great mood. Once dressed, she decided to head downstairs to make breakfast. When she got to the kitchen, Elisabeth stood at an old stove frying bacon while Jonathan sat at the table with his nose in the newspaper.

Jonathan looked up and said, "Good morning, Morgan. How are we today?"

Morgan smiled and answered, "We are lovely. How are you two?"

Elisabeth turned from the stove with the hot pan in her hand and said, "We're delighted you can join us."

Morgan noticed the table was set for three with a plate of cinnamon toast and another with scrambled eggs in the center. "Everything smells fantastic. Is it possible for me to have breakfast with you?"

"Sadly, no," Jonathan answered and made an exaggerated sad face as Elisabeth served him. He quickly forgot about Morgan and ate the best breakfast that kitchen had witnessed since the Wilkersons lived there the first time.

"I don't understand the details, however, you cannot eat with us yet—we can share your food and drink, but it doesn't work both ways. The most important thing is that we can still enjoy each other's company," Elisabeth said as she put the pan back on the stove. Morgan pointed at the stove, but Elisabeth and Jonathan relished their breakfast in peace with plenty of smiles for her. The stove Morgan bought for the kitchen was not the one Elisabeth cooked on. Elisabeth's stove was an appliance from the 1940s and stood in the same spot as Morgan's present-day stove.

Frustrated, she stood, went to the stove, grabbed Elisabeth's teakettle, and took it to the sink to fill with water for tea. When she turned on the water, her teakettle appeared in her hand, and when she set the kettle down on the burner, the stove became her own modern stove with no evidence whatsoever that breakfast had just been prepared there on an antique appliance by a long-dead ghost.

"Well, as long as we can get the guidelines straight about what time period we're in, I think I'm okay with this arrangement. I mean, if we do live together, it's better to know all the rules, right?" Morgan was wide-eyed as she stood by the stove and spoke to Elisabeth and Jonathan at the table.

"Come, fear not you; good counselors lack no clients," Jonathan said between bites.

Morgan narrowed her eyes at Jonathan and chewed her lower lip. Elisabeth looked at him, turned to Morgan and said, "Jonathan loves to quote Shakespeare. He said that wise people never lack company. We hope to entertain you as much as you entertain us."

Morgan stood by a chair and stopped before she sat down. "What do you mean by entertain?"

"Oh, your choice of music and television and ..." Elisabeth said.

Jonathan spread his arms and shouted, "Well, happiness to their sheets—"

Elisabeth interrupted and said, "Again that's Shakespeare. He means that he hopes you find someone to have a wonderful time in bed with—no matter whom you choose."

"What? You watch when I have dates stay over?" Morgan sputtered as she stood ramrod straight at the edge of the table.

Jonathan choked scrambled eggs all over the kitchen as Elisabeth tried to calm him.

"Now, now, dear, please. Morgan, please relax. Whenever I'm aware that Jonathan is inappropriate I make him leave the scene immediately."

Jonathan hung his head as Elisabeth spoke.

"What? What? I don't want either of you to watch. Ever." Morgan struggled to breathe as she stared at her ghosts.

"There, there, old girl. There hasn't been much to see for quite some time now," Jonathan said and curled his bottom lip under in an exaggerated pout.

"What? What? You're here in my kitchen casually mentioning my sexual dry spell?" Morgan sat down hard in her chair.

"Jonathan, darling, perhaps you should exit the room now. Morgan needs to absorb this information. You know this is all new to her and we've had many decades to adjust," Elisabeth said as she patted her husband's arm.

Jonathan disappeared with a *blip*. The chair was empty and his plate and cup were also gone.

"Where did he go?" Morgan asked as she looked around. The lingering smell of the food made her mouth water. The kettle boiled so Elisabeth stood and went to the stove, which was once again Elisabeth's stove and kettle. She poured a cup of tea for herself and brought it to the table.

"Oh, he's off to debate some intellectual or have some innocent fun with his friends. Let's get to know each other. You go first." Elisabeth smiled and nodded for Morgan to start.

"Apparently you already know me, Elisabeth. I can't believe this is what the afterlife is about—voyeurism. Pure and simple voyeurism. That's sick."

"Calm down and we will discuss this as best we can," said Elisabeth as she stirred her tea.

"How come I can't see through you? I thought ghosts always looked faded and filmy. You look real. Sometimes only half of you shows up, too. Why is that?"

"We are as real as you are, but we're in another dimension. The vibrations are much higher, whatever that means. I've also been told that not everyone can connect with our dimension, therefore, they can't see us at all. In those cases, darling, there are no issues." Elisabeth finished her tea from the china cup and stood to get her kettle from her stove.

"So, if a stranger came in here right now, they would not see the tea kettle move and float in the air? They wouldn't see you at all, right?" Morgan held her head in her hand.

"That's what I've been told. It seems silly to me but, apparently, that's how it works when I function in your dimension," said Elisabeth as she shrugged.

"What does it feel like to be dead?"

"That's a very good question and doesn't have an easy answer. It doesn't feel different at all. Certainly, I'm not like you, but I do what I want, when I want. I eat, drink, share affection with my husband, read books, and go to the movies. It's not the same as your life, but it is an existence. I don't bleed when I get scratched, but I still get scratched. I'm careful about injuries since they don't heal the way they used to and they scar far worse."

"But what if you die from a car accident and your body is all messed up or all withered away from some disease? Is that the one you have for all eternity when you're dead?"

"No, gosh, that would be awful. You get to pick how you want to look. Do I look like a ninety-year-old woman? That's what I was when death knocked at my door."

Morgan's cell phone rang from the hallway and worrying that it might be the hospital, she excused herself and hurried to get it. She looked at Elisabeth and said, "Please don't move, don't go anywhere. I want to finish this conversation, but I have to take the call and make sure it isn't work."

Elisabeth was left at the table with her chin in her hand and her gaze a million miles away.

"Good morning, Morgan," Savannah almost purred on the phone. "How was your date yesterday?"

"It was fan-damn-tastic," Morgan answered as she walked back to the kitchen. "We spent the day together and he went home about 11:30 p.m. or so last night. Is there anything wrong at the hospital?"

Savvy ignored her question and asked, "He didn't spend the night? I'm stunned. Seemed like a sure bet. What did you do, Morgan? Did he see your table manners? Did he meet the Wilkersons?"

"Thankfully, no, he didn't and, by the way, Dr. Cranky Pants, my table manners didn't bother him in the least. Well, maybe they did a little because he bought me another T-shirt to cover the one that got all the stains on it. I'll break the news about the Wilkersons on the next date."

Savvy wanted more details so Morgan filled her in on what happened the day before. She glanced back at Elisabeth who grinned as she admired the flowers in the backyard. "Savannah, hang on a second, would you?" Morgan held the phone against her leg, cleared her throat and asked, "Elisabeth, didn't you tell me that you have always been in my house and I only discovered you after my head surgery?"

"Yes. I believe that's true," Elisabeth said as she stood again and went over to the counter. She looked around and reached for the bread and pointed at the bread and toaster to ask if Morgan wanted some, as well. Elisabeth then smacked her forehead remembering that Morgan couldn't eat their food. She popped the bread into a toaster from the 1930s and the wonderful aroma filled the room.

Morgan put the phone back to her ear and concentrated on Savannah. "I'm sorry, but Elisabeth is here with me. Are you up for a trip over here later to join us?"

"Elisabeth Wilkerson is there with you? And you're getting friendly and having a conversation?"

"Yes, Savvy, she's here with me and we're having tea. It's a little more complicated and we each make our own, but you get the idea." Morgan smiled at Elisabeth.

"I am tired and had a rough shift yesterday. I had to pull a double when one of my illustrious colleagues had too much to drink at a fundraiser and felt that he needed to lay low. Truth is, I heard he was busted for a DUI and called from the jail to cover his sorry ass at work." Savannah sighed and continued, "The doctor on duty called me, so I don't have proof of where the drunken doc was, but I will investigate and find out. Let me repeat what you said—you're sharing tea and toast with Mrs. Wilkerson?"

"Yes, ma'am. Right here in the kitchen with me."

"Oh my. I'll be there as soon as I can. I don't want to

miss this. Make sure you have decent coffee for my arrival."

With that order Savvy hung up. Morgan clicked off her phone and heard Cary Grant's voice speak a line from one of his movies. It was gone before she could identify which film it came from. She shrugged, looked around, and knew that Elisabeth was no longer in the kitchen.

To the empty room, Morgan said, "I thought I heard Cary Grant's voice. Now, there's a ghost that I would really like to have in the house." The lights flashed in the kitchen and Morgan knew Elisabeth agreed.

Two hours later, Savannah arrived with a bag of groceries. "Where is Mrs. Wilkerson?" she asked.

Morgan answered, "She vanished when we finished our phone call. I think she'll be back at some point."

Savannah sighed, went to the living room, and surfed the channels until she found an old movie. Morgan joined her and stopped to pay attention to the television.

"I don't know if you'll believe this or not, but the first line he spoke when I walked in here was the same one I heard him say this morning after I talked to you." Morgan rubbed the back of her neck.

Savannah settled on the couch to watch the movie—complete with a bowl of popcorn, hot coffee, and a very large chocolate bar, all of which she had brought. She held the remote in her right hand as the channels changed every two to three seconds.

"Didn't you want to watch that movie?" Morgan asked as she got comfortable on the other end of the couch.

"I'm not the one who's changing the channels, my friend. Here's the remote." Savvy held up the device with two fingers and wiggled it. "It changes channels all by itself." Savvy's eyes opened wide as she dangled the device again. "Wait, did you say the real Cary Grant was here earlier today?"

"No such luck. I said that I heard the line from the movie that was just on the first channel you had. You know how you get a few words from a song stuck in your head? That's what I mean. I heard him speak this morning and now I see the same movie with that line on TV later the same day. A weird coincidence? I think not."

The channels continued to change every two to three seconds.

"Jonathan, knock it off. I mean it, this is an irritation." Morgan glanced around the room and spoke to the ceiling.

Savvy frowned when the channel stopped on the Cary Grant movie.

"Thank you, Elisabeth," said Morgan.

Morgan went to the computer and booted it up, but it didn't start. She tinkered with keys and it still didn't start.

"Looks like that's dead, too," said Savannah. "What are the odds of that? Although, I would guess that electrical appliances, both large and small, have a hard time with the Wilkersons in residence."

"That never happened before and the Wilkersons have been here for years," Morgan answered as she plugged and unplugged the cords.

"They never used energy to materialize before, now did they?" Savvy said as she batted her eyes.

"No, I guess it's different now. Crap." Morgan slapped the keyboard and the lights came on and the computer hummed.

Savannah said, "This is all a mystery, however, I want every jagged little edge accounted for and explained. If we have proof there are really ghosts among us, imagine the headlines."

"Does any of this make you uncomfortable?" Morgan asked as she snuggled into the chair at her desk.

"I don't feel afraid, Morgan. Startled at times, but not like I'm in any danger."

Morgan rolled her eyes and concentrated on the computer.

"Wow, I just got a big whiff of stale tobacco and a musty attic. Like an old wet dog who has taken up cigarettes," said Savannah, immediately jumping up from the couch. She then shouted, "I'm also sorely out of practice, but I could swear someone just felt up and down my thigh."

On the couch, next to where Savvy had been sitting—the outline of a person began to materialize, but just as quickly it disappeared.

"Did you see that?" Morgan asked.

Savannah took a big gulp of her coffee. "I have not had enough sleep and I'm hungry. I thought I saw the outline of a man. Did I?"

"Savannah, c'mon. You know perfectly well that my imagination cannot materialize a man for you. I would have done that long ago if that were the case."

Morgan smiled at Savvy and received the stink eye in return. Savvy turned back to the couch—feeling it all over for heat or cold. "Ask your friend to show himself or herself. Right now, I'm ready and want to see one of these so-called people up close."

"Okay. Elisabeth, are you here?" Morgan spoke to the ceiling.

"Why do you always ask the ceiling?"

"Well, there isn't a particularly good reason to speak that way, but it seems more respectful than the floor. That might hint at hell rather than heaven," Morgan said, shrugging. She added, "I don't really know the etiquette for this situation."

"They aren't in heaven or hell, Morgan. They're here in your house."

Savvy walked around the room, looking behind chairs, under the couch, and behind a framed picture, which caused Morgan to cringe.

The front door opened and slammed followed by Elisabeth Wilkerson coming in from the hallway. She entered the room without opening the French doors. She wore short denim overalls, a pink gingham blouse and a large white hat.

"Yes, dear, what on earth is wrong? You scared me," said Elisabeth as she looked at Savvy and then back to Morgan.

"The remote changed the channels non-stop again and I wondered if you were here or if Jonathan was here," Morgan replied and closely watched the two women.

Elisabeth leaned against the bookcase and looked adorable in clothes that were the height of 1944 fashion.

"That's it? I thought you were in danger." Elisabeth sighed.

"Well, Savvy *is* here." Morgan smiled.

Savannah pursed her lips and remained silent. Elisabeth and Morgan turned to look at her.

"I'm not sure what I expected, but every hair on my entire body is at attention," said Savannah. "I believe I need to sit down."

Still standing, Morgan commented, "Well, you've never met in person, but you have communicated through the automatic handwriting."

"I also witnessed half of the couple dancing from a distance," Savvy said primly.

"Well, then you're practically family, right?" Morgan tried to make light of the situation but it was awkward to watch worlds collide. "Let's see if we can all sit and get to know one another better. How does that sound?"

Before anyone made their way to the couch—all three women heard water rush from the floor above into the hallway. Looking up, there was a gaping hole with water streaming down.

"Just watch, the earth is going to part and snatch us up." Savvy moaned. "This is the end of the world as we know it, Morgan."

"I'm pretty sure it's just a broken pipe or a leak, Savvy, not the apocalypse," Morgan grumbled as she stepped around a huge puddle forming in the middle of the foyer. Savvy was behind her and Elisabeth brought up the rear.

"Where is that coming from?" Savvy asked.

"The master bathtub upstairs. I think that grand old clawfoot has had a full life and needs to go to the junkyard. It's gonna cost a fortune, but I think it has to go." Morgan raced to the kitchen to turn off the water to the house and then bolted up the stairs to confirm the source.

A few minutes later she came back down the stairs emphasizing her words with every step. "The pipes are rusty and break often enough that it's gonna do some real damage if I don't get a plumber in here and fix the bath. I'll have to get it re-tiled, too. Bye-bye pink."

"That old claw-foot tub you have up there? Don't you think there must be some use for it? It's an antique." Savvy was at the foot of the stairs as Morgan came down.

"You can't get rid of that tub," said Elisabeth, standing behind Savvy and looking up at Morgan. "Please, you can't, you just can't. Your friend is right, you have to find another plan."

Morgan looked at Elisabeth. "I don't understand your concern about the tub. Do you have some sentimental attachment to it or, God forbid, still use it?"

"No, why would you ask that?" replied Elisabeth as she wrung her hands.

"Then why are you so upset—if I may ask?" Savvy turned to Elisabeth and smiled.

"Because you can't just remove a beautiful antique and throw it to the curb like trash," Elisabeth said with her chin held high.

Savvy opened her mouth, closed it, and asked, "Wait a minute, the other night you looked like a hologram and today you look real. Why is that?"

"I am real, but in another dimension," Elisabeth answered.

Suddenly a loud *thump* came from the library across the hall. All three women looked in the door in time to see a bright orb bouncing around the room. It circled, hovered, and then plopped down on the chair. They watched silently as it sparked, fizzled, and finally enlarged. The light became so bright Savannah and Morgan turned their heads away to protect their eyes just as Jonathan's outline formed on the chair. This time he had a dog in his lap.

"Oh, Jonathan, you brought Freckles," Elisabeth squealed and clapped her hands. "I hope you don't mind, Morgan. Freckles was our treasured cocker spaniel."

No, I don't mind. Douglas may object, but I don't mind," Morgan answered absently as she watched Savvy's face turn an odd color.

"For the first time in my life, the words 'whiter shade of pale' make sense to me," Morgan whispered. "I never knew what that meant.

Ignoring Morgan's comment, Savannah gasped, bent over, and put her hands on her knees to steady herself.

Jonathan and Freckles disappeared with a *popping* noise.

CHAPTER 13

"All righty then, this seems like the right time to break the ice for everyone. Elisabeth, I would love for you to know that Dr. Savannah Holt is the medical director of the emergency center where I work. Dr. Holt is a board-certified emergency room physician and one of the finest in the area." Morgan smiled at Savvy's dirty look and continued, "One of the finest in the nation. Dr. Holt, I would like you to meet Elisabeth Wilkerson, master gardener and wife of the famed professor of literature as well as sometimes actor and full-time performer, Jonathan Wilkerson, who just a moment ago sat with their dog on his lap."

Savannah stuck her hand out and Elisabeth took a step back, which prompted Morgan to intervene immediately. "Whoa, ladies. Different time periods with different ways to greet strangers. Elisabeth, ladies today shake hands. Savannah, ladies in the 1940s did not shake hands as we do now—it was most definitely not part of the customary ritual. Let's just be polite right now and not worry about convention. Okay?"

Elisabeth turned to Morgan and asked, "Ladies also shake the hands of gentlemen they are not familiar with?"

195

"Yes, we do. We may have to race to the bathroom to wash our hands more often, but it's more of an issue of equality," replied Morgan.

"It's less awkward that way," Savannah said as she offered her hand out for Elisabeth, who shook it very gently.

Elisabeth looked directly at Savannah and remarked, "You're very beautiful, Dr. Holt. You are a medical doctor?"

"Yes, I am," Savvy answered.

"I think it's wonderful that women are able to be educated as well as men. I would have loved to have been a doctor or a veterinarian," said Elisabeth wistfully.

"Today you can be whatever you want. You still can't expect to make the same money, but equal pay is closer than ever before. But you were a wife, and I assume you were also a mother," Savannah said.

"Why yes, Dr. Holt. Jonathan and I had six children. Perhaps if I had a profession outside the home, I would not have had so many kids." The women shared a giggle and stood quietly.

"Mrs. Wilkerson, are you responsible for Morgan's beautiful flowers and shrubs?" Savannah moved over by the window and pulled back the curtain to expose the yard.

"Why, thank you, Dr. Holt. Yes, I am," Elisabeth beamed. "I try to take care of them, and this year they're better than ever. I don't know if it's the electricity or persistence."

"I bet it's a mixture of both." Morgan moved over by the window and looked at the bushes, shaking her head in disbelief.

"I planted most of the trees in this yard. One for each of my children," said Elisabeth.

"Why did you move? It sounds like you were very happy here," Savvy asked.

"Oh, we were very happy here for a long time. Then Jonathan wanted to live closer to Detroit and the nightlife.

He wanted to be around more theaters and entertainment venues. The drive became more congested with traffic and he didn't like long drives unless it was the weekend and we were out in the country." Elisabeth looked at the floor as she spoke. "Being closer to the city also gave him the opportunity to be around more women, and that's when our real trouble began." Elisabeth looked embarrassed and disappeared.

"She didn't even say good-bye," Savvy said softly.

"I guess she's not comfortable talking to us yet. So, what do you think about seeing her up close?"

"Through all of the years in all of the emergency rooms I have worked in, I have never ever had an experience like this. Oh, I've had silly premonitions and hunches galore, but never have I had the pleasure of openly communicating with someone who has passed on. Do you understand how hopeful that is? This really isn't all there is," Savannah said as her eyes teared.

Morgan moved closer to hug her friend and said, "I don't know why this has happened to me, and I'm in the awkward position of being a hostess to the other side, but here it is, and I genuinely enjoy her company. Elisabeth is kind, patient, and so intelligent. She is a pleasure to have as a friend. I guess I can call her a friend. Roommate might be more appropriate."

"What's the husband like, other than his obsession with the naked you?" Savannah asked as she blotted her face with a tissue from her pocket.

Morgan answered, "Jonathan, even though he seemed a bit shy today, was here the other morning and read the newspaper at the kitchen table while Elisabeth made breakfast. He quotes Shakespeare quite a bit and likes to spend time with his men friends. He is drop-dead gorgeous, though, pardon the pun. I mean that he is seriously handsome."

"Does your food actually disappear from the fridge when they eat?"

"No, come to think of it, it doesn't." Morgan frowned. "In fact, I don't keep a lot of food around here in the first place and some of the things she serves at breakfast smell phenomenal. I know damn well I didn't buy those groceries. Like the potatoes O'Brien and link sausages. My mouth waters thinking about the way the kitchen smells when Elisabeth cooks."

"How do you explain that?"

"I don't have a clue."

"Let's make a list of questions for Elisabeth," Savvy suggested as she looked around for pen and paper.

Morgan got a pad and pen out of the desk drawer. When she sat down her hand got very hot. She took the pen and held it to the paper and wrote: *We have our own supplies.*

"Here's the answer to your question," said Morgan as she showed the tablet to Savvy.

"Well, that makes sense, I think. Here's another question for her, why does she write notes instead of appearing and talking to us directly?"

Again, Morgan wrote on the tablet and showed it to Savvy: *It's a difficult concept because we don't have electrical outlets to plug in and recharge, but believe it takes a tremendous amount of electrical energy or force for us to appear. We have only so much and must practice training more or borrow it from humans in your dimension. That's why you sometimes only see parts of us. The more we appear, the easier it gets. Please be patient.*

Savannah asked, "What is the point of all this?"

Morgan's hand moved with a flourish as she wrote: *Each incarnation is a lesson to be learned. One must experience different people at different times to be most efficient in the educational process. Various tasks would not be learned if we simply repeated our lives exactly with the same partner each time. Our lives may be filled with spirits we have known before and loved but the arrangement will be different so the outcome can be enriched.*

Again, Morgan held the pad up for Savannah to read the long message. "That isn't Elisabeth—that's Jonathan."

The lights in the room blinked. "See, I told you so."

Do you understand what I have shared with you?

"I think so," Savannah said to the ceiling. "Why do I direct my conversation to the ceiling now?"

"No idea, but doesn't it seem like you *should* do it that way?" asked Morgan as she shrugged.

My love to you both. And just like that the pen fell out of Morgan's hand indicating the end of the conversation.

Savannah sat on the couch with a goofy grin on her face and said, "Do you have any idea how many scientists and researchers would give their beady little hearts to experience what just happened here?"

"No, not really, but probably quite a few." Morgan stretched her hand and arm trying to relieve the tension and pain. "So, we agree this isn't a matter of imagination?"

"This is very real, and we are very, very fortunate. Don't you feel hopeful, Morgan? Don't you feel invigorated because of what we need to learn? We have friends on the other side and friends on this side. Do you understand what a joyful prospect that is?"

"I'm beginning to see everything in my life from a different perspective. So, yes, I'm excited about this adventure, but I've also learned that anything too good to be true usually isn't, and I'm waiting for the other shoe to drop."

Savvy nodded and replied, "I understand that completely. We are not young girls, and we've seen our fair share of death and dying. This is a new depth for us. The only thing that has changed was your brain surgery. The only way I can make sense of this is to say that the psychic activity now is the result of you being used as a vessel by the dearly departed and they couldn't do that before you were rewired. They are using you to participate in this dimension. It'll be interesting to find out how this all works and if you can see into their dimension."

"Uh, I'm not sure I'd be interested in that."

"But sometimes the cosmos align and magic happens. I

can't wait to see what the future brings," Savvy said as her stomach growled.

Morgan nodded and said, "Oh my gosh—are you hungry, Savvy? I can order a pizza if you'd like. I'm starving." After a pause, she added, "If you're not too tired."

"Don't be silly. The caffeine in that coffee gave me a second wind and the adrenaline rush from an encounter with Elisabeth, Jonathan, and their dog could keep me up for days. I don't remember if I've ever been this excited before." Savannah spread out her hand, stretched it across her chest, and patted herself. Her face was hot pink and glowed.

Morgan called the neighborhood pizza place for a large double pepperoni with garlic crust. "They swore to me that it would arrive within half an hour."

Too excited to care about the pizza, Savannah sat at the computer and searched the Internet. "Were you physically abused as a child?" Savvy asked.

"Why would you ever ask me that?"

"I believe that this psychic phenomenon is all relevant to your brain surgery, but as a scientist, I must ask one last question. If you have no history of abuse as a child, then there is one and only one explanation for the experiences you're having, and I'm a small part of. However, if you were abused, we'd have to investigate that. I would think you would have had psychic abilities as a child if you were abused. They wouldn't manifest now so *many* years later."

"No, I was not physically abused as a kid, but wait a minute—whether I was or not, both of us are in the middle of this experience. So, you've shared my trauma or I've shared yours? C'mon, Savvy. Two of us sat here and talked to the woman who used to live in this house and died years ago. My childhood has no connection to this."

"That would be a no, then." Savvy was pecking at the keyboard.

Just then the doorbell rang and Morgan picked up her

wallet from the hall table and hurried to the door.

"Maybe it's your over-active imagination," Savvy said to her back as Morgan left the room.

"I think it's more likely to be the guy from the pizza place," shouted Morgan in reply.

As they ate, Morgan's cell rang and she looked around the room until she spotted it on the bookshelf. She picked up and saw that it was Caleb and answered it so fast she almost hit herself in the face with the phone.

"Hi." She was sure she sounded a tad too enthusiastic.

"Hi yourself," Caleb said. "You sound pretty happy."

"I'm eating pizza, which is like experiencing heaven on earth. And Savannah has been here for a while."

Savannah heard her name and nodded as she returned to the computer.

"I wanted to call and let you know that there was a warrant issued on a guy named Kirk Chester. He was brought in last night after an assault. Rosemary from X-ray identified him as her attacker and the police hauled him away. He was arrested for aggravated assault on another woman and Rosemary will add to the charges. She said to make sure I let you know."

"Ohmigod. Now I'm a crime solver for sure. Two in a row. Wow. That is fantastic."

"It's really busy here right now and I have to get back but thought you should know. Let's make plans for next weekend. Maybe dinner and a movie like a conventional couple."

"That would be nice, Caleb."

"If I don't see you at work, I'll call you later in the week and we'll discuss details. Thanks again, Morgan. It's an advantage that you share my work. That's very important to me."

"Oh, that's so nice. I was thinking it's an advantage that you share my work."

"Oh, little girl, I haven't even started to make nice comments to you yet."

With that remark, Morgan instinctively felt her face to see if she had drooled.

"I need to go now, Caleb. Savvy hasn't had much sleep and she's all worked up on the Internet." Morgan glanced over and saw Savvy pacing in front of the keyboard.

"Okay, we'll talk later, I have to get busy. Bye."

"Bye, Caleb."

Again, her knees felt weak. She clicked off the phone and noticed the blob of pepperoni and cheese on her shirt. She picked it off and ate it.

"If anyone had warned me six months ago about all the changes in my life, I would have laughed, and it would be, no doubt, a cynical laugh. Instead, here I am uplifted by what Savannah said about hopefulness and goodness." Morgan muttered to herself and rubbed her eyes. She stood behind Savannah and tapped her shoulder trying to move her friend from the keyboard, but Savvy wouldn't budge, choosing to clutch at the desk instead.

"Do you want to spend the night here in the guest room?" Morgan pulled on Savvy again. "You are far too strung out to drive over to the eastside."

"You know, I think I'm too worked up to drive home. May I please spend the night here tonight, Morgan?"

"What a great idea. Sure." Morgan aimed her friend toward the hallway.

"Please, don't go to any trouble on my account. I will sleep right here on the sofa."

Before Morgan could argue Savvy had sat, thrown her head back, and made sounds similar to the horn on an ocean liner. Morgan got a blanket and pillow out of the window seat and put them next to Savvy on the couch. If her friend woke up cold or stiff—she could rearrange the linens on her own.

"Douglas, c'mon. You need to go out before night-night."

Douglas hurried to the kitchen and scampered out to the backyard. Morgan looked up at the stars.

"I don't know, maybe I never looked up before, but it all seems different now," Morgan whispered. The lights in the kitchen flashed twice, causing her to smile.

Finally, Douglas came back inside. She locked the door and stopped at the living room door to check on Savannah, who was out cold on the couch. There was no reason to wake her. Doctors learn very early in their careers to sleep where and how they can. No one in the house stirred until the clock went off at 4:30 a.m. the next morning.

CHAPTER 14

The morning had been slow in the EC, giving everybody the chance to get caught up on paperwork. Ellen, Savannah, Nancy Clark, one of the part-time nurses, and Morgan stood around the nurses' station. At the same time, they all saw Maxine enter the EC—no one moved or spoke.

"Well, it looks like someone should be busy around here," Maxine snarled at Savannah.

"I thought that, as well. So, don't you have some piddly chore to do somewhere else, Maxine? Some scut work that you can call your own?" Savannah studied the papers in her hands and spoke without looking at Maxine.

"I have plenty to do. You people are the ones who just stand around." Maxine pointed at everyone in the area.

"Ah, so because you're in motion, that's proof that you're busy?" Savvy smiled, shook her head and added, "I don't think that's how it works."

Maxine glared at the group, turned, and left the unit.

"That woman will never change. I have no idea why she still works here," Morgan said.

"Administration loves her because she spies on people, has no conscience whatsoever, and she's a pathological liar. Those are all endearing qualities to the penny-pinchers of this hospital who care more about the bottom line than providing the best care," Savvy said while peering over the top of her reading glasses. She added, "What? I know this is a business and has to be run like a business, but the only ones making money are the insurance companies—not the hospitals." She sipped her coffee and continued reading the papers in front of her.

Sensing that Savvy could go on a tirade about insurance companies, which she referred to as the 'true evil in healthcare,' Morgan spoke up, "So, ladies, who knows about the haunted VIP rooms on the seventh floor? I've been dying to find out since I first heard about them."

"Well, what do you want to know? I used to work up there. What's your question?" Tiffany took some of the papers away from Morgan and put them on the desk.

Savannah looked at Tiffany and asked, "Are those rooms truly haunted, as in we could see some real evidence?"

"Well, they're strange, I can tell you that for sure. I heard noises and noticed smells that no one could explain," Tiffany said, reaching to answer the phone.

"Why do you ask about such things? It's most likely a rumor, isn't it? I mean why would the hospital allow that to go on?" Ellen asked as her phone rang and she scurried away to an exam room.

"I told Morgan about the so-called rumors, and she didn't believe me. Our girl here has never even heard anything about those rooms," Savannah said.

"How could I work here so long and never hear about any good rumors like that?" Morgan asked.

"Well, the hospital did keep it pretty quiet. They were concerned about how it would look to the public. Truth is, I don't think there have been any new incidents in years," Nancy added as she sipped her coffee. "It's quiet. Why don't you go look for yourselves? I can handle this."

"I think that's a mighty fine idea. Tiffany, you can go

with us since you used to work there. It's like a morgue down here and our only corpse, namely Ms. Maxine, left," Savannah said while tugging at Morgan's arm. "We shall return shortly, Nancy. Call me if you need us."

Tiffany stood and looked at Savvy, who barely nodded her approval. Tiffany nodded back and walked around the desk to join the other two women.

"This could be a waste of time," Morgan muttered just as Gloria Vanderveer strolled by with a pan of cinnamon rolls heaped with sausage and scrambled eggs on top.

"Breakfast is the best meal in this place," Gloria said as she stood in front of Morgan. There was food debris all over her chin and the hospital lab coat she wore over her designer suit. Morgan stared without saying a word.

"Of course, this could also be another adventure," Savvy drawled.

Morgan whispered, "Can you see her, too?"

"What are you talking about?" Savannah whispered as she hit the elevator button. "Do we have company from your house?"

"No, don't be silly," Morgan whispered. She would have to find out why Savvy couldn't see ghosts at work but could see them at her house. Maybe it had something to do with mindset and Savvy being more open to possibilities when off-duty. She'd have to think about that but was pretty sure this was not the time to tell Savvy that the EC was also haunted. Suddenly a hot pain shot through Morgan's head near her surgical scar. This had happened before, but she was surprised by the intensity of the ache. It had something to do with nerves reconnecting and the healing process. She shook her head and remained quiet.

When the elevator arrived, three women and one ghost entered.

Once in the elevator, Morgan held her forehead and rubbed it. "My head feels like it's full of bumblebees," She said, shaking her head a couple of times to clear away the sound.

Gloria balanced the pan of food under one arm and grabbed Morgan's arm with the other. Tiffany leaned over and punched the button for the seventh floor.

"You shouldn't go up there," Gloria said to Morgan. "You should spend your talent on mysteries and crimes, like my murder. My sister did it, you know. She wanted my life, so she took it away from me."

Savvy and Tiffany were making small talk about the history of the haunted floors and whether there was any truth to the rumors. So, they wouldn't hear her conversation with Gloria, Morgan turned to face the far corner of the elevator.

"I need solid evidence before I can go to the police," Morgan whispered with her head against the wall and face downward. The buzz still hummed in her head.

"Here's evidence. She bought the gun that killed me with my own credit card. Have the cops investigate the recently purchased guns, and they'll see that my sister bought the ballistic match." Gloria became distracted by her collection of foods and said, "Just tell them." She disappeared in a mist before they reached the seventh floor.

Morgan moaned and turned to face the front. She watched the red numerals of the elevator's digital readout rise with each floor passed and the buzz in her head got louder. She turned to look at Savvy and Tiffany over her shoulder but the pain in her head and neck were so fierce she could not focus.

When they arrived on the unit and exited the elevator, Tiffany walked straight to the nurses' desk to speak to the women she knew. Savannah stayed behind and hissed, "Morgan, what is it? What did you see downstairs?"

Before she could answer, the room went black and Morgan was back inside the elevator. The door reopened and she stood on the seventh floor again, but it wasn't the same seventh floor. This time it was dimly lit—the scene was straight out of a war movie. There was light fog in the room. She could hear the buzz of the saws, bang of the hammers, and moans with an occasional tortured scream. There was a doctor in his shirtsleeves pouring alcohol on the leg of a man who screamed until he passed out. Another man stood next to the bed with a saw poised over the man, waiting to place the first cut. Blood was splattered on the walls and floor and dripped from the table where the man was held down by two other men. His blood formed a thick, dark red pool next to the surgeon's left foot.

"Talk to me," Savannah demanded with fear in her voice.

Morgan realized her hands were pushed against the closed elevator doors. The elevator was gone, but she could not move away.

"This place smells like rotten flesh and old blood mixed with infections and dirty r-r-r-rags," she stuttered.

"Morgan, tell me what you see. Wait, first, let me tell you what I see. I see the desk where a clerk sits and answers phones. I see a spotless hallway where patients walk around the unit as they push their IV poles. Everything seems normal. Morgan, now tell me what you see," Savannah said in her practiced, professional tone.

"B-b-b-blood," Morgan stuttered.

"Okay, you see blood. You've seen lots of blood, Morgan. Why is this blood different?" Savvy asked.

"Everywhere," Morgan said.

"Okay, blood everywhere. I understand. Keep telling me what you see," coaxed Savannah.

Another man's screams rang throughout the halls, and Morgan fell to her knees and covered her head. Savannah was hanging on to her when Tiffany returned and stood behind Morgan. Together they stood on each side of their friend, pulling her so she could stand.

"Should I go get a wheelchair?" Tiffany asked. Savvy nodded and turned her attention to Morgan.

"Please don't be afraid," Savvy said. When Morgan looked in the direction of Savvy's voice, she saw a man saw off the arm of another soldier on a different table—he swigged the alcohol, poured a little on the arm, and sawed as his sweat dripped into the open wound. The patient passed out or died, Morgan wasn't sure which, but he stopped the wretched screaming.

Tiffany returned with a wheelchair and they helped Morgan get seated. With Tiffany pushing the chair, the women slowly made their way around the nursing unit.

"Can't you see them?" Morgan whispered.

"See who?" Tiffany asked as she bent down so her ear was next to Morgan's mouth.

"The soldiers. All of the injured soldiers." Morgan gagged and covered her mouth and nose.

Tiffany pushed the wheelchair next to a bench in the hall, ran into the supply room, and returned with a plastic kidney-shaped pan for Morgan to vomit in.

"Good idea, Tiffany. Morgan, when you feel like you can do it, bend over so your head is between your knees," ordered Savvy.

"I had no idea it was so bad for you," Tiffany said as she placed her hand on Morgan's shoulder.

"It's all part of a recurrent dream that Morgan has struggled with since her unfortunate brain surgery. The dreams have manifested from her post-traumatic stress disorder," Savannah said.

"Right, uh-huh, PTSD." Tiffany looked directly at Savvy with doubt written all over her face.

"Look, not everyone needs to know about this," Savvy answered. "Obviously, you've been around her enough to figure out what's happening."

Tiffany nodded. She spotted the patient kitchen and went to the refrigerator. She came back with a cold ginger ale from the nursing unit stock of snacks. She opened the tab and handed the small can to Morgan who drank the pop immediately. She soon settled down.

After a few moments, Morgan said, "Let's go to room 720."

"Do they keep it locked?" Savannah asked as they got closer to the room.

"No, not anymore, it's always open," Tiffany said and pushed the room's door wide open once they reached it.

"I can't believe they leave it like this so just anybody can wander in," Savannah said.

Tiffany went in first and turned on the light. "It looks like a standard hospital room to me."

Savannah was next into the room and Morgan followed last, leaving the wheelchair in the hall. She struggled to open her eyes all the way and hold her head still as the bumblebees hummed again at a fevered pitch.

The women stood there for a moment as the door slammed shut behind them.

"That was a little creepy, don't you think," Tiffany said.

"Did you slam it?" Savannah asked.

"I didn't. It did that by itself," Tiffany answered. "Why would I try to scare us?"

Before Savvy could say another word, the essence of the room changed. A breeze began to whirl slowly around the space and after two or three rotations it formed a smaller tighter circle that picked up strength and velocity with every revolution. Orbs sprayed in an arc around the room before the room became dark as night.

"Savvy, maybe we shouldn't be in here." Tiffany held her hands out to feel the wind.

"Can you hear that? It sounds like a woman crying somewhere. Or maybe it's some poor little kid down in pediatrics," Savvy said. "It's like we're in the eye of a hurricane. A tropical hurricane."

The cries and the wind became louder and louder.

"I can hear her now and she's saying her husband died. She's so upset I can't understand all of what she's saying," Tiffany shouted above the bedlam.

Morgan stood perfectly still near the window.

"There's a strong smell in here, like gardenias," Savannah said softly. "Like my grandmother who always smelled of gardenias."

The lights in the room blinked on and off.

"This is a little on the creepy edge." Tiffany turned to Morgan who still held her head in her hand. Pulling Morgan's arm, they walked out of the room into the bright and quiet hallway. Savannah smoothed her hair and peeked into a mirror in the kitchen, making sure she did not look disheveled. They left the room as they found it and walked by the nurses' station, gave their thanks, and moved on to the elevators. Morgan followed behind them silently.

"I need to go put that wheelchair back where I found it," Tiffany said.

"Let it go," Savvy said, blocking Tiffany and hitting the down button. "They know where it is, they'll get it."

The elevator appeared immediately. No one else was around.

"Well, that was certainly interesting, don't you think, ladies?" asked Savannah.

Morgan leaned against the back of the elevator and sighed. When they reached the first floor and got out, Savvy felt Morgan's head and took her pulse. Tiffany hurried back to the nurses' station to relieve Nancy.

"You will live, Morgan. You scared the hell out of me up there, but you will live. Mind you, it's only because I've allowed you to live that you will continue to live," Savvy whispered as they walked down the hall back to the EC. "You will calm yourself down and tell me in exact detail what you saw. We're close to the EC, so please pretend that you have all of your faculties."

"Why are you irritated with me? This was all your idea, Dr. Holt. I had never even heard of a haunted patient room, remember?"

Morgan went directly to the bathroom, and Savannah sat at the other end of the desk away from Tiffany. When everyone had cleared away Tiffany leaned over to

Savannah and asked, "Do you think we tampered with the devil?"

"It wasn't the devil, it was my maternal grandmother. When I smelled the gardenias, I knew that woman was there," Savannah said, straightening her lab coat. "She was a scary, formidable woman, and I do recall there were times that we believed she could give the devil himself a really good scare if she were in the mood."

Tiffany giggled and went back to her chair and computer.

"Did you see anything, Tiffany? A ghost or clues to some mystery?" asked Savannah as she rested one arm on the desk.

"No, Dr. Holt, I can't see ghosts. I can sense an entity around me, but I have never actually seen one. Today was different, and I'm not sure what it was. You?"

"Yes, I have, but I've never had an experience as scary as the one we had upstairs. Never anything like that." Savannah stood from the chair and stood at the desk as Morgan returned from the restroom. "Just exactly what did you experience?" Savvy asked, leaning back against the desk with her arms folded.

Morgan shared what she had seen, heard, and smelled in detail while Savvy listened without interrupting.

"I think I need to make a log of all of these incidents," Savvy whispered as she checked the messages on her phone.

Ellen came to the nurses' station. "So, was it haunted?"

"Who knows?" Savannah said as she put her phone away. Losing interest, Ellen shrugged and went down the hallway to check on patients.

Savannah, Morgan, and Tiffany stood quietly as they thought about their shared experiences.

"There's probably a lot more out there than we can even imagine. There's likely a whole world that we don't even know exists. But whether you talk about it or not has no effect on its existence," Tiffany said softly. "Don't think of me as an expert. I know about as much as you two do on the subject."

Morgan asked, "Savannah, did something happen to you in that room?"

"Yes, I believe my grandmother hugged me while we were in there," Savannah whispered as tears filled her eyes.

"How do you know for sure it was your grandmother?"

"Gardenias." Savannah sighed.

"It could have been Billie Holiday." Morgan smiled.

Savannah laughed and said, "Ms. Holiday would not have hugged me."

"No, not without a proper introduction."

"It doesn't matter. We shouldn't discuss this right now, besides, what on earth is on the front of your shirt?"

"Looks like either tomato juice, ketchup, or strawberry jelly. Excuse me while I go change tops." Morgan went to her locker to grab another shirt. Savvy went down the hall and Tiffany sorted the orders on the desk.

Later that afternoon, a fifty-ish, handsome gentleman transferred in from another hospital by helicopter. The man was taken into an exam room and moved to a trauma bed. The X-rays showed he had suffered multiple broken bones and injuries from a man versus tractor accident that had happened earlier in the day. He was first taken to a small hospital up north where he was stabilized before transferring him to Good Sam for treatment.

The face sheet with all of his information was right on top of the chart. Morgan looked at it and realized that he was from the same general area that Caleb was from.

"Hi, sir, can you tell me your name?" asked Morgan as she entered the man's room.

"Talbot. Eric Talbot," he said. "My head is fine. It's my left arm and leg that are in trouble."

"You're right, Mr. Talbot. The X-rays from St. Francis Hospital show quite a few broken bones. They sent you here to get these breaks fixed. Are you in pain right now?" Morgan asked as she checked the patient's monitor, read the notes in the chart, and wrote his name on the whiteboard.

"No, not bad pain. They gave me a shot in the ambulance," Talbot answered.

"Well, Mr. Talbot, we have a new doctor on staff in the EC from your part of the state," Morgan said.

"Yeah, I heard. Caleb was a good kid and grew into a good man. We like him. Figures that a pretty girl like you knows him already." He laughed but quickly winced with pain.

"Dr. Holt will be in shortly to see you," Morgan said. She hooked the monitor to his arm and checked blood pressure, heart rate, and oxygen saturation with a clamp on his finger. "Dr. Holt will get your care arranged with the orthopedic trauma surgeons who are already in the OR."

Mr. Talbot nodded, and by the looks of his elevated blood pressure, he was very likely in a great deal of pain. Morgan did the preliminary once-over of his physical examination to save Savannah some time and get him to the OR as fast as possible. The EC was busy, and she would appreciate the extra steps.

"Ring that button I showed you if the pain becomes worse, Mr. Talbot," she said opening the door to the hall.

Morgan stepped out of the room and Gloria was standing there smiling. The beautiful ghost chewed on a chicken wing, which she waved at Morgan as a greeting. She also had a bag of potato chips in her lab coat pocket.

"I saw him before you did. He's a nice man, but he's part of a big secret," Gloria said. "I sense danger all around him."

Morgan watched her eat and said, "What kind of danger?"

"I don't know. I'm not good at this yet, but I'm developing skills and, in time, I will learn finesse. I'll make rounds with the residents, and maybe I can pick up some of the jargon and get a feel for this racket. This is not a bad place at all to spend eternity since it's never dull—that's for sure. Besides, I like the food here. My compliments to the chef," Gloria said as she saluted with the chicken bone.

Morgan stared at her, shook her head, and returned to the nurses' desk. On the way down the hall, she glanced back and saw Gloria waving and smiling. How did she eat when most of her middle was gone? There was something different about the other dimension without a doubt. Morgan shook her head again and saw Savannah going into Mr. Talbot's room.

Morgan charted the information she had gathered into the electronic medical records. In the old days, only paper charts with printed pages were used, but today electronic medical records with monitors and keyboards in every room and the mobile COWs simplified notes for the records. Being old-fashioned about this, Morgan still liked to settle back at the desk and write her notes in the charts. Not to be misconstrued, she was all for technology, but electronic charts didn't feel right, in fact, it was incredibly uncomfortable filling in an electronic page right in front of a patient. Vital signs readily available in your notes made so much more sense, especially when the computers didn't work right. She picked up some scrap paper to write herself a note about one of the patients and instead wrote: *Check the waiting room. Be careful. E.*

She took the note, folded it, and stuck it in her pocket. She went down the hall to find Savannah outside Mr. Talbot's room.

"Call Dr. Larson down here," Savannah said. Larson was the orthopedic fellow on call for the EC. "This man will likely go to the operating room for open reduction and internal fixation of his fractures but we need Ortho to do the paperwork."

"Are you gonna go tell the family in the waiting room or do you want me to do it?" Morgan asked.

"It would be nice if you have time to do it. I could use the help," Savannah said as she wrote notes on her own little pad—she had the same objections to the electronic charts.

"Yeah, sure, I can do it. I mean, how dangerous could it be?" Morgan said as she turned toward the waiting room.

"Why would it be dangerous at all?" Savannah asked.

"I don't have a clue what I meant by that," Morgan said and left.

This was not the right time to share with Savvy that she had a note from Elisabeth. Savannah was supportive as long as it didn't involve the EC directly, and it appeared that Elisabeth had been there.

"I don't even know what I want the damn note to mean, but I have to find out," Morgan muttered on the walk to the waiting room. "Two people have warned me now."

When she went into the waiting room Morgan thought about Gloria Vanderveer's sister again. The public computer was open for anyone's use, so Morgan sat down and typed an email that explained what Gloria had said. She looked up the police email address and sent the message very quickly. No one could trace that message back to her. Hundreds of people used the PC in this spot every single day. Now maybe Gloria would have peace and her husband would be released from jail.

She sat back, patted herself for the exceptional email, and saw two men enter. Both were dressed in overalls, and they went over to the opposite corner of the waiting room. One was in his eighties and appeared to be Eric Talbot's father. The other was a young man, maybe thirty, and could easily be the patient's son. Both stood when Morgan acknowledged them.

"Are you gentlemen here for Eric Talbot?" Morgan asked, wondering if they were the danger Elisabeth warned her about, since she thought they looked harmless. They were salt of the earth, good guy types. Clark Kent could have been related to these men. What in the hell did Elisabeth's note mean? Maybe she was wrong or confused. She was pretty old if you thought about it. Sure, Elisabeth was dead, but she was still up there over ninety years old and that had to have some effect on memory and perceptions. Morgan snapped back to attention and shook hands first with the young man. He was a cute guy and said his name was Robbie Talbot. Morgan noticed there was quite a bit of blood on him and thought he very likely helped get his dad to St. Francis Hospital up north.

The older gentleman held his hand out and said, "My name is John Talbot. Eric is my son." Morgan shook his hand and the room flashed and bright lights appeared everywhere. Her vision blurred and then cleared, revealing the series of photographs that flipped very quickly creating a video for her mind's eye. There was a young couple who held hands as they walked by a river. They stopped to kiss and the young man felt her breast. Obviously uncomfortable with the man's actions, the young woman pushed him away, but he resisted, pushed her back, and tore her blouse.

"You're a prick tease, Maryanne. I won't put up with it anymore," the young man shouted.

"You think I'm gonna just give it to you, John? You're not good enough. You'll never be more than a poor farmer like all your people. Oh yeah, you're handsome, but you'll never amount to a hill of beans," she spat at him.

He pushed her once again, and this time she fell to the edge of the river. John kneeled next to her. She laughed at him and called him a white trash cracker. At those words, John turned bright red and seemed to explode. That's when Morgan saw John turn Maryanne over like a rag doll and held her face in the water—he sat on her legs and held her down until she was motionless.

John stood and looked down at Maryanne's face. He panicked and looked around for a large rock. He could barely pick it up, but he used it to smash the left side of her head. Blood was everywhere. Breathing heavily, he removed her shoes and dragged her into the river. He dropped her shoes in a grassy area and lifted her body. With all his might, he threw her into the river, hoping if someone found her, they would assume she had an accident in the water. John ran for his car, started it, and hurried from the scene. There was a newspaper on the back seat with the date of August 31, 1959.

Morgan's vision cleared and the old man's grip felt like a hot coal scorching her hand. She shook loose and wiggled her fingers.

"Wow, quite a handshake, there, Mr. Talbot. You're a very strong man," Morgan said.

"I've been a farmer all of my life," he said slowly. The expression in his eyes sent chills down her spine. "That work makes you strong if it doesn't kill you."

"Same is true for nursing," Morgan said and smiled. "Your son will be on his way to the operating room very soon for repair of his broken arm and leg. You can stay here, if you like, but you're both welcome to go to the hospital cafeteria to get a bite to eat before heading up to two south, which is where the operating rooms are located. There's also a lounge there that you can use and be closer to the action."

"Oh, thank you, thank you," said John Talbot. "My boy will be all right?"

"He's in good hands. It may take some time for him to heal, but he'll be good as new in a few weeks. For now, these are complicated breaks and it's best to use screws and devices to stabilize the bones. He's gonna be fine," Morgan said and backed out of the waiting room.

"Don't disappoint us, missy," John Talbot said. His cold smile was meant to scare her, which it did.

Morgan hurried to the supply closet so she could call Caleb. She pulled out her phone and punched redial for his number.

When he finally answered, Morgan explained the conversation with John Talbot as calmly as she could. She also told him what she had seen in the vision.

"Morgan, this is a crime that might have happened more than sixty years ago? I know the Talbots. They are pillars of the community and you want me to call the police chief to arrest the patriarch for a murder from six decades ago that may or may not have been real?"

"Yes, what's the problem with that?" Morgan placed the palm of her hand on her forehead and rubbed.

"Well, evidence for one. I can't tell the police to go get a warrant based on my friend's visions."

"Caleb. Please, find out if there's a cold case from August 31, 1959. A murder that was never solved or was deemed an accident. Please. Everybody may have thought it was an accident or a suicide. And her name was Maryanne."

"I know what a cold case is, Morgan, and I'm pretty sure that if there were an open murder case back home, I would have heard about it at some point." Caleb paused and continued, "I'm also sure the police department doesn't have enough people to investigate a cold case. Look, I promise to speak to a friend of mine on the force but don't expect any quick answers. Other than that, it's nice to hear your voice."

Morgan blushed and looked down at her shoes. She grinned into the phone.

"You don't have a snide remark to say about that?"

"Oh, I have them, Caleb. I have plenty to say but can't think of a single word right now."

"Look, you've been pretty accurate so far. I'll dig and see what turns up, but don't say a word to anyone. I mean that, Morgan. Don't say a word to anyone. If this is a first-degree murder case, I don't want any leaks. Promise me that you will keep this quiet."

"Not a word, Dr. Lightfoot. I'm a good girl," Morgan said and saluted the phone. "Besides, the old man scared the stuffing out of me."

"I hope to hell that's not true." He laughed and said, "Bye, Morgan. I'll call you later in the week."

Morgan said good-bye and hung up. She rubbed her arms and shook them as she grinned from ear to ear. She opened the door of the closet and looked directly at Savannah.

"Why were you in the closet?"

"I was on the phone with Caleb and wanted some privacy."

"We have every exam room filled and you hid in a damn closet to talk to one of my staff members?"

"Yep. I have no defense. I'm guilty as hell."

"Well, good for you. Other than that, you've certainly had a fecal-filled day. Now, wipe that grin off your face and get busy. Get out there and save lives and stamp out diseases. This is a hospital, not a social circle," Savvy lectured as she walked away.

Morgan daydreamed the remainder of the day as she searched for lab results, checked vital signs, prepped patients for surgery, and kept everyone intact.

By the time she got home that evening, exhaustion had taken over. She didn't have enough energy to stop anywhere and get dinner and was too tired to eat anyway. She thought a cup of tea and a piece of toast would be all she could handle, plus it was simple to make and eat, which was a bonus.

Opening the door, Douglas was thrilled to see her and had his legs crossed—eager to go into the yard. She filled the teakettle with water and sighed as she placed it on the stove. She waited for the water to boil and grinned again as she thought about Caleb. He genuinely amused her. When the water boiled, she filled her mug and went to the door to watch Douglas. He was playing fetch with his invisible friend as if it were an Olympic event. The stick would be thrown and Douglas would fetch. She laughed out loud because bulldogs don't fetch. You threw it, you get it is their code to live by. She thought it was likely that the invisible friend was Jonathan but it could also be Elisabeth. They both loved dogs and neither one had ever hurt Douglas—so what if nobody could see them? It was a minor detail in the scheme of things.

For years, Morgan came home to an empty house after work and never minded until now. She looked around and hoped to catch a glimpse of Elisabeth. "Good grief, the Wilkersons are turning me into a social being, and I'm not ready for that," she said aloud. "What's next, I'll take up sewing and crafts?" The light blinked on and off. "No way," Morgan said, grabbing a beer from the refrigerator. No damn way."

CHAPTER 15

Morgan let Douglas back into the house, turned around, and saw Elisabeth as a hologram making hot water for tea.

"Hey," Morgan said softly. "You guys get thirsty?"

"Hello, Morgan," Elisabeth answered smiling. "A cup of tea really isn't about thirst, is it?" When she spoke, she appeared as a three-dimensional person.

Elisabeth was a beautiful woman and her clothes were different every time she appeared. Today she favored a short-sleeved Katherine Hepburn sweater and slacks. The pants looked well-tailored with cuffs—they fit her loosely in the legs.

"No, tea really isn't about thirst. It's all about comfort," Morgan said.

"What was your mother like?" Elisabeth asked as she got a teacup out of the cabinet. The mug was still on the counter and she placed both items on the table with Morgan staring at the teacup, not having seen it before.

"Please, Morgan, what was your mother like?"

Morgan continued to examine the teacup, then put it down on the table and leaned back in her chair. "Why do you want to know?"

"We are so very different, and I love the topic of nature vs. nurture. It fascinates me that your biology can determine who you are just as much as the opportunities and choices you may be presented with in life. From my vantage point I can also see how women have changed in the past hundred years, and that's so interesting."

Morgan thought about the question and smiled. Elisabeth had all the time in the world, but she got down to brass tacks with no waste of time.

"Well, the women in my family were not all that friendly when I was young. My mother tended to be depressed and angry, intermingled with depressed and paranoid. My grandmother was on a far more even keel and remained angry all the time with murderous overtures. My sister, who was quite a bit older than I, seemed preoccupied with boys and freedom. My father and grandfather dealt with life through deep dives into alcohol of various flavors." Morgan smiled as Elisabeth joined her at the table.

"What did that do to you?"

"The result of all of those family bonds left me with trust issues and a problem with commitment. Savannah and Ellen are the closest people in the world to me, yet even with them I'm not comfortable enough to completely spill my guts. Although, I must say that despite being opposites in personalities, I do like that neither one is a girly-girl."

Morgan's teakettle whistled and she stood to make another mug of tea. Elisabeth motioned her to sit down and poured the mug full of water from Morgan's kettle on the modern stove. Then Elisabeth's teakettle whistled and she made her tea from her kettle on her stove. Morgan stared as Elisabeth completed these chores. Elisabeth took a bow and grinned.

"When did you learn to cross dimensions so expertly?"

"I've been working on it and practicing every chance I get. I mentioned to you that it's all about electrical energy, and I'm getting better at it," Elisabeth said sitting across from Morgan.

"Now, what's a girly-girl?" Elisabeth asked.

"Oh, a female guided by emotion and not intellect or reason. They are utterly feminine and love dolls, cuddly toys, and long talks about boys. I don't have the patience to deal with fluffy conversations about dresses and shoes. Those of us who are not girly-girls take a more masculine approach to life and sex," said Morgan as she stirred her tea bag around the mug.

"I might be a girly-girl," Elisabeth whispered.

"Maybe, I would guess that you are, but I can't tell for sure yet," Morgan said and patted the woman's hand. "No harm, but it's good to know that ahead of time in case an emergency arises. You want the non-girly-girls to be at your side in a crisis. They're more action-oriented."

"How much of that is nature versus culture?"

"That's a great question, and it's probably a combination of both. I'm not an expert and can't really tell you, but I do think that culture has a great deal to do with behavior. On the other hand, if it isn't in your nature to cry at a movie then it's also equally likely that you are action-oriented. I may have to study this topic at some point because I find it as fascinating as you do. How do we get to be who we are? If I go back to school, I'll share my books with you."

"If you go back to school, I may go with you." Elisabeth giggled. She looked around the kitchen and added, "Are you in a hurry to go to bed this evening, Morgan? I would really like to have some female company."

While waiting for a response, Elisabeth took the mug and teacup over by the stove and put a tea bag in each. She started the kettle again and returned to the table while it boiled.

"Ah, you know, I'm not really busy tonight," answered Morgan. "While we're at it—it's odd to have this kind of conversation with a ghost. Are you sure you don't have friends over there on your side that you'd rather spend time with?"

The kettle whistled and Elisabeth went to the counter, poured the water, and brought the tea back to the table.

Elisabeth answered, "Oh, I can chat with them anytime. You're far more of a mystery to me."

Morgan stirred her tea and looked at the ghost across the table and said, "You told me that you don't use my groceries. How does that work?"

"I don't know how that works, but I do come with my own accoutrements. Our refrigerator is always stocked. Fortunately, we are not a burden on you, and I will try to leave some sustenance for you as well."

"Your consumption of food is not a burden. Your husband's behavior scaring or fondling me is a burden." Morgan frowned at Elisabeth as she spoke.

"Oh, Jonathan is a scamp, he surely is. He's a good man and always worked hard for our family. If he touches the occasional beautiful, young woman while she's in the shower, I don't complain." Elisabeth sipped her tea.

"Are you serious? I'd have his skin ... if he has any skin anywhere. Why would you put up with that?" Morgan sat up straighter in her chair, folded her arms, and waited for an answer.

"Boys will be boys."

"What? Are you out of your mind? That's so dismissive of you and your emotions. Kick his ass to the curb, Elisabeth. He doesn't deserve you. He's a grabber, and you can't change or trust a grabber. Ever, obviously," Morgan snorted.

"I'm sure you speak from experience, Morgan, but times were different when I learned about men. Now, be honest, he has only touched you, correct? He hasn't been inappropriate other than some light touches?"

"True, but touch is touch, Elisabeth. He has grabbed, felt me up, and peeped at me naked. The man has been *in* the shower with me. He has seen more than he should and used his grubby hands more than allowed."

"Morgan, I don't think he's a threat or a danger." Elisabeth laughed lightly.

"You don't care if he does this?"

"No, I don't care. Jonathan loves me as best he can. He may flirt, touch, and look. Just because he's on a diet, it doesn't mean he can't read the menu." Elisabeth cocked her head to one side.

"Look, women today have started to openly fight off these men and make them pay for the anguish and pain they cause. He reads a menu that is apparently printed in braille on my ass, Elisabeth. Boys can only be boys with partners who let them—otherwise they are felons. Please understand that it's wrong, and you can't condone behavior as if it's biological and he is forced to do it. Our culture has let it go on long enough." Morgan watched as Elisabeth stood and walked around the room, wringing her hands. She added, "Oh, so that's why you brought up the topic of nature versus nurture? Has nurture allowed men certain privileges rather than nature allowing those privileges? Excellent question. I can see us taking classes, and how funny would that be? We could cheat and no one would know. You could find the answers to tests and never get caught. There are endless possibilities with this notion. Good thinking, Elisabeth."

Morgan shut her mouth and concentrated on her tea, but not for long. She couldn't stand being quiet anymore and said, "One more thing, Elisabeth, you're from the generation who believed they had to tolerate that crap. If he insists on being a boy as you call it, you can equally feel free to head out there and grab your own male friendliness."

Elisabeth smiled broadly. "Well, if that Caleb man comes back, I might grab a little bit of him to make it a fair playing field. He's quite handsome, and far better than you've brought home before, certainly."

227

Morgan couldn't resist and laughed along with her ghostly friend. "Caleb is one fine specimen—no doubt about that. Why didn't *he* try to find some braille on me?"

"Oh, I'm sure he will. His work comes first, and there wasn't time the other night." Elisabeth fanned herself.

"You watched?" Morgan shivered.

"Not for long—remember, you were promised privacy. I did take a quick peek before I skedaddled." Elisabeth grinned and added, "He looked like a charmer."

"Yeah, he's pretty handsome. He has a great ass, too, and that's usually a good indication of how he'll be in bed. You know, it's the engine," Morgan said as she pumped her arm.

"No, I don't understand."

"Oh, come on, Elisabeth. You had a houseful of kids—you certainly know about sex. It's not like you haven't been around the block at least six times, let's say."

"Don't be ridiculous, Morgan. I know you mean s-e-x. But what do you mean his rear is an indicator? We always believed it was the arms. The arms can tell you if a man will be good in bed or not."

"Arms? What do arms have to do with it?"

"Well, they hold him up. Good arms mean he can hold himself up and not crush you."

"How does that show he's any good in bed? It just means that he won't send you to the hospital after?"

"That's the point."

"Wait a minute," Morgan held up her hand to stop the conversation. She gathered her thoughts and continued, "Okay, it's my turn to be shocked. To your generation a man was good in bed if he didn't knock the wind out of you? What about orgasms?"

"Well, if you were lucky enough to experience a so-called 'orgasm,' and most nice women didn't, believe me, you didn't talk about it to anyone, not even your doctor. That could only cause hostility and resentment from your friends. You know, they cannot be happy for you, because they are not as fortunate." Elisabeth paused before adding, "You look horrified, but this is the best explanation I have—nice women didn't like s-e-x."

"Ohmigod, you poor ladies. That's right, I remember when I took a women's studies class in college. You had to worry about birth control, injuries, and infections every single time and never could enjoy yourself. I always thought your generation had the same information we have and just didn't get into it. Now I understand that you had no clue about intercourse and the bar for male performance was unbelievably low because they controlled the bar. If they didn't cause permanent injury, they got away with whatever they did. Wow, that's tragic."

Both women remained quiet and sipped their teas. Morgan pulled on her lip while deep in thought.

"Well, it was our responsibility to practice birth control and keep our bodies healthy. Young women today are very lucky indeed," said Elisabeth.

"Indeed." Morgan shuddered as she went to the fridge and grabbed a beer for herself and one for Elisabeth. She placed the bottle in front of the ghost who stared at it as if she had never seen one before. Morgan lifted the bottle and twisted off the cap before handing it to Elisabeth.

"You are very strong. Obviously not a girly-girl."

"Naw, it's a twist top," replied Morgan.

"Oh. I don't know if I have the power to drink this."

"Give it a shot. I think you need it after that conversation."

Elisabeth reached for the beer and held it tightly as the cold sweat from the bottle wet her hand. She marveled at it for a few seconds with Morgan grinning as she watched.

"I like your life, Morgan. You've chosen to have a career, no husband, and no children. You take care of the house by yourself. I like that about you."

"Well, thank you, Elisabeth. I like that about me, too. Truth is, I never wanted to be tied down because it makes me claustrophobic—this way I can do what I want when I want."

"Sometimes we sense what's in the house and don't actually visualize what you're up to." Elisabeth turned the beer bottle in her hands studying the label. "It's all about quantum physics, you know. Certainly not my best subject in school, but when we're in our dimension we can't see or hear your dimension. We have to make the concerted effort to enter your dimension and we do sometimes for entertainment and to refresh memories. Does that make sense?"

"Yes, it does. Is that why I sometimes dream about parties here … and I actually think I saw one once?"

"What do you mean?"

"I've had a recurrent dream about parties in this house. The other night, the party woke me and I sneaked over to the stairs and watched. Everyone was dressed in black and white and there was a piano."

"What else do you know about your recurrent dreams, as you call them?"

"It's a cocktail party and no one will say a word to me. I feel like an intruder, but it's not clear whether or not they even know I'm there."

"I think it might be our little get-togethers. We still have quite a few, and I had no idea that they bothered you."

"You have parties every night?"

"Well, in your timeframe, yes, it could feel like every night."

"So, I'm the party crasher?" Morgan asked as she held her beer not far from her mouth.

"Yes, I guess you are." Elisabeth smiled and asked, "Morgan, are you going to remove the claw-foot tub?"

"Well, very likely, why? If you still like to use it, I can get one of those huge soaker tubs that are just as good. Maybe better if I get one with jets."

Elisabeth shook her head, put the beer on the table, and clenched her hands together. "You don't understand."

After a pause, Elisabeth continued, "I didn't want anyone to ever know, but I've hidden some letters between the tub and the wall. They're tucked away out of sight behind the wall tiles near the floor. I put them there when the new tile was installed."

"Letters from Jonathan?" Morgan took another drink of beer—savoring it as she waited for Elisabeth's answer.

"No, from someone before Jonathan." Elisabeth stared at her hands as she spoke.

"I think I understand. Do you want me to seek and destroy them?"

Elisabeth took a long pull on the beer, hiccupped, and burped. "Excuse me. That wasn't very ladylike."

Morgan laughed and snorted through her nose. Both women laughed and settled back into a serious tone.

"Please destroy the letters, Morgan. I don't want them around to haunt me anymore," Elisabeth whispered.

"Odd choice of words, but you better be sure that's what you want. I'll rescue them for you, and we can play it by ear for now. When they're gone, it's forever. I can keep them safe until you're absolutely sure you want to get rid of them."

Elisabeth nodded before adding, "I have to go now before Jonathan gets worried." With that, she took one last chug of beer and placed the empty bottle on the table.

"I am seriously impressed with your beer talent," Morgan said. "But be careful, since you're not used to this."

"I know but, damn, it tastes good." Elisabeth smacked her lips and wiped her mouth with the back of her hand. They nodded at each other as Elisabeth stood.

"Where do you go when you leave my sight?"

"Into the other dimension. I'm really here all the time in a way, but I'm able to move in and out of your world and mine."

"I'd like to see your world."

"Oh no, not for a long time, missy. Tonight, you go to

231

bed like a good girl and get some sleep. You're going to have a busy week." Elisabeth was fading.

"Wait a minute, can you tell the future?" Morgan jumped up and felt for cold air in the spot where Elisabeth had been but found nothing. Morgan finished her beer and smiled as she cleaned up the table.

"You're a pretty cool woman, Elisabeth. Even if you're dead and never burped before in front of another person."

Morgan put the bottles in the recycle bin kept in the pantry. She glanced into the fridge and saw there were still three bottles of beer remaining. She was more tired than she thought because she was sure she had taken the last two. She went straight to bed and didn't wake until the clock went off in the morning.

On the way to work the next day, Morgan had extra time and stopped at a coffee shop for a large chai tea to start her glorious day. As she waited in line the handyman called her cell to confirm the repairs on the bathroom. Morgan told him the neighbor would let him into the house to make the repairs and asked if he found the letters to please give them to the same neighbor. She assumed Jonathan would snoop if the letters caught his eye in her house, but they'd be safe with Mrs. Toland. The handyman didn't mind and agreed to be there around mid-morning. Morgan got into her car and sipped the hot drink. She started to call Mrs. Toland but decided a text would be safer. She didn't think Jonathan could intercept cyber messages, but he could hear a phone conversation if he's in her car. At the next light she texted Mrs. Toland and confirmed the call from the repair guy. One tiny orb darted around the back seat of her car.

"Jonathan, is that you? Elisabeth?" asked Morgan as she drove. "Have you run away from home? Why are you in my car?"

The frenzy from the orb increased. She stopped at another light and watched the mirror. It looked like one spastic orb, so she decided it was Jonathan.

"You have to stay in the car while I'm at work," she said as she kept an eye on the light. "You can't wander around the hospital or the garage or any place where you could get lost or scare somebody. Promise me that you'll stay in the car."

There wasn't an answer. Morgan parked at the hospital and got out so she could open the back door. She looked around the interior but couldn't see or smell Jonathan. She leaned in and whispered, "Jonathan. Promise me that you will stay in the car or I swear I will turn this vehicle around and take you back home."

There was silence.

She locked the door and knew full well she didn't have a prayer of keeping him in the car even for a minute. She muttered about this to herself as she walked to the hospital from the deck. She balanced her tea, purse, and utility bag, then stopped at the curb before she crossed into the main door of the Emergency Center.

The area always bustled with trucks, cars, ambulances, and people in and out of the hospital, but on this day, it was very still and quiet. Morgan blinked and suddenly the world turned black and white. She looked around and saw lots of lights flashing as they entered the campus to the EC. Ambulance after ambulance pulled up to the doors until there were six emergency vehicles lined up. Each one had a critical trauma victim inside. She could see blood on the patients as they were removed from the backs of the vans. She looked away and closed her eyes. When she opened her eyes again the entrance was in color and there weren't any ambulances queued at the doors. She exhaled and walked into the EC with her head down.

Savannah was there and barked orders at a lab tech.

"Where oh where is *my* tea?" Savvy wailed when she saw Morgan.

"Savannah, I'm so sorry, I should have gotten one for you but I was completely self-absorbed this morning. I can go to the coffee shop in the hospital if you want me to."

"Oh, never mind. I don't need the damn calories anyway. Even my fingernails feel bloated, and I don't need more sugar and fat. But you're sweet to offer."

"Mostly because I don't want you to take mine," Morgan answered as she walked around the desk to the lockers.

"You do look peaked. You look like you've seen a ghost, and please do pardon the expression. No disrespect was meant by that."

"Savvy, I had a premonition a few minutes ago, and I think there will be an accident today. Bigger than usual, you know. I saw half a dozen ambulances outside in the bay and everybody was covered in blood." Morgan put her coat in the locker and moved her tea closer to herself on the table. "I heard someone say there was only one DOA." She quickly rubbed at the twinge in her chest.

Savannah looked heavenward and said, "Morgan, my mother is on her way for a visit. That premonition you had is really the universe revolting as my mother packs her designer bags for a visit to Detroit. It is not a major accident. Besides, how do you know it wasn't a flashback? A scene from the past?"

"The age of the ambulances and cars indicated it was present-time. Are you sure it was just your mother planning a visit?" Morgan frowned as she picked up her tea and sighed.

"My mother is a powerful creature. No one else on earth makes me feel so small and vulnerable."

Everyone at the EC knew the stories about Savannah's mother, but none of the team had ever met her. Mrs. Audrey Peabody Whitlock lived alone in a mansion in the Buckhead district of Atlanta. She visited her daughter in Grosse Pointe rarely since Savvy made several trips each year to Georgia to commune with her mother and keep the woman out of Michigan. Savvy insisted that it was safer for everyone that way.

Morgan looked at Savvy and laughed. "Are you

honestly afraid of your mother?"

"I have told you that my mother is of the psychic persuasion. That did not bode well for a young lady who certainly enjoyed being entertained by eligible young men. That damn woman knew everything I was thinking and feeling. She damn near ruined my young adult years. She knew things that I barely gave thought to, yet she prevented me from going forward."

"That sounds like good parenting, Savvy."

"From this point of view, yes. But I also cannot keep a secret from that woman—not one mean word or devilish thought without being called out for it. No one should have to be perfect every waking moment."

"I can understand that, but you're lucky to still have a mother."

"I know, I just wanted to raise a little bit of hell in my youth. She wanted me to be flawless. That's a huge order for a young girl with gumption."

"I understand, and it was years ago. You need to get close to her before she's gone."

"I know, but I get angry so fast, the visits are usually traumatic for both of us."

"Savvy, maybe this trip can bring you two closer together."

"I gave up hope years ago."

"Don't ever give up on family, Savvy. That and good friends are all that matter." Morgan continued, "On another note, what do we do about a major accident that may or may not happen?

"If, indeed, there is an accident, and I do hope you're wrong, we can't stop it. We have no control," Savvy said as she patted Morgan's shoulder. "We're the best trauma center in the region, so whatever will be, will be. We have plenty of supplies, medical staff is here or close by, and there are no shortages of blood or medicines. We're good as far as I know." Savannah left the desk and walked down the hall pinching her nose with her index finger and thumb. Her aura was shooting yellow lightning bolts in every direction, which had become a sure sign Savvy was stressed.

"You are really afraid of your mother," Morgan taunted the stately doctor and saw Savannah stagger a couple of steps, regain control, and continue her rounds with her head held high.

It was a regular day with asthma cases, respiratory infections, gallbladder attacks, and broken bones. Close to one o'clock, Morgan went to the fridge to grab her lunch when she found Maxine elbow-deep in a search of the lunch bags and containers.

"What did you lose?" Morgan said, stepping behind Maxine with the intention of startling the woman. It worked, and Morgan smiled as Maxine jumped.

"Maxine, what you're doing is dangerous. Edibles are sacred down here in this department. We eat every precious bite we have, and there isn't enough to share."

When Morgan reached for the refrigerator door, Maxine moved and she brushed against the woman's arm. As soon as her arm connected with Maxine—she saw an accident. An overpass caved in and demolished numerous cars that traveled underneath. It looked like one of the older overpasses still used in the city. The GPS on the dash of one of the cars was locked on today's date and the time was four o'clock. Three hours from now.

Maxine squawked like a wet chicken about getting a lawyer to file charges of physical assault. She then added, "You just wait, Morgan Cutler. You think you pee port wine, but I have news for you—you're not even half as good as you think."

"Be quiet, Maxine. I have to think. What time do you get off work today?" asked Morgan.

"That's none of your business."

"Seriously, don't toy with me here. Humor me and tell me what time you get off work today or I'll grab your other arm and stuff it back in the fridge," threatened

Morgan.

"My shift ends at five, but today I have to leave at three-thirty, not that it's any of your concern. I work plenty of overtime and I can go to a doctor's appointment when I need to."

"Oh, crap. Your doctor is down at the medical center in Detroit, isn't he?"

"Yes, and that's none of your business either."

"Oh crap." Morgan knew in her heart that miserable Maxine would be right under the overpass about the time it was due to collapse later today and she was the DOA. Morgan closed her eyes to think. She couldn't tell Maxine about the premonition because Maxine would claim she was a witch, unfit, should be fired, and needed the help of a team of psychiatrists. If she were wrong, she would upset everybody for no reason. There was no way to get Maxine to cooperate by telling the truth. Maxine was hopelessly narcissistic, arrogant, and incompetent, but still a person.

It was almost 1:15. She pulled on her lip as she paced. How could she stop Maxine's death? If she delayed the woman for ten or fifteen minutes, that could be enough. Of course, ten or fifteen minutes with Maxine was like an hour underwater with no air. Morgan sighed and rolled her eyes knowing what she had to do and hoping that it would not set off cosmic disasters because she tampered with the future.

At 3:25 Morgan called Maxine and explained that there were numerous discrepancies between the report from the computer on physician orders and the actual electronic medical records. There were always differences, but Morgan knew that Maxine wouldn't have a clue about that. Generally, the desk clerk or the nurses made the corrections and moved on.

"You're the only one with the authority to alter the electronic medical record," Morgan told Maxine. "You have to come and fix this right away."

Maxine sputtered and muttered, but she couldn't resist

a call that insisted she was needed. She stormed into the EC at 3:30 on the dot.

"You've done this on purpose, Cutler. You want me to be late or miss my appointment. It'll be your fault if I do and I'll be sending you the bill. Now, that said, what do you want?" Maxine scoured the room for an audience. No one else was around, and when she finally realized this, her beady little eyes stopped their ricochet around the EC.

Morgan showed her the charts and the documents on the screen. She showed Maxine the problems related to previous visit information and the critical medication lists and allergies. She walked the administrator through which orders were written and which ones needed to be added. Maxine stood there and listened. Morgan was almost positive that Maxine did not have a clue what she babbled about. Maxine looked at her watch several times and screeched, "You know I have an appointment and I have to go."

Abruptly at 3:50 she said, "Look, Maxine, you're right, don't let this hold you up. Go, get out of here—we can discuss the issues tomorrow."

Maxine hissed, "You knew that when you called me down here, you, you … I'll get you for this."

"My pretty. You forgot to say, 'I'll get you, my pretty,' and then cackle and threaten my little dog, too," Morgan said without looking up as she shuffled papers.

Maxine snarled and raced out of the department. Morgan figured the dreadful woman was safe by ten to twenty minutes. As far as she could tell, the other accident victims would be fine with minor to moderate injuries overall. She stood at the computer and deleted the charts created for the charade.

Savannah appeared at the nurses' desk and asked, "Why the Cheshire cat grin?"

"I think I just saved Maxine's life," Morgan saluted at Savvy.

"Those are grounds for immediate dismissal, Ms.

Cutler. I could fire your sorry ass and have you escorted to your car for such conduct."

"I know, and that's part of why you love me. Look, I planned to leave at four today, but it makes more sense to hang around and help out."

"Fine, but why? Are you still convinced there's going to be an accident?" Savannah said as she looked at the emergency communication console used to keep in touch with ambulances and police. The first of many high-pitched warning signals chirped from the system. Within twenty minutes, the six ambulances were queued up in the bay.

As Savvy triaged, Morgan and the other nurses identified patients and verified injuries. None of the victims were the *lovable, charming* Maxine.

KATE MACINNIS

CHAPTER 16

When Morgan finally got home at midnight, she took care of Douglas and flopped into bed. At 5:00 a.m., the scrumptious smell of breakfast woke her. She showered, dressed, and hurried down the stairs.

In the kitchen Elisabeth was as filmy as a hologram but stood at the stove and fried bacon, eggs, and made toast. Jonathan, also very faint, sat at the table and read a newspaper. The headline was about World War II and there was a picture of FDR on the front page. Coffee brewed in some sort of machine Morgan had seen once in an old movie. The couple looked relaxed and content.

Morgan walked directly behind Elisabeth in order to get to the table. Elisabeth visibly shivered when Morgan passed behind her. This time, Elisabeth didn't acknowledge her as she had at breakfast the other day.

"I just got the coldest chill." Elisabeth turned from cooking and spoke to Jonathan.

"Someone just walked on your grave, darling," Jonathan answered without taking his eyes off the paper.

"You know how I hate that phrase. My mother used to say it all the time and it's so harsh." Elisabeth placed the bacon on Jonathan's plate. She put the empty pan on the stove and went over to the fridge, which was an early model from the 1940s. She opened the door and there was a glass bottle of orange juice, cardboard cartons of eggs, bowls of assorted fruit, a loaf of bread, glass bottle of milk, and meats wrapped in butcher paper—there were no visible plastic or Styrofoam containers. Elisabeth poured a glass of orange juice, walked back to the table, and placed it in front of Jonathan.

"Will you join me, darling?"

"No, dear, I ate with the children before they went to school." Elisabeth sat next to him at the table and picked at the newspaper sections he had finished already.

"What's up with you?" Jonathan kept the paper in front of his face as he peeked at her over the top of the page.

"I don't know, but the house feels funny. Like we're not alone." Elisabeth looked directly at him through the newspaper.

"Whatever do you mean?" Jonathan glanced at his wife over a corner of the paper that he had folded down with his fingers.

"I don't know. Never mind, I'm silly." She stood and brushed crumbs off the table with a dishrag.

"Women. Your moods always change. I swear it must be tied to the phases of the moon." Jonathan sniffed and continued reading his newspaper.

"I'm sure that's it or this place is haunted," Elisabeth muttered as she rubbed her arms.

Their food smelled great, and Morgan checked out the fridge to see if there was anything easy for her to grab and eat. When she touched the handle, it became her modern, French three-door refrigerator. When it opened, there was no question to whom this appliance belonged. It contained a chunk of moldy cheese and expired milk with part of a leftover sandwich stuck in the door. The inside of the fridge smelled stale and sour. When she turned back to the table the Wilkersons were gone and so was their breakfast. Morgan realized they must have been completely in their dimension and she was the voyeur for a change.

"Well, that was cool," Morgan said out loud. She locked up the doors, got in her car, and drove straight to her favorite carryout window. When she finally arrived at the hospital, Ellen and Ted were at the nurses' station in a heated discussion. Her phone dinged with an email message from Ed Hill and she opened it immediately. Morgan smiled at the chief's message and put the phone back in her pocket.

"Do you honestly think there's sex after death? I mean, why would there be? It's meant for procreation. You probably shouldn't procreate when you're dead, you know. Cover the earth with little zombies or whatever they would be," Ellen sputtered. "I bet lots of churches would be against that in a big way."

Ted replied, "Sex is a gift of pleasure. It's only procreation when you're alive. When you're dead, it's pure pleasure."

"That makes no sense whatsoever, Ted. I mean it. You're off the wall a lot, but this one takes the cake."

"Hi, Morgan. Will you tell this guy that he's nuts and doesn't know what he's talking about? Sex in the afterlife is one of the dumbest things I've ever heard of," Ellen said as her phone rang in her pocket. She looked at it and hurried down the hall.

Ted sighed, "She has no sense of adventure."

Morgan smiled and asked, "Do you believe that? That sex goes on after you're dead?"

"Why not? I want to believe it." Ted received a message on his phone and left the desk.

"So do I," Gloria said. She had been standing behind Ted holding a one-pound tub of cake frosting that she dipped into with a large spoon. "I would love to find out that there's sex in the afterlife. How great would that be? No muss, no fuss but intimacy of a sort."

"I need to talk to you privately," Morgan covered her mouth and whispered to Gloria.

"Hey, Tiffany, I'm going into the supply room to make sure that we have what we need. If anyone is looking for me, please come and get me, okay?" Morgan spoke as she turned and bobbed her head for the dead woman to follow.

Tiffany looked up from the computer and said, "Does this have anything to do with a gunshot wound victim?"

"Why, it could, but it's hard to say," Morgan said as she led the ghost down the hall.

Once they were alone, Morgan whispered, "You won't believe this. I sent that tip to the police chief that you gave me about your sister's gun. She confessed last night and your husband is free." Morgan reached to hug her but stopped as Gloria's face scrunched up and she wailed as loud as she could.

"Shhh, shhh, someone might hear you."

"No one can hear me, I'm deeeeaaaaaaaddddddddd."

"I thought you'd be happy."

"So, did I, but I'm not—I'm still dead. Nothing has changed for me."

"You could go into the light and pass to the other side," Morgan said softly.

"I don't want to. I don't know what's over there and neither do you."

"I've heard it's another dimension, and once you go, you can use your energy to visit this dimension whenever you want to."

"I'll think about it," Gloria said through a mouthful of frosting. She disappeared with a *popping* sound.

Morgan left the closet, went back to the desk, and sat next to Tiffany and asked, "Did you see her?"

"No, but I sensed it was her. Did the conversation go well?"

"Nope, it did not." Morgan laughed.

Ellen returned to the desk and said, "Savvy called to remind us that she won't be in today. She'll be off a couple of days with her mother in town. I think her mother must be very strict because Savvy said she would prefer to work but her mother wants her home."

"I'm not sure if she's strict or not, but I do think that Savvy is afraid of her. All three of them laughed at that.

Ellen shivered and said, "Yikes, how scary is that woman?" She continued to shiver as she walked down the hall.

Turning to Morgan, Tiffany said, "Line two is that police chief, Ed Hill. He wants to talk to you."

She nodded and answered the phone. "Hi, Ed, what's up?"

"Hey, Morgan. I wasn't sure if you got my email or not and wanted to let you know that we arrested Gloria Vanderveer's twin sister for her murder. The husband was released last night when she was picked up. After the interrogation barely started, she broke down and confessed to the murder. Turns out, she was a wreck and insisted that her sister was haunting her. She had to tell us so she could get some sleep."

"That's fantastic, not the haunted part, but the arrest. I did get the email and told ..." Morgan caught herself and recovered with, "That was good police work, Chief. Congratulations."

"Yeah, about that. We got lucky with a damn good lead about the gun in an email. Strange clue, though, since we traced the email to the PC in the waiting room right there at Good Sam EC. Any idea who could have sent that to us, Morgan?

"Oh, Ed, c'mon. Do you know how many people are in there on any given day of the week? Hundreds, my friend. Take the credit for your detective work and don't worry about who sent it. We don't even have a sign-in sheet for anybody on that PC. We guard the remote control for the TV far more than the computer."

"Yeah, well, I thought you'd like to know," Ed said. "Maybe coffee next time I come up?"

"You bet. Especially if you come without Thornton or

whatever his name was."

"Oh, that guy transferred out of here already. He seemed to think that I was a dirty cop and when his plan to destroy my career and take over as chief backfired, he ran. So, it'll just be me."

"That's even better. See you next time."

Later that afternoon Morgan's cell rang. Savannah was on the other end and said, "My mother wants to visit your house. She is curious about the activities that go on there. I do understand what an imposition this is and, if you would like, I will tell her that you have other plans."

"Are you serious? You said your mom is a psychic so bring her over. Shall I make dinner for all of us? Make a night of it?"

"With your culinary skills, it would serve my mother right, but no, we shall dine first at the early bird hour of 5:00 and then be at your house by 6:30. Does that work for you?"

"Of course, of course. I'll grab a bite for myself on the way home. I'm excited, I can't wait."

At exactly 6:30 that evening the doorbell rang. Savannah stood at the door looking exhausted. Next to her was a woman nearly a foot shorter but just as beautiful and elegant. Mrs. Whitlock wore a red cape and matching red fedora with a giant gray feather stuck in the brim. Her curly white hair peeked out from under the hat and was perfectly coiffed. Her porcelain skin was nearly wrinkle-free and she had Savvy's shimmering green eyes.

"Why, Morgan Cutler, I would know you anywhere," Mrs. Whitlock purred.

Savannah rolled her eyes as she entered the house, guiding her mother along by the hand. They stopped in the foyer and Savvy said, "I would like you to meet my mother, Audrey Peabody Whitlock. Mama, I would like you to meet my very good friend, Morgan Cutler."

"It's a thrill to meet you after all these years, Mrs. Whitlock," Morgan gushed as she reached to shake hands with the woman.

"Oh, child, I assure you, the pleasure is all mine." Mrs. Whitlock leaned to hug Morgan. "Please, allow me to walk through your lovely home. I would like to get a feel for it before we sit down and chat."

Morgan nodded and got out of the way. Mrs. Whitlock shed her cape and handed it to Savvy, who tossed it on the hall table. She turned around slowly in the foyer and then glided from room to room throughout the house. Savannah and Morgan waited in the foyer watching the tiny woman move around.

"I'm sure the buzzards have circled your house, and I do apologize for that," Savannah hissed as her mother went into the kitchen.

"She seems adorable, Savvy. Why do you make such awful comments about her?" Morgan asked.

"She's still angry that I married a low-life auto executive from Grosse Pointe and moved up here into Yankee territory and renounced my Georgian citizenship. That's why," whispered Savvy. "She never accepted the fact that I loved Gregory and moved to him and away from her."

Mrs. Whitlock disappeared and reappeared occasionally as she seemed to float throughout both floors of the house before rejoining Savvy and Morgan in the foyer.

"Ladies, would you please join me in this delightful room?" Mrs. Whitlock said as she gestured toward the library. "This is my favorite room with the beautiful bookcases."

Morgan saw a tiny orange light flash in one corner of the ceiling. The orb had a solid pulsating rhythm and hovered by the top of the bookcase. With each beat, it got bigger and bigger. A distinct shape formed from the light as the illumination became so intense, the entire room radiated a bright orange. The women held their hands over their eyes for protection as they turned away. When it dimmed, the outline of a faceless head in the center of the light emerged then disappeared.

Mrs. Whitlock moved to the center of the room and spoke first. "We are friendly, dear spirit. Do not fear us."

"The damn spirit *isn't afraid of us*, Mother. It's showing off, and he almost scared the *shit out of us*." Savannah spit her words through clenched teeth.

Mrs. Whitlock glared at her daughter for a full minute before saying, "I do not know who you are. My daughter, my glorious daughter would never speak to her mother with that tone or content. I do not know you, stranger," she replied and turned her back to Savannah.

"Oh, Mama, stop it. He put on a performance for you. As I've already told you, if that was Mr. Wilkerson, he likes to write notes, not talk. He's an actor, a melodrama devotee. Isn't that right, Morgan?" Savannah turned to Morgan and whispered, "I swear this is one of the most exhilarating experiences of my life, but damnit, they make me angry when they scare me. I sincerely thought the house was going to catch on fire."

"W-w-well," Morgan stammered. "I thought the house would burn down, too. I've had several conversations with Elisabeth and Jonathan, and I don't like it when they frighten me either. Nothing bad has happened, but that doesn't mean that it can't."

Mrs. Whitlock beamed. "I knew I would see evidence. There is a very strong link to the spirit world in this house, and I am pleased to have been a witness." She smiled at Morgan and glared again at Savannah.

Outside on the sidewalk an older woman walked her dog until the animal stopped in front of the house and barked wildly while the woman struggled to maintain control of her pet.

"Petey, Petey, stop it. What on earth," she said as she pulled the dog's leash. Petey settled down but kept an eye on the house as he passed by.

"Why don't we go into the kitchen and I'll make some tea for us," offered Morgan. Mother and daughter glared at each other but followed their hostess to the back of the house.

From the kitchen door Morgan saw the fleshy Wilkersons as they kissed in front of the sink. Elisabeth wore an apron and Jonathan nibbled her neck while she giggled.

"Do you see a couple engaged in passion?" Mrs. Whitlock whispered.

"Yes, ma'am," said Savannah. "But I can only see the upper halves. The bottoms of them seem to be gone."

Morgan nodded in agreement. There they were clear as day right down to the tops of their thighs.

"You are the most enchanting woman in the universe, my Elisabeth. I will always love you," Jonathan whispered as he rubbed her waist and down her thigh or where her thigh would be if it were there.

"I will always love you, Jon," Elisabeth answered and kissed his neck tenderly. He tilted his head back to allow her to continue.

Jonathan took her hand and placed it somewhere in the vicinity of his penis. She smiled and looked up at him. Elisabeth didn't see the other women at all.

A strong wind blew inside the house knocking Mrs. Whitlock's hat off her head and landing on the floor near the Wilkersons. The curtains flapped, pages of the notebook on the counter turned rapidly in one direction then turned rapidly in the opposite direction. The wind stopped abruptly—it became so quiet Morgan could hear the kitchen clock ticking.

"Savannah, dear, I believe I would like to sit down for a spell," Mrs. Whitlock muttered. Savvy moved quickly to steady her mother as the elderly woman sat at the kitchen table.

"Morgan, as you know, this house is haunted," Mrs. Whitlock said slowly. "I also believe we just experienced a time slip. That's where the ghost is locked in one era and we are in another."

"Yes, I'm pretty sure about ghosts in this place, Mrs. Whitlock. I've had some fairly animated conversations with Elisabeth and she knows I'm here. Yet at other times, she's far away and has no idea that I exist," replied Morgan.

"That's a time slip, as well. She slides in and out of your time but she's also in hers. You may just have to learn to live with it. Let them do what they want, and they'll let you do what you want." Mrs. Whitlock fanned herself with an embroidered handkerchief.

"Have you ever seen ghosts before?" asked Morgan.

"Yes, but not quite so passionately," Mrs. Whitlock answered.

Savannah was rummaging in the cabinet. She found the bourbon and poured a shot in two teacups, one for her mother and a large one for herself before taking them to the table. She tipped the bottle to Morgan and indicated she would pour some for her, as well, but Morgan shook her head.

"Mother, I told you that the ghosts wrote the other day that they want to help Morgan with her new skills. They want to protect her from evil spirits on the other side," Savvy said after she downed the liquid in one swallow. Mrs. Whitlock drank her bourbon in one gulp and shook the glass at Savvy to pour another.

Savvy looked in the cabinet again and found the bottle of peppermint Schnapps. She added a touch of that to her teacup and a little bit to her mother's. She looked at Morgan and raised her eyebrows in question. Again, Morgan shook her head in refusal and Savvy tipped a little more into her mother's tea and grinned.

"Mrs. Whitlock, how can evil spirits on the other side actually hurt me? Is she talking demonic possession or something like that?" asked Morgan.

"Yes, in a sense. When you become a medium for conversations between this world and the next, your energy and thoughts are expended making you vulnerable.

You struggle to maintain your strength and separate from the entities so you may recharge. An evil spirit may not want to let you recharge—he or she may want to use you full-time." Mrs. Whitlock held her cup to Savvy for more liquid.

"Okay, well the Wilkersons and I have to make this work out somehow. I won't leave my home, I love it here."

"Consider this a precious gift, girl. Very few people are blessed to have decent individuals as neighbors in this life. You have wonderful people from a previous life available for conversation, companionship, and counsel. Life is made up of circles that intersect, and these people are part of your past as well as your present and future. Cherish it and enjoy. It will be fun and quite an adventure." Mrs. Whitlock finished her drink, which was causing her cheeks to turn a hot pink. Savvy picked up her mom's hat and plunked it back on her head, and in thanks, Mrs. Whitlock made kissy noises at her daughter.

"Unless you have more questions, I'm going to get my mother home and tucked in for the night," Savvy said as she drained her cup. "C'mon, Mama. Enough ghostbusters for one night. Morgan has to work tomorrow." Savannah helped her mother stand and walked her to the front door. The tiny woman moved in a zigzag motion.

"I want to thank you for an enlightened experience," Mrs. Whitlock said. "Oh, I almost forgot," she added, pulling a small box out of her purse. "This is a good luck charm from a jeweler friend of mine in Atlanta. Please keep it with you and your luck will always be positive."

Morgan opened the box and laughed at the entwined figures of a couple dancing. "This is perfect. Thank you so much," she said, hugging Mrs. Whitlock.

Savvy turned and air-kissed Morgan as she guided her mother out to the porch. Even with Savvy's size and strength, Morgan couldn't imagine how she would get the slightly intoxicated, diminutive woman into her SUV, but

Savvy was a well-trained professional. They walked to the car, Savvy opened the door and sort of tossed her mother into the front seat before getting in on the driver's side. Mrs. Whitlock smiled as she glanced at herself in the visor mirror and saw her hat was askew and clothes were jumbled. Nonetheless, she looked completely pleased and radiant as she waved good-bye.

Morgan returned the wave and stretched. These encounters were exhausting every time. She went in the house, and after taking care of Douglas, went up the stairs, unbuttoning her blouse on the way. In the bedroom, she scanned the room to make sure she was alone. Again, she felt as if she were being watched and she checked to make sure the blinds behind the curtain were closed so no one on the street could spy. There wasn't anybody under the bed or in the closet. She removed her blouse, jeans, and bra and slipped into an oversized T-shirt to sleep in.

"Jonathan, are you here?" Morgan asked the empty room. Out of the corner of her eye there was a tiny whirlwind of bright lights. Morgan watched and said, "Jonathan, I believe in my heart of hearts that you're not the only one who watches me. Have you brought along your buddies?"

The orbs began a frenzy of activity. Morgan got into bed and covered herself up to her neck. As she dozed off, she swore she heard a faint "thank you" somewhere in the corner.

The next morning Morgan hurried down the stairs and saw an old-fashioned vacuum cleaner move across the library carpet with no one behind it. She watched for a minute and realized that she was late and had to get to work.

"Thanks, Elisabeth. If you want to clean the house for free, it's a win-win," Morgan shouted as she went out the front door. On the way to work, her cell phone rang and she answered.

"Did I wake you? I have this image of you asleep in the

nude and the phone is cradled somewhere naughty."

"Get serious, Caleb. I'm bumper to bumper on Woodward Avenue trying to get to the hospital. Besides, if I cradled the phone anywhere, I couldn't take time to talk and you wouldn't like that."

"Depends," Caleb answered. "I've been here for two days because of sick calls with flu and Savvy's well-earned days off. Forgive me if I'm not coherent.

"I will be there in a few minutes if you want to have coffee."

"I'm on my wait out. I remember now why I called—how about a date on Friday?"

"Sure. With you, or did you have someone else in mind?"

"Me, I guess. I'm new in town and don't know that many people. I'll figure out later what we can do."

When she arrived at Good Sam, she checked the board and went to see her first patient. Caleb had left, and without Savvy there, the EC felt empty. She spent the day taking care of broken bones, food poisoning, and urinary tract infections. She found herself keeping an eye on the clock or checking her wristwatch every few minutes. After lunch, she was convinced that time was going backward. When the day was finally over, she wanted nothing else but to take a long, hot shower since she had wallowed in the stench of Betadine and urine most of the day. Curling up on the couch with a good book and then going to bed early sounded heavenly.

When she arrived home, she went upstairs and turned on the water in the shower. She stripped off her stinky clothes and noticed the house was exceptionally quiet. She looked at the ceiling and silently prayed for a solo shower. She stepped into the shower and adjusted the massage head to the right pressure—feeling the tension ease away from her back.

While rinsing, a hand was placed on her shoulder, making her freeze in position. It felt like a real hand, and it wasn't a light touch. She glanced behind, but no one was there. She turned off the water, threw on a bathrobe, and checked everywhere in the room. A real person was not there lurking in the corners.

Morgan sat on the closed toilet and tried to calm her heart as it pounded against her ribs. She finished drying, went into her bedroom, and opened the window for cool, fresh air.

"If you're here with me now, Jonathan, prove it," Morgan whispered to the ceiling. After a few moments, the digital camera on the dresser flashed. She walked over to the camera and picked it up. The camera screen showed a picture of Morgan. There was also a photo of Morgan as she removed the clothes worn that day. The next picture showed her naked from behind as she showered. The next picture was taken when she lathered in the shower. She looked at each photo and gasped at the images of herself asleep, working in the garden, bathing in the shower, and making tea in the kitchen. Someone had been very busy with the camera.

"I know you're here, Jonathan, since you left quite a bit of evidence." Morgan clicked the delete button to get rid of the entire batch of photos. When she finished, the hushed sound of a man laughing echoed through the room, causing her to jump and scream. She searched the room and found no evidence of Jonathan.

She sat on the side of the bed—trying to come to grips with the situation. After a few minutes, Douglas ran into the bedroom. "Let's go sit in the backyard, handsome," Morgan said, waving Douglas to go into the hall.

She dressed quickly and they went outside. Douglas romped around the yard and Morgan sat on the porch with feet on the first step and elbows on her knees. She was relaxing in the fresh air and realized this new life was filled with entertainment, even if it frightened her at times. Mrs. Whitlock said that the ghosts were a gift, in which case, they could keep her attention in a twisted sort of way.

Maybe a ghost could be like another pet. A psychic pet who could warn her about danger and perhaps what fashionable clothes to wear. Yeah, that would be nice. Her very own distant family to keep her up on all the latest news and events without any of the fights. Win-win. Elisabeth was always dressed well and quite tastefully. They were about the same size, so this could work out. Elisabeth would have to make more effort with current news but it seemed like a good idea.

Her cell rang and before she spoke, Caleb said, "Hey, how's the world's greatest nurse?"

"Oh, tired and stressed. I'm in the yard with Douglas and we've contemplated how difficult it would be to go back in the house to get a drink. It's pretty far away, you know."

"Hmmm, you shouldn't drink alone."

"I'm not. Douglas is here."

Caleb laughed softly and told her about his day so far. He arrived at the EC to cover the night shift after she left work. She listened to this funny man recount the odd cases he had seen that evening.

"I need to pay more attention to the phases of the moon," Caleb said and struggled with a yawn.

Morgan felt warm and relaxed listening to his voice. She felt that twinge in her chest and knew for certain Caleb would be part of her life for a very long time. This relationship, such as it was, was not like the other times she met someone new. She didn't feel the urgency to please or to stay quiet, and if she didn't see him for days, she wasn't worried that he was with other women. They had been on one non-date to the antique flea market and certainly were not in a committed relationship. But it was completely different than any other with no rush.

Morgan stood to go inside and find a snack when Elisabeth suddenly appeared in the yard throwing sticks for Douglas to retrieve. She did this several times wordlessly. When she finished, she hugged Douglas and kissed the top of his head. She turned to look at Morgan on the porch.

"Are you his invisible playmate?" Morgan sat back down on the porch.

"Yes, most of the time. I love dogs." Elisabeth sat next to her.

"Sometimes I see you and Jonathan and you have no idea that I'm there."

"Sometimes we see you and you have no idea we're there." Elisabeth threw another stick for Douglas.

Morgan nodded and said, "What's wrong? You seem weary."

"The letters behind the tub. I owe you an explanation." Elisabeth scratched Douglas's head and around his ears.

"No, you don't. It's none of my business." Morgan frowned at Douglas as he rolled his eyes in pleasure from the backrub Elisabeth was now giving him.

"No, I do. I've carried this burden for decades. It's easy to forget just how long it really has been."

"Go ahead then and be assured I won't repeat any of it. I'm a vault." Morgan made the gesture of turning the lock on her lips and throwing away the key. "By the way, my neighbor Mrs. Toland has about twenty of your letters. I haven't had the chance to tell you."

Elisabeth smiled, nodded, and sat back against the pillar. "Jonathan was not my true love. I gave myself to a boy who was killed on the beaches of Normandy. I found myself pregnant and unmarried on the very same day his parents called and told me that he was dead. My life, as I knew it, was over. I didn't know what to do or where to turn."

She looked at the stars and continued, "Jonathan had been a good friend since high school. He was from a prominent family and promised to marry me and raise the baby as his own. No one would ever have to know that the child was not his. I really didn't have any choice and married Jonathan before I began to show with the child."

"Oh, Elisabeth, how *awful*. You spent your life with a man you didn't love? And now you must spend eternity with him, as well? Good grief, that's awful. Is that hell?" Morgan reached out to hold Elisabeth's hand.

"It's wasn't so bad. It started out just fine, but as the years passed and the rest of the kids came along, I ignored Jonathan more and more. That's when he began his quest for women who would pay attention to him. Jonathan wasn't like that in the beginning. I think in his mind he only acted that way to make me jealous, but I was so wrapped up with the house and kids, I didn't even notice that he lingered too long at the fair." Elisabeth put her head down and studied her fingers.

"If you had not married Jonathan, what would have happened to you?"

"Very likely, I would have left town, bought a simple gold band, and then made up a story in a strange city about the loss of my husband during the invasion of France. If I kept the child, he would have grown up with only one parent and that parent would never have been around because she had to work to support him. He would have been raised by a neighbor or daysitter." Elisabeth rubbed her hands together. "Most likely, my parents would have disowned me or forced me to give up the baby for adoption so I could return home with a clean slate."

"You chose the lesser of three evils."

"Jonathan desperately wanted to be a Shakespearian actor. He traveled the country and appeared on Broadway as well as some other very prestigious theaters here and abroad. When we married, he gave up show business for the solid security that teaching provided. He never once complained and he kept his promise to me and my baby. He never treated Alex as any less than his own flesh and blood. He truly is a good man."

"Aww, you had a boy."

"Yes, a blond, blue-eyed boy."

"The letters from behind the tub are all you have left

of…"

"Gabriel. The father was Gabriel. Yes, the letters are the only personal property I have left of him other than his son. At first, I had one of his shirts and wore it around the house every day while I cleaned and Jon was at work. It made me feel close to Gabriel, and I swear I could still smell him on it. I wore it until it completely fell apart and had to throw it away." Elisabeth's eyes teared at the memory as she looked up at the night sky.

"What would you like me to do?"

"I told Jonathan years ago that I had forgotten about Gabriel and didn't keep any material possessions of his. Jonathan made a great sacrifice for me, and it feels disloyal to keep the letters written in Gabriel's own hand. I kept them to remember him and my love for him. I realize now that the silly letters had nothing to do with my emotions and memories. I think of him every single day and believe that Jonathan would be devastated if he knew about the letters. Please take them and throw them in a fire. It's silly to be sentimental after more than seventy-five years."

Morgan nodded. "I understand, but there is no way on earth that I will let those letters be destroyed. I'll put them in a safety deposit box at the bank before I'll let them be harmed."

Elisabeth sighed and tried to hug Morgan, but her arms went right through her. "Sorry. Some days I'm better than others with contact." Elisabeth put her hands in her lap.

"Why don't you try to find Gabriel in your dimension? You could spend eternity with him."

"I owe it to Jonathan to stay by his side because he saved my life. Jonathan wishes adamantly to spend most of our time here in this dimension. Besides, I can check on my children and grandchildren often. It takes a great deal of energy to visit from the other side of the light every time."

"I'm so sorry, Elisabeth."

"Don't be silly. It has worked out for the best."

Elisabeth stood and straightened her skirt. "I need to move along now." Elisabeth disappeared with a soft *popping* sound.

Later, when Morgan was in bed, tears stung her eyes as she thought about the letters and how devastating unwed motherhood must have been. She wondered if it was safe to keep the letters knowing Jonathan was capable of getting into everything including a safety deposit box. Damn, she'd have to come up with something to preserve the letters and Jonathan's ego. These were her thoughts when she finally drifted to sleep.

CHAPTER 17

The entire next day at work was spent in meetings that forced Morgan to listen to presentations about budgets and overtime. Then she had to endure Maxine's view of how an efficient emergency room should run—it would have worked, too, if patients were not involved. After that she spent hours learning more about electronic charts and all the fabulous advantages of the system—until the computers were down and everything was frozen in place. She acknowledged again that those in the back office have no idea of what it's like on the frontlines and vice versa. These worlds never merge.

When she got home after work Morgan went into the living room and noticed the television was on—only it wasn't her television, it was the black and white model that belonged to the Wilkersons. There was a funeral procession on the screen and Morgan sat on the edge of the couch to watch. A riderless horse with the boots turned backward appeared and she knew it was the funeral of JFK.

"It still makes me cry," said Elisabeth as she formed on the other end of the couch. Her eyes were riveted to the TV.

"It's been nearly sixty years."

"Oh my, that long?" Elisabeth hugged her arms tightly. "I was never one to watch much television. The kids loved it far more than I did, but when the president was shot, I sat here hour after hour for several days. My heart ached as it hadn't for nearly twenty years—since Gabriel."

"My mom used to talk about it," Morgan said, "I can't relate, because there really hasn't been a president since then that everybody loved that much. Maybe Obama."

"JFK was a charmer." Elisabeth stood and pushed a button on the face of the TV to turn it off. When she did, her television disappeared and Morgan's TV reappeared with its attached cable boxes, speakers, and DVR.

"Are you anything like your mom?" Elisabeth turned on the couch to face Morgan.

"We weren't close, really. I think we cared for each other but just didn't understand each other. She meant well, but her life didn't go the way she wanted. As I've told you, she was sad, depressed, angry, and it didn't help that she held it in." Tears welled in Morgan's eyes and she added, "I wish I could talk to her again now that I'm smarter and older."

"I'm sure she knows that you loved her." Elisabeth reached for Morgan and connected. The touch was gentle and compassionate.

"I don't know. I was always short-tempered with her because she was upset one-hundred percent of the time. Never had fun, always worried. I just didn't understand and felt so much anger. It was like I didn't belong to that family—we didn't have a common thread. But now I need to tell her that I'm sorry I was so mean." Morgan wiped her eyes.

"Maybe you'll get to someday. I'm sorry I brought it up, but you have good family now with your friends at work and you have us here at home." Elisabeth patted Morgan's arm. "It doesn't have to be a bond built with blood to be family."

Morgan remembered a bottle of rosé in the fridge. She also grabbed two glasses and went back to the living room with the wine. Elisabeth was still there and Morgan placed the glasses on the coffee table and turned on the television.

Immediately there was a commercial for erectile dysfunction. Elisabeth asked, "What exactly do they mean?"

"A lot of men have issues with acquiring and maintaining significant penile erections," Morgan answered in her clinical voice.

There was a guttural sound from the chair and suddenly Jonathan appeared. His face was red as he choked and said, "Whaaaaat? That's inappropriate in the presence of ladies."

"There's a pill for most ailments now, Jonathan, and they let people know with these commercials. They also broadcast information about private lady parts, too," Morgan said softly as he shook his head violently and covered his ears with his fingers and eyes with his thumbs.

Morgan poured the wine in the two glasses and offered one to Elisabeth. She nodded at Jon and Elisabeth shook her head. Jon turned and looked the other way.

"Well, what's the fuss, Jon? We all know the story of the birds and the bees, so why not be honest? No man or woman wants to deal with a willy-nilly if there's a pill that can fix it." Elisabeth sipped her wine and smiled.

Jonathan's mouth formed a perfect circle and he disappeared with a loud *pop*. His exit included the same guttural noises as his entrance.

"He's really quite dramatic, isn't he?" Morgan leaned over and asked Elisabeth.

"Oh, yes, he's a doozy," Elisabeth said. The women shared a laugh, and when Morgan turned to speak to Elisabeth again, she was gone, as well. Her empty glass was on the table.

There was still wine in the bottle and in Morgan's glass, so she wandered out to the backyard to finish it. The cool night air felt good on her skin. Douglas played with a chew toy he had brought from inside. She placed her feet on the bench of the picnic table and sat on the top, which made it easy to see the backs of several homes in the neighborhood. The lots were small, but the houses varied in size. Most were dark or had few lights on as the owners readied for bed. It was a peaceful place on Melody Lane— a sanctuary in the middle of the city. Morgan wondered if this was the "happy" she had always heard about.

A strange, prickly sensation was spreading from her legs, to torso, arms, and head. She imagined that she was balanced at the edge of an abyss as all consciousness floated away. She envisioned warm nights in the arms of a man who loved her and held her close. Her brain flashed on dresses, faces of children and fractured scenes from a life together. The memories were vague and foreign, as if from another time. She strained to catch them before they were gone into the vast chasm of her memory, but she was too slow. Just as fast as it started, the sensation was gone. She made a mental note to ask Elisabeth if that was a past life regression or time slip or what. If it was, Morgan had a ton of research to do.

Douglas was ready to go back inside and Morgan placed her feet on the ground when her cell phone rang.

"How you doin'?" Caleb asked.

"I'm great now." She walked a few steps farther from the house and looked up at it as she listened. A movement from her bedroom window on the second floor caught her eye. The curtain pulled back and then was dropped into place. Someone was watching, but Morgan wasn't afraid anymore. They talked for a while and Morgan told him she would be off the next day. She looked forward to the time alone with no plans and a chance to recharge. She might even go to the grocery store, which was a shock to her own mind.

They hung up, and she truly looked forward to the dinner date.

Her cell rang at close to ten o'clock the next morning.

"Hello, sunshine," said Savannah. "Did we have a good night?"

"Actually, we had a great one and once again slept alone," Morgan growled.

"Hunh, well, are you up for breakfast, lunch, and-or some company?"

"Sure. I've already been to the grocery store and ran some errands. I'm ready for company and some food. What's up?"

"My mother finally left for Atlanta and I'm due for a celebration. My migraine is gone and life is good."

"Nice. Hurry, so you can tell me all about it."

Morgan went back up to her room and noticed that her dirty nightshirt was not by the dresser where it was dropped earlier. She went into the bathroom and saw it—clean and folded on top of the hamper.

"Thank you, Elisabeth," Morgan said to the ceiling.

After changing her clothes, she trotted down the stairs and saw Douglas scratch at the front door. She opened it and Savvy was there on the porch sipping a coffee brew of some sort while balancing a small bag of bagels in her arm. She grabbed a large tea from the porch railing and held it up to Morgan.

"You didn't call from your house," Morgan said as she accepted the drink.

"Nope. Called from your driveway."

Douglas barked and paced back and forth.

"What's got him all riled?" Savvy nodded toward Douglas and handed over the food.

"Beats me, I thought he was asleep." Morgan sniffed the fresh bagels and peeked inside the bag.

Douglas stood his ground and barked his most serious threat. Savvy was standing in the foyer and Jonathan was in the open doorframe reaching for her behind.

"No, no, don't you dare do that," Morgan yelled while grabbing at his hands.

"What did I do?" Savvy stopped short.

"You dirty dog. I will tell Elisabeth if you don't stop this behavior. You can't grab every woman who comes in this house."

Jonathan disappeared, but his deep, masculine laugh could be heard which caused Savvy to gasp and protect her coffee at the same time.

"What did he plan to do?"

"Just a friendly grab of your fanny," replied Morgan as they walked into the kitchen. They saw the back door open and Douglas going outside.

"Who opened that door?"

"Very likely Elisabeth." Morgan reached inside the drawer for a bagel knife. "Did you get some cream cheese?"

"Of course, I did, and it's in the bottom of the bag. Are the Wilkersons around here enough that you can be cavalier about their visits?"

Morgan noticed that Savvy's aura had faint yellow lightning bolts.

"Yes, they are, and I am desensitized. Jonathan has improved a great deal and appears as a complete body more often so I'm not frightened by random parts," Morgan spoke as she smeared cream cheese on a bagel and handed it to Savvy who took it and sat at the table.

"My mother said this house was very linked to the other side and freakishly busy. She said that you seemed to be enjoying the Wilkersons. Is that true? It seems to be true."

Morgan nodded in agreement.

"Can you still do the automatic handwriting?" Savvy asked as she nibbled at her bagel.

"Not so much. I don't need to because Elisabeth and Jonathan feel comfortable and drop in often for a visit or for company. I just realized how completely insane that sounds."

"Yeah, but if there aren't problems, so what?" Savvy

asked as she sipped her coffee.

"Oh, Jonathan is a bit of a grabber still, but he's a work in progress." Morgan bit into her bagel.

Elisabeth entered the kitchen and waved.

"Would you join us, Mrs. Wilkerson? We are having bagels and cream cheese this fine morning," Savvy said as she leaned her elbows on the table.

"This is peculiar, don't you think?" said Morgan.

Savvy responded, "I suppose. But I really like it. We can't tell everybody about this, but we really don't need to, do we?"

Elisabeth smiled as she dug through the bag of bagels and looked for one that pleased her. Morgan sipped her tea and turned to Savvy and said, "So, tell me about your mom's visit."

Savvy cleared her throat to speak. "Well, she was intrigued with your little house here and felt that two spirits live here with you. She said they were quite gregarious and had frequent parties with lots of their friends."

Elisabeth said, "Oh yes, that's quite true."

"I overheard their parties and that's why no one knew me in my dreams," Morgan said. "I was not invited and the celebrations were in another dimension. That makes sense to me now."

"My mother also said that there will soon be an important man in your life. I think he's already here, though, don't you?" Savvy raised her eyebrows.

"Maybe. I'm not totally sure," said Morgan.

Elisabeth said, "Oh yes, Morgan. Dr. Lightfoot is an old, dear friend of yours from a past life. He was also a lover of Dr. Holt's in a previous life."

"Whaaat?" Morgan almost choked. "Are you serious?"

"What is wrong with that?" Savvy asked and grabbed Morgan's hand. "She said previous life, Morgan. I don't remember it."

"You were lovers with Caleb in a previous life? I can't

believe this," Morgan said as she turned directly to Elisabeth.

"He doesn't look the same, and besides, you were there, as well, working as his assistant. In this life, he wants to be with you." Elisabeth grinned.

"Where do you get your information?" Savannah asked Elisabeth.

"Well, it's history, and we all know it," Elisabeth answered and picked at her bagel. "Besides, we get to pick when we return to earth to learn more lessons. It's not uncommon to come back and click with old friends from previous lives."

"Do you also know the future?" Savannah asked as she sipped her coffee.

Jonathan sauntered into the room and went directly to the coffee pot. Morgan assumed it was Jonathan because Elisabeth smiled at the man but the body was headless.

"What would you like to know, dear lady?" Jonathan spoke in his most perfect stage voice.

"Will I ever find true love?" Savvy asked and covered her eyes with her hand.

"Come here right now, woman," Jonathan boomed.

Morgan laughed and patted Savvy's arm. She looked humiliated.

"Sweet, sweet angel of mercy, of course you will find love in this life. A loyal man. A man who loves you and is not threatened by your intelligence, beauty, or dedication to your noble profession." Jonathan's head appeared as he moved over by the table and held her hand.

"It better happen soon. I'm running out of years," Savannah said to him.

"All in good moments, fair lady. All in good moments. You couldn't possibly stay alone with the amount of charm you possess. He will be the one with whom you will build a fine life. You two will be so close, you'll have to remove your watch to tell the time." Jonathan bowed when he finished the last sentence.

Savannah replied, "Well, I think this warrants a conversation with my mother, and she will love hearing this."

"Please, Savannah, tell your mother that she will also meet a man and marry once again. They will be quite happy for fifteen years."

Savvy had tears in her eyes. "My mother told me last night that she met a man at the grocery store. Can you believe it? She is in her eighties and met a man at the grocery store. She said I would also find love, but I didn't believe her. Mothers are supposed to say that."

"Love is everywhere," Elisabeth said.

With that comment, the Wilkersons left.

Savannah looked around the kitchen and said, "I think I'm ready to go home now. You are a good friend, Morgan, and thank you for this entire experience. I can't possibly ever do the same for you."

Savannah and Morgan walked to the front door. They hugged good-bye and Savvy left.

Morgan's cell rang and she heard Caleb say, "Did you remember that we have plans for dinner tonight?"

"Hmmm. I remember that you'll be here later. Not sure what the details were exactly."

"I'll be there at six. Be ready for all possibilities."

Later, Morgan was ready and the doorbell rang right on cue. Caleb entered the foyer and whistled. Morgan twirled so he could get the full effect. Her little black knit dress with the right pump always hit the mark. No matter what she weighed, the dress made her look perfect—both slim and curvy at the same time.

When Caleb touched her arm, Morgan felt the heat go up, turn, and head to her nether regions.

"Before we get going, I need to tell you something. My friend back home said that there weren't any cold cases but there was an accidental drowning death in 1959, in fact, the only one in the township at that time. He was curious to find out how I knew about it. I told him that I'd heard a conversation in the cafeteria. He said he'd check into the file but no promises. I did my part as you asked."

"Thank you. That gets us both off the hook and we did our best. All your friend has to do is re-read the autopsy and he'll see that she was choked. You're a good guy, Dr. Lightfoot." Morgan smiled and put her hand over his as Caleb's gaze locked on something over her head. She turned and saw Elisabeth standing at the top of the stairs.

"Excuse me, I didn't know you had company."

"Company?"

"Well, the beautiful woman at the top of the stairs." Caleb nodded in the vicinity of the stairs.

"OHMIGOD. You can see her?" Morgan put her hand over her mouth.

"Of course, I can see her. Can't you?" Caleb looked at Morgan as if she had two heads.

Elisabeth glided down the stairs, and when she reached the bottom, she held her hand out to Caleb—but he didn't react. He blinked a few times and remained quiet. Elisabeth frowned at him and glanced around the room.

"I guess I forgot my legs." Elisabeth giggled as she stood in front of the couple without the bottom half of her torso. Caleb finally took a step back and looked at Morgan.

"What the ..." He gasped.

"I'd like you to meet Elisabeth Wilkerson. She's the previous owner of this home," Morgan answered.

Elisabeth held out her hand again and, this time, Caleb shook it. Elisabeth laughed and said, "I'm sorry if I startled you. You look like you've seen a ghost."

Caleb's mouth hung open as he studied every detail about Elisabeth.

"You look real except for the parts that aren't there," he said.

Elisabeth cleared her throat and her legs materialized. "I did that for effect. I have a playful sense of humor, especially with handsome men," Elisabeth said and batted her eyes.

"Oh my, you hussy," Morgan whispered. "Do not touch him."

"There is much to be envied about life. Warm flesh and intimacy are two of them," Elisabeth purred and laughed at Morgan. "Can't you take a joke, Morgan? I wouldn't flirt with a man barely half my age."

A mist appeared next to Elisabeth and in a few moments, Jonathan formed—putting his hand on his wife's shoulder. Caleb saw him and moved back another step.

"How many of these do you have?" Caleb asked Morgan.

"Only these two." Morgan then introduced Jonathan and added, "For now, anyway, until they have another party."

"Would you care for a drink?" Jonathan asked and hurried to the kitchen.

"No. Yes. Maybe. Sure," Caleb answered.

Jonathan returned with a small glass of dark brown liquid.

"What is that?" Morgan asked.

"Damned if I know," Jonathan answered.

Caleb smelled it and drank it in one swallow.

"Don't worry, it's watered-down Coke," Caleb answered as he made a face of disgust.

"Why did you add water?" Morgan asked Jonathan.

"I thought it was needed," Jonathan answered. "It was too sweet otherwise, and you certainly don't have any lemon or lime to cut the taste." Jonathan looked at Morgan with disdain before he disappeared.

"Will your friends be with us all evening?"

"Don't be silly. Why would they go with us to dinner?" Morgan asked innocently. "Although the possibility of stowaways on this date hadn't occurred to me."

Morgan looked around for her purse and to make sure that Douglas was tucked away and safe. She looked at

Elisabeth and pointed a warning finger. She mouthed, "Make Jonathan stay out of this." Elisabeth nodded and smiled.

"Let's go. It's all under control here now," Morgan said and put her hand on Caleb's arm. He still looked a little shaken as they walked outside.

"Maybe you should drive. I knew you could see auras and wisps of smoke. Why didn't you tell me that you could see the ghosts? They obviously live here, and it's apparently a very friendly arrangement," Caleb said as he walked slowly down the sidewalk. Morgan took his keys and opened the door for him on the passenger side of the SUV.

He continued, "I mean, you only hinted at it, but to actually see them and talk to them is mind-blowing. It sounds cool, and I'm comfortable with my own sixth sense, but this is more than I ever dreamed. They look like real flesh and blood."

"Would putting your head between your knees be helpful? You don't have very much color in your cheeks," Morgan offered as the engine of the SUV purred to life.

"Air. Yes, I need lots of air. Your friends don't need air, do they?" Caleb asked and tilted his head.

"We don't discuss such details. It's a mystery to all of us, and we want to keep it that way. You would go crazy if you always looked for logic, and I've learned that sometimes you just have to believe."

"You look great tonight by the way," Caleb said. He rolled the window down and let the air hit his face.

"You look fantastic yourself. Well, at least you did before you met the Wilkersons. I see touches of green in your complexion right now."

At the first stop sign, Morgan adjusted the seat, the mirrors, and got comfortable behind the wheel. "You want to tell me where we're going?"

"Just head south straight down Woodward. How long have they been there?"

"Well, off and on for a few decades, and I met them in the past few days."

"You do realize that no one will believe you, right?"

"Yeah, I'm pretty sure that it won't make it to the nightly news any time soon." Morgan kept her eyes on the road and Caleb remained very still.

"What about an exorcist?" Caleb asked and pulled out his phone.

"Do I really need one?" Morgan pressed the gas pedal a tad harder. She wrinkled her nose at a hint of mustiness in the car. Looking in the rearview mirror she saw a glimpse of a faint layer of fog in the back seat. "Jonathan, if you're in the back of this car, so help me, I will turn around and take you home." The mist disappeared.

Trying to hide her anxiety, she fired questions at Caleb. "So, are you a big sports fan? Detroit is a huge sports city and we have them all. Hockey, football, baseball, basketball, and the fans are terrific …"

"Sports are fine, Morgan. I'm a guy and like them best from the couch with a beer in my hand. Listen, is it going to be a problem having ghosts in your house?"

"Problem for whom? Right now, they're the only family I have besides work family and we're getting used to each other. What's wrong with it? Technically, they've been there for years and I didn't have a clue that they were there. Now the only difference is that I do know because of my head injury." Morgan paused and added, "Why can't I keep them? Who says they have to go? I don't need a license or shots for them. They're quiet most of the time."

When she glanced in the mirror again, she could see Jonathan's outline. At least he was alone. Elisabeth was probably angry and frantic with worry. She knew there was nothing she could do to stop the man from being a stowaway.

"Does Elisabeth know that you left the house?" asked Morgan.

"I think so," Caleb answered. "But why would she

care?"

"Not you," Morgan answered and nodded toward the back seat. "I'm afraid we have company."

Caleb turned around in the seat. "I see parts of a man, I think. Some of him isn't there."

"Jonathan, I will warn you once more and that's it. Go back home to Elisabeth or I will turn this car around and take you back myself," Morgan said.

There was a groan heard from the back seat and then a hiss. Morgan watched in the rearview mirror and when it was quiet, she smiled.

"We're alone," she said to Caleb.

"Well, this is a first. I don't see how I could ever be bored when I'm with you and your entourage, and this is only our second date." Caleb laughed and patted his chest.

"It might level off some after we've been around each other more. Besides, it's a lot of laughs or will be someday."

"Yeah, it's that, for sure."

She pulled in front of the restaurant that Caleb pointed at and the valets hustled to greet them. The old restaurant was a very large, yet quaint, English cottage. Built in the 1800s, it had once been a horse livery for those who traveled Woodward Avenue regularly. There were several cozy dining rooms with a fireplace in each. The wood was dark, warm, and every room was painted a dark blue or rich dark green with red accessories. The artwork, lights, and furniture were more than one hundred and fifty years old. The smells of steak, garlic, and potatoes from the kitchen made their mouths water when they went inside. Other diners were dressed in black ties, lots of shiny jewels, and cocktail dresses.

"I thought it would be a great place because they supposedly have a haunted private dining room in the restaurant," Caleb said in a low voice as they waited for the maître d. "I'm not so sure that's clever now."

They were seated and had an exceptional dinner with

no ghostly appearances by residents or visitors. Afterward, Caleb drove them down Woodward to the Fisher Theater. Once inside the Fisher Building, they both marveled at the exquisite art deco design from 1928. The marble floors and light fixtures were works of art. With a copper rooftop and offices and stores located throughout; the Fisher was one of the first skyscrapers in Detroit and retained its sophistication and charm through the years. Historical photos confirmed that it was far more beautiful now than when it was built almost ninety years ago. Known since then as "Detroit's largest art object," the Fisher had a timeless refinement and strength of design that whisked visitors away to another era.

The elaborate Fisher Theater is located on the first floor of the Fisher Building and always has stellar entertainment—often a Broadway hit during a cross-country tour. With thirty minutes before curtain, Morgan and Caleb took the elevator up several floors and walked hand in hand around the beautiful space. They got into one of the many bronze elevators and Caleb pushed the button to go down to the theater. The door opened again and Jonathan stood there in a costume appropriate for Henry VIII.

"Are you here to chaperone us?" Morgan asked as Jonathan got on the elevator.

"Don't be silly, you're both practically senior citizens. I'm here to revel in the greasepaint and the roar of the crowd. How could you go to dinner and then the theater and not even consider an invitation for me to tag along?" Jonathan sniffed as he gazed at the mirrors on the ceiling of the elevator.

"It was an oversight, Mr. Wilkerson. It won't happen again," Caleb answered and kept his eyes glued to the floor indicator.

"Oh, dear boy, Jonathan is fine. Let's not be formal. I'm sure we'll learn lots more about each other before the night is over," Jonathan said with a wink.

Caleb's head snapped in the direction of Jonathan. "What do you mean by that? How much do you see?"

"That which is not hidden."

"How do we hide that from you?"

"You can't, dear boy. You can't."

"Jonathan, do you watch me in the bathroom other than the shower?" Morgan asked with the whites of her eyes showing all around the iris.

"You'll get over that," Jonathan said matter-of-factly.

"Well, what if we decide to, er, um?" Caleb asked awkwardly.

"I shall serve popcorn," Jonathan said and looked down his nose at Caleb. "Give me some credit, old boy. I do have a shred of decency left. If you ask for privacy, then privacy you shall have."

Caleb closed his mouth and eyes for the remainder of the ride. They exited the elevator and hurried to an usher at the door of the theater, who led them immediately to their seats. Before the curtain went up Caleb shook his head and looked heavenward.

"Where did Mr. Wilkerson go?" whispered Caleb.

"I saw him going down the hall to the dressing rooms," answered Morgan.

Caleb nodded and sighed. They were able to enjoy the performance except for a few minutes during the second act when Caleb was positive he could see Henry VIII backstage in the wing. After the show, the drive back to Morgan's house was very quiet and they both assumed that Jonathon found enough entertainment that he didn't need to ride along. When they arrived at Melody Lane, Caleb walked her to the door.

"Would you like to come in for a drink?"

"How could I possibly resist?"

When they stepped inside the lights were dimmed and music from the big band era played softly from Caleb's radio in the library.

"Yep, there's a fire in the fireplace and snacks on the

coffee table." She pointed to the food.

Caleb followed and sat next to her on the couch. He put his arm around her and leaned in for a kiss, which caused heat to flush up and down her entire body. They sipped the wine, nibbled the cheese and crackers, and looked quietly at each other.

"Where's your bedroom?" Caleb asked.

"I'm not that kind of girl," Morgan answered.

"But you are that kind of woman. Tell me before I throw you down in front of the fire."

She pointed upstairs and they walked up together and went into the bedroom.

"Can they watch us in here?" Caleb asked.

"Well, let's see. Elisabeth, do you have Jonathan under control?" Morgan spoke to the ceiling.

The lights blinked twice.

"Will you give us some privacy? Now and for the rest of the night?" Morgan asked.

The lights blinked twice again.

"You're good to continue," Morgan said to Caleb.

Caleb wrapped his arms around her and looked into her eyes. "Listen, I don't know what this is or what it will turn out to be. I also know that we barely know each other, but I want you in my life, Morgan. We'll just have to figure out how to include the Wilkersons, within reason."

"I want this, too. Let's take it one day at a time and see what happens. This could be the start of a beautiful relationship."

"Or a very strange family," Caleb kissed Morgan and the lights went out in the room.

"I think there will be company at breakfast tomorrow," Elisabeth whispered in the hall outside the bedroom door.

"This gives me ideas, my beautiful wife." Jonathan squeezed her hand and they disappeared with a *pop*.

KATE MACINNIS

ABOUT THE AUTHOR

Michigan-born and raised, Kate earned a Bachelor's Degree in Journalism at Oakland University and Master's Degree in American Culture at the University of Michigan-Flint. As a professional writer for more than 20 years, her career has been primarily in health care, particularly hospitals. This provided an opportunity to hear many stories from nurses, doctors, visitors as well as her own family members about unusual activities and miracles that occur without a clear-cut, scientific explanation. She also claims to have personally had a few unusual experiences, some of which she shared in this book.

Kate is married to the love of her life and has two grown sons and three grandchildren.

webpage: Katemacinnis.com
email: authorkatemacinnis@gmail.com

Made in the USA
Monee, IL
13 January 2021

55367122R00163